NOBODY LIKES

Anthony Appian

Constable · London

First published in Great Britain 1994
by Constable & Company Ltd
3 The Lanchesters, 162 Fulham Palace Road
London W6 9ER
Copyright © 1994 by Anthony Appiah
The right of Anthony Appiah to be
identified as the author of this work
has been asserted by him in accordance
with the Copyright, Designs and Patents Act 1988
ISBN 0 09 473300 7
Set in Palatino 10pt by
CentraCet Limited, Cambridge
Printed in Great Britain by
St Edmundsbury Press Limited
Bury St Edmunds, Suffolk

A CIP catalogue record for this book
is available from the British Library

Nobody likes Letitia

The eminent barrister and amateur sleuth Sir Patrick Scott and his novelist wife, Virginia, are asked for Hogmanay by the rich laird of Sealsay, Colin Rundle, who, with his wife Iona, lives on the tiny island across the Firth of Lorn on the west coast of Scotland.

The assembled guests include a large gathering of relations spanning the generations – one, a very nasty small boy – a nanny and an au pair or two, a ravishing and flirtatious editor of a magazine financed by the laird himself, and the solitary, reclusive, socially graceless, Letitia Rundle, Colin's sister.

As the preparations for the forthcoming festivities get underway, Sir Patrick notices that almost everyone is behaving peculiarly: it is as if Sealsay House has been invaded by demons. This aura of threat and danger becomes a reality when Letitia is seen leaping from a cliff top into the raging sea below. Pandemonium ensues, as coast guards, crofters and guests frantically search for the missing woman.

She is found, however, not drowned in the sea, nor smashed on the rocks, but in the most bizarre of places, and Sir Patrick becomes convinced that he hasn't a suicide on his hands but a cold blooded killing.

Family secrets long hidden, the facts of a priceless inheritance, the undiscovered revenue from a pseudonymous writing career, the barely disguised display of an illicit love affair – all are finally laid bare in the unmasking of the murder by the astute Sir Patrick in the finale to this elegantly written, gripping and tragic story by the author of *Avenging angel*, Sir Patrick's previous investigation.

Also by Anthony Appiah

Avenging angel (1990)

1

An hour out from Oban, on the choppy late December waters, I decided that breakfast had been a mistake. The problem was not the weather: the grey-black clouds scudding across the face of a reluctant sun were not yet a storm, and in any case we Scotts have always had fine sea-legs. No, the problem was the fried egg that had swum across my plate in the company of a piece of soggy toast half an hour earlier, and was now being churned about my interior as I bestrode the narrow deck staring east towards the isles. I tried not to think about the egg. But each time the sun appeared, that ochre circle of pallor brought it back to mind. As the boat heaved clumsily on towards the empty horizon, I drew back my left sleeve and glanced down at my watch. 10.13. Another two and a quarter odd hours to go. I shook my head briskly to clear it, took a deep breath of the salt air, and turned back to face Arran. And there was Jinny, with a teacup full of what looked like frothing water. 'Patrick,' she shouted over the flapping sounds of the wind and the grinding of the engines, 'Patrick, I think you ought to take this.'

Since we were on our way to see in the New Year on Sealsay, I should have known that Jinny would have brought along an armoury of pills and potions designed to combat the gastric consequences of excess. I did not ask her what it was. She did not even for one moment suggest, not even by the mildest of reproaching glances, that she had been right to urge against breakfast. And as I obediently gulped down the cup – Eno's Fruit Salts, perhaps – I delivered up one of my silent prayers of thanks to the Almighty.

*

Sealsay, to which, as I say, we were bound, is an accident of geography that history has made into a tiny social experiment. The island is no more than twelve miles long, and at its widest point it would probably take a sober crow a flight of a mere mile or so to cross it. The land rises steeply from the shoreline to a spine of hills which runs from north-east to south-west along most of Sealsay's length, and, without the benefit of wings, crossing from the northern to the southern shores is more easily accomplished by following the single road that winds slowly up to Ben Moray, and then unwinds down to the other shore. At the peak of the little mountain are the ruins of an old stone tower, a relic of days long gone, when the monks of Sealsay had a reason to keep an eye out for strangers from the north. The island's few square miles are occupied by a dozen or so crofts – small tenant farms, with a scattering of sheep, the odd cow, and (so far as I can gather) a hefty subsidy from the European Commission and the Highlands and Islands Development Board – where ageing couples, their children largely lost to the mainland, struggle to keep alive an old way of life. Then, there are a few holiday cottages, occupied in the summer by professional people from Edinburgh and Glasgow, who want a place to swim and fish and walk; and, last but not least, come the home farm and the rambling Victorian baronial monstrosity of Sealsay House, home of our hosts, Colin and Iona Rundle.

Colin's family had owned Sealsay for only about a hundred years. His great-grandfather, the first Rundle laird of Sealsay, turned a fortune made in the mills of Lancashire into a baronetcy and, in choosing Sealsay for his summer home, he gave his natural misanthropy full rein. Josiah Rundle was as businesslike in pursuing his private obsessions as in his life in the mills: he built Sealsay House with a magnificent home farm, had one of the island's small lochs landscaped, extended and stocked with trout, and employed a small fishing boat to trawl the waters off the island to keep the house supplied with mackerel, of which he never tired. And all this on an island with two hundred and fifty inhabitants who could easily be persuaded to keep out of his way.

Colin, whom I had known since we were up at Cambridge, inherited the island twenty years ago; and once Gavin, their youngest, had been packed off to prep school, Colin and Iona moved there more or less permanently.

Colin and Iona had several dependants installed on the island. There were the Wrigleys, who ran the hotel, and a doctor by the name of Crawford, in his late sixties, whom I had never met. And then there was David Mackintosh, who managed the home farm. Known, as many of the islanders are, by the name of the land he farmed, he and his wife Fiona were always called David and Fiona Sealsay.

Peter and Wendy Wrigley, Colin and Iona and their household, the Mackintoshes, Dr Crawford, and fifty or so crofters and their families, dotted about the island; these were the island's only permanent residents, and they made up a rather strange community.

I have been to Sealsay off and on for more years than I care to number. The first time, Colin and I were undergraduates and he asked me up for the summer of '40. I spent a marvellous couple of weeks of tennis, swimming, fishing, walking and, above all, eating. Colin's mother, Lorna, had died in an accident a year or so earlier, not long after his brother Alistair was born, and his grandmother, Maud, Lady Rundle, who was still alive, maintained an extraordinary table, complemented by the wines from her late husband's cellar. All of which felt very queer in the first summer of the war.

Next summer we were to take our degrees. I went into my war work in Intelligence and Colin set off for a distinguished career in the Scots Guards. For the rest of the war, we were in touch, on and off. I knew that I would go to Sealsay again.

That summer nearly fifty years ago was also when I met Letitia, Colin's sister, three years older than he; a strange, tall young woman, with long black hair in a single braid, who kept her own company and her own counsel, appearing only for the evening meal, where she insisted on sitting silently between her father and her brother, eating heartily, but acknowledging no one outside her family. Once, all those years ago, I returned from a solitary walk and came upon Letitia as I rounded a corner in the path through the rhododendrons behind the house, almost crashing into her. She stared at me with an unhurried frankness and then, as I mumbled an apology, she said in a clear, confident, contralto voice, with no hint of shyness, 'Mr Scott, I do not care for strangers.' I can still remember being overwhelmed by a sense that I had slipped out of the real world; by the oddness of her; by the fact that her tone was polite and her manner friendly as she spoke these impolite and unfriendly words. I never mentioned this episode to Colin, of course, and when, next term, he spoke of her once, and I gave him a querying look, he moved on to another topic, and seemed grateful that I did not press.

In the years after the war Colin developed something of a reputation as an explorer. He travelled up the Amazon and into the rain forests of Borneo; he made a much-bruited trip to the South Pole; he met remote tribal peoples in Highland Burma. He always took along with him all the apparatus of an old-fashioned scientific expedition – botanists and zoologists and anthropologists – and was always lavishly covered in beautifully photographed stories in European and American magazines. In each of the articles he would describe himself somewhat self-deprecatingly as a member of a remote clan from a remote island on the western limits of Europe visiting other remote peoples. Occasionally cynics would observe that most remote peoples did not have millions of pounds in the stock market. But usually he would charm the reporters who wrote about – and sometimes travelled with – him, and those whom he did not charm were charmed by Iona, who stayed at home, shuttling between London and Sealsay, looking after the children and dabbling in the best of good works. No one ever mentioned Letitia, or drew out the strange paradox that this famous British explorer, who once said he regarded the whole globe as his home, should have a sister who lived almost all of her life in a geographical circle more circumscribed than that of the Yanamano Indians or the forest tribes of Sarawak.

But, of course, Colin always came back from his global home to Sealsay. And often, when he was there, both before his father died and later, in the 1970s, he asked me to join him for a week or two of fishing in the spring or sailing in the early summer or shooting in late August. I suppose I went to Sealsay a dozen times over the twenty years after the war and Letitia was there every time but one. That was also, as it happened, when Virginia came once for a few days for her only visit; Letitia was making one of her rare visits to Edinburgh. Jinny couldn't see the point of Sealsay, and so, when I did go again, I went by myself.

Once, in all those years, I remarked to Colin that Letitia had hardly ever spoken to me. 'Count your blessings, old man,' he replied; and then he looked away, embarrassed by what he had said. Those words shaped my response to her. Over the years it was borne in on me by occasional remarks from various Rundles that the members of the family (to whom she *did* speak) were not overfond of her. One rarely saw her about the house, except in the library. If you did see her in the grounds or walking in the hills, she was almost always reading or scribbling away in a notebook. And every evening she sat silent in the drawing-room knitting over a book. 'Reads a lot, Letitia, doesn't she?' I said to Colin many years ago when the two of us caught sight of her as we were walking up to fish in Loch Gaver. 'Yes, she tells me she's making her way through the entire *oeuvre* of Walter Scott for the third time.' Colin's tone did not suggest that the intelligence had raised her in his estimation.

Colin's son Gavin had summed it all up succinctly a few weeks ago, when we had bumped into him at a dance at Lincoln's Inn, in the company of one of the string of young women whose unsuitability so distresses his mother. After the introductions, I asked after his family. And Gavin, whose head had never, I think, been very strong, responded in a drunken mumble, 'Pater's pootling about in boats at Sealsay; Mother is sublimely beautiful as ever; the sisters are preoccupied with the vast diversity of sex. And you can't care to know about Aunt Letty. *Nobody* likes Letitia.' Tacked on at the end like that, the remark seemed particularly mean-spirited. It was hardly the most nephewish thing he could have said. But it was, I suspected, true enough.

And yet, there was another side to her. Gavin's careless and uncaring observation led me back in memory to the summer my father died. After the funeral, I spent some time walking the island alone; and that summer Letitia spoke to me again, this time after seeking me out as I sat fly-fishing in the stream that wandered along the fields to the west of the house. 'I'm sorry about your father,' she said, in the same voice I had remembered all down the years. 'Family is so very important.' And then, before I could reply, she walked back to the house.

It was our second conversation and it was oddly affecting. But I cannot say it made me eager for more of these tête-à-têtes.

In the twenty years since my father died, I had been to Sealsay rather less often, almost always for a few days when Virginia was unapproachable in one of her fits of writing. Colin and Iona had become more fully Scottish when they took over the island, though Jinny and I had had them to stay a couple of times in the seventies, after they gave up their London house. When they first established themselves they had asked us routinely to join them for one of their house parties every summer, and, routinely, we had been busy with something else. My father's death, for one thing, had left us spending more time at Chewton Ampney, where I had grown up, looking after my aged mother and an even more aged and decaying house.

But this time they had asked both of us for Hogmanay. At our age, as one grows into what the Sunday magazines have taken to calling prettily one's 'sunset years', one's friends gradually drop away . . . and, in the end, mere longevity, the fact that one has known people for decades, begins to count for something. Together one can 'summon up remembrance of things past', as the bard has it. More and more, the depth or the intimacy of friendship matters less than its extent. And so it felt right to re-establish contact with Colin. I was looking forward to playing an active part in this most energetic of festivals.

I had been once before to Sealsay for the New Year, when I was a very young man. Then, for the first (and last) time in my life I had drunk enough whisky in enough of the island's crofts with enough of the islanders I had met at the laird's gathering to pass out and lose all memory of the occasion. Colin's son Gavin had vouchsafed to me once, just after he came down from Oxford, on one of the few occasions we had met on Sealsay, that my exploits that night were the stuff of island legend. I had not encouraged him to provide details, but I remembered enough of the earlier part of the evening to know what to expect: at eleven, once the family and their guests had dined, the islanders would gather in the great hall of the house, already, most of them, a little the worse for wear, and begin to dance the New Year in with reel after reel, to the accompaniment, of course, of the bagpipes. 'Do let's go, Jinny,' I had said to my wife. 'You've hardly ever been and Hogmanay is enormous fun.'

I mentioned my memory of the pipes on the telephone to Colin when I called to accept the invitation, and he told me that David Sealsay, who had won many a prize at the Highland games for his piping, would play the New Year in for us. All in all, it seemed to me, as we packed our suitcases in London, that there was plenty to look forward to.

But approaching the island, with the dark clouds gathering from the north and the storm rising, and my stomach settled by Jinny's potion but still queasy, I felt less confident that we had made the right decision. Reeling and drinking and eating to excess are, on the whole, activities for the young; and, as we docked at the pier, I wondered if we should not have spent the New Year quietly at Ampney with Sebastian and our new granddaughter.

Now the waves slapped the boat up against the dock and we staggered down the gangway on to the pier. The enthusiasm with which I had begun the day in our hotel in Oban was replaced with a dark sense of foreboding. When Colin strode towards us, his mass of unruly white hair blowing in the wind, a windcheater open over his dark blue jersey, hands thrust deep into the pockets of his plus-fours, I tried to muster at least a simulacrum of excitement.

As always on the island, he was dressed without formality, but also without even the most negligible nod to fashion. Colin was comfortable here, and it showed. 'Patrick,' he said. 'Good to see you. Jinny. Welcome.' He leaned down from six foot and three inches of height to kiss her. When he straightened up, he gave the pair of us a somewhat forced smile and set about bustling us on our way. 'No need to carry your cases any farther. Jock'll take 'em.' He waved vaguely in the direction of a middle-aged man in a tweed suit, with a pipe-bowl showing from his top pocket. 'Jock, here we are: Sir Patrick Scott and Virginia, his good wife.' Jock, whom I had known for years, tugged at his tweed cap in greeting; but there was no smile of welcome. He was the dourest of kirk-loving Scotsmen. 'Could you pop their cases in the boot? And now, let's go up to the house. Iona will be waitin'.'

Colin had weathered well the years since I had seen him last. His skin – which had borne the bright sun reflected from the polar ice caps, the endless humid heat of jungles, and the desiccation of the desert – had looked weather-beaten for decades. But it had not changed. The lines reflected not age but the range (and the rigour) of the environments he had known. And he still had that great mane of hair. White now, it had greyed early, so that that too seemed to have changed little.

Colin moved like a younger man. He was always fit from his physical exertions: the daily sailing through much of the summer; the long walks, often accompanied by Iona, up into the hills.

And yet something was not altogether right with him. The occasional, unfamiliar, twitch in a face that had always been strong and calm; an equally unfamiliar undercurrent of hostility beneath his febrile friendliness: his whole manner was subtly, but distinctly unexpected.

Jock drove us in the Range Rover up off the pier and on to the narrow road. We passed the ruins of the old kirk in silence and made our way along the coast road that runs, half a mile further on, past the hotel. Somebody waved from the door of the bar, though I couldn't make out who it was through the drizzle. 'That's Mrs Wrigley,' Colin said, turning from his place in the front passenger seat to address Virginia and me. 'They've done tremendously well. Don't know what we'd do without 'em.'

The Wrigleys ran the small hotel for Colin and Iona. Its major function was to house Sealsay's bar. But they also managed the island's only shop. Peter and Wendy Wrigley were one of Iona's projects. I had met them a decade earlier, when they first came to the island, one summer when I was sailing with friends off the west coast and had dropped in on Colin and Iona for a day or two. Peter had been a pop musician in the seventies and had become, at some point, a heroin addict. He ended up eventually in a clinic in Glasgow that Iona had decided she and Colin should set up and support; and Wendy was a nurse who had fallen for him. At the moment when Peter finally came off the drug, the Lindsays, who were running the hotel and shop previously, were thinking of retiring. So Iona offered the job to Peter and Wendy. 'After all,' she told me, laughing, 'there's not much of a heroin trade on Sealsay.'

Colin obviously felt that now we had started talking we had better continue. He asked us about our journey and the Christmas holiday, without managing to maintain the pretence of interest. He was plainly distracted. Every few minutes he ran his hands through his hair, like a stage lunatic. When he turned to address us, his eyes skittered hither and thither. As we were chatting desultorily half-way along the three-mile drive to the gates of Sealsay house, we struck a pot-hole rather too fast and Colin snapped at Jock, 'Be careful, man. Watch where you're goin'.' It was thoroughly out of character, and Colin seemed immediately to regret it, smiling ruefully back at us, and patting Jock on the shoulder. Each time he glanced back, the tension in his jaw showed in the shadows cast by the pale winter light; he was chewing feverishly at his lower lip. The truth was that Colin was more strained and tense than I had ever seen him. Jinny gave me a questioning look, and I squeezed her hand. I didn't feel very able to reassure her. Obviously something was wrong: the holiday season on Sealsay was not exactly brimming with goodwill.

The first roar of thunder broke as we reached the gates of the long drive, and the sky dimmed to an almost nocturnal darkness. By the time we reached the house there was lightning streaking the sky above the great west tower of Sealsay, and the vast stone dragons were displayed in hideous relief. 'Pity about the weather. We could be in a winter storm in Southern Peru,' Colin said, smiling vaguely.

The effect was extremely disconcerting. *'Nam risu inepto res ineptior nulla est,'* I thought. Nothing dafter than a daft smile. Horace or Catullus, I couldn't remember. But it was what came to mind. What came to Virginia's mind, as she told me later, was Mrs Shelley's *Frankenstein*; even without a ghostly figure outlined on the tower, Sealsay seemed grimly forbidding.

By the time we arrived at the front door, the unsettled feeling in my stomach was no longer the result of my ghastly breakfast.

2

Sealsay House is a handsome enough building in the high Victorian manner. At the far end of each wing is a tall, square tower with battlements, intended to evoke the martial spirit of the days of Ivanhoe. On the flagpole on the west wing, a red pennant sometimes flies, with the Rundle arms etched in white; but today, in the pouring rain, the pole was bare. Atop each of the four corners of the east and west towers is a large stone dragon, rampant, carved by Italian craftsmen brought here for the purpose by Sir Josiah. Nothing, so far as I could see, had changed since my last visit. Even the ivy that clambered up the stone face of the centre of the house looked exactly as I remembered it.

'Don't you worry, darling,' I whispered to Jinny as the car drew up noisily on the gravel in front of the house, 'I'm sure that whatever's eating Colin, Iona will be fine.'

This was not one of my more reliable predictions.

Things began normally enough, though. Parsons, the butler, opened the door, dressed in his apron, ready to carry up our bags. His few remaining hairs were plastered firmly in a grey mass atop his bald pate. At the other end of his face, so to speak, there was an alarmingly luxuriant mousy-grey beard, whose effect was to underscore the relative glabrousness of his scalp. As usual, he tugged at his beard nervously from time to time as he spoke. 'Good afternoon, Sir Patrick, Lady Scott. Sir . . .' (this last addressed to Colin).

Jock brought our cases into the hall, while Parsons collected our raincoats. 'Might I hang these in the drying room for a period?' Parson's vaguely Midland accent, with its exaggerated consonants, and the occasional intrusion of a refined Scots vowel, all combined with an understated singsong intonation and a slight burr borrowed over the years from the islanders to produce a completely original effect. Since he had been with the family for only a dozen years, Jinny had never met him. I could see that, while I had prepared her for these vocal oddities, she was still having some difficulty in restraining a giggle.

There were signs of preparation for the forthcoming festivities. The huge carpet from the library, where the dancing would go on, was gathered in an enormous untidy roll in the corridor that led towards the kitchens; and there were dusty chairs arranged around the hall – obviously up from the cellar where they had languished since the last New Year – waiting, I suppose, to be cleaned off.

The hall itself is a cavernous Victorian affair, plainly meant to suggest the room at the heart of a great medieval house. Its walls are rather randomly endowed with coats of arms, antlers, and a couple of huge unprepossessing paintings of island scenery, painted by Maud Rundle in the 1890s. At the centre of each canvas was her husband, Sir Josiah, in a MacIver tartan, engaged in an improbable piscatorial feat. In the painting over the great fireplace with its enormous flaming fire, he was struggling to land a salmon the size of a new-born whale, somewhere in the stream that falls from Ben Moray and passes down between the home farm and Sealsay House. Colin told me that, so far as he knew, there had never been salmon in that stream, an entirely artificial affair created by Sir Josiah's landscape gardeners. Every Rundle I knew agreed that these paintings were ludicrous. But they were grandmother's (and, by now, great-grandmother's) and so they stayed.

Parsons disappeared with our coats and Colin shouted for Iona. She came from the drawing-room into the main hall to greet us, handsome as ever, in a comfortable tweed suit. As she came near, Colin mumbled, 'Hallo, darling, here we are, then.' But Iona affected not to hear. She walked straight past her husband, looking through him completely. It was as if he was a wraith, visible, for some reason, only to us. Her face, which had always been pale, was even more drained of colour. She had her hair cut tidily short. (I found myself wondering for a moment if there was a hairdresser on the island.) The whole effect was gamine. She looked like a defenceless urchin, scrubbed and tidied to meet the governors of the orphanage. More than anything else, she looked tired. This was not the Iona I remembered.

'Jinny, my dear, I'm so glad you could come. And Patrick; marvellous.' She offered her cheek for kissing. Iona was intent on being civil to us while ignoring her husband. 'You're in the Green Room, as usual, and Parsons will bring up your things as soon as he gets back. You must go up and change and then we shall have lunch.' Overlooking the tension between Iona and Colin, I made the best of the warmth of Iona's welcome, and breathed, as it were, an inward sigh of relief.

'Iona, I'm sure we could just wash down here and join you all almost at once,' Jinny said. 'It's rather after lunchtime and we wouldn't want to keep the others waiting any longer than we have to.'

Colin began to say what sounded like 'Good idea,' but was cut off by Iona. 'I've told Mary we shan't eat till half-past one, so there's plenty of time. Come and find us in the drawing-room, when you're ready. It's only family . . . and Emma Gale, of course . . . and she, like you two,' Iona added with an unnaturally sweet smile at Colin, 'is practically one of us.'

At this moment I chose to divert the conversation by remarking breezily, if irrelevantly, upon my many pleasant memories of Sealsay. This tactic had a surprising and unintended effect on Iona: she burst into tears and fled off down the corridor towards what I knew was her office. Colin muttered in embarrassment, 'I'm afraid Iona's not terribly well.'

'That, Colin, is an out-and-out lie.' Letitia's voice, the same voice I remembered down the years, aged a little, but still clear and strong, came from out of the library, followed in a moment by Letitia herself. Save for the greying of her braid, Letitia had not changed at all. 'Hallo, Patrick,' Letitia added in my direction. 'You have explained to your wife, I expect, that I don't speak to strangers. God, where did you get that dress – the Salvation Army?' she went on, as she surveyed Jinny.

'For Christ's sake, Letitia, do shut up,' Colin muttered, his irritability breaking through once again (this time with more cause). Letitia did not respond, gliding off towards the dining-room, her tall figure swathed, as always, in a long dark dress. 'Do hurry,' she added as she turned the corner in the corridor, 'we're all famished.'

Letitia's remark about Jinny's dress was more than discourteous: it was astonishingly off the mark. It will no doubt sound like the boast of a doting husband, but the fact is that Jinny has always had impeccable taste in clothing and she combines it with the capacity to look wonderful even after the sort of long, uncomfortable and wearisome journey that had brought us to Sealsay. It was as if Letitia had planned a nasty remark for Jinny's arrival ages ago and not bothered to adjust it to the evidence of her eyes. But then, I thought, Letitia is not exactly your English rose and her own clothing – in this case a vast shapeless flower-print frock in blacks and browns that looked as though it had seen a good three decades of wear – came off as eccentric at best.

Colin spoke again. His drawl was unnaturally calm. 'It's too bad of Letitia; she doesn't really mean these things she says. I'm afraid, Jinny, that she's in one of those moods where we shall all have to try and ignore her. I *am* so sorry.' The smile was charmingly apologetic, the tone sincere. His temper was back under control.

Virginia and I were soon rushing about the room changing out of our travelling clothes. Parsons had deposited our bags a few minutes after we had arrived, his manner deferential but utterly unrevealing as always. We tried to take stock.

'It's all a question of attitude,' Virginia began firmly when he left us. 'We must just set out to enjoy ourselves, whatever happens, and we shall infect the others with our *joie de vivre*.' The voice she adopted for this last phrase was that of Miss Jean Brodie – or rather of Maggie Smith as Miss Brodie 'in her prime' – and while the effect was comical, I took her point.

'Righty-oh,' I said. 'But just before we set about pretending that all is well, would you mind telling me what exactly I said to make Iona burst into tears and run off like that?'

'Really, Patrick, it's quite egomaniacal to think it had anything to do with you. Obviously she was upset when we got here.'

'Granted, oh wise one, but still I must have provided the occasion for that display.'

'Well, what you *said* was "I have so many wonderful memories of this house", and so, I suppose, her response meant that *her* wonderful feelings about this place are *only* memories. But never mind Iona. With her husband in that mood, any woman would be a bit edgy. What about your chum, Letitia?'

This was not the kindest way of phrasing the enquiry. I know that I had told Virginia endlessly how blissfully happy Colin and Iona were, and that Letitia would probably not speak to us, but sarcasm, on the order of 'your chum' said in that particular tone of voice, was not, I felt, warranted. In fact, I had been more surprised when Letitia had said hallo to me for the first time in her life than by anything else; and I was, frankly, at first at a loss to explain it. Not only had she greeted me, but she had gone on to utter more words in my presence than I had heard from her in the nearly five decades of our entire previous acquaintance. True, they were exactly the sort of unpleasant words that Gavin and his father had led me to expect. But it was the first time I had heard her say anything that was more offensive than it was odd.

Virginia's challenge however got the grey matter active and I found myself replying coldly, 'She's never said hallo to me before. So I expect she was just deliberately controverting what she knew I would have told you about her. She's rather inclined to that sort of thing.' And, as I listened to myself, I thought that sounded like the right explanation. Annoyed at Virginia and pleased with my own insight, I retired to the bathroom to attend to my tie.

Frazzled as our nerves were by the generally unpropitious turn of events, tension between the Scotts, while not yet of the spectacular level displayed by the Rundles upon our arrival, was, shall we say, building. So I suppose that when I returned to the bedroom and Jinny remarked that my neckwear did not exactly match my jacket I should have held my tongue and quietly exchanged my Clare College tie for another. 'Don't nag,' I said. 'It's quite bad enough without your nagging.' And I walked out into the corridor muttering, 'See you downstairs.'

I slammed our bedroom door behind me. A moment later, a small child, with a freckled face and an enormous mop of red hair, darted out from behind the end of a large armoire in the corridor and towards the stairs. 'Are you having a row?' the boy asked when he reached the top of the flight. And then, before I could think of an answer, he leapt on the banister and slid out of view.

'Out of the mouths of babes,' I muttered to myself. I had to return to the bedroom. 'I'm sorry, Virginia,' I said. 'But this is all very disturbing. I wish now we hadn't come. But since we *are* here, can I take you up on the offer to make the best of it? Pax. Let's try the Brodie line.'

'I'm not really a nag, darling; your tie simply looks extremely silly with that jacket. But if you *want* to look silly, I shall defend your appalling taste like a loyal wife.'

It did not seem necessary at this point to say anything. I changed my tie and kissed my wife and we set off down to lunch together, reconciled.

'Why is this the Green Room?' Jinny asked as we left it. 'Not a green thing in it.'

'Green was a friend of old Josiah Rundle's. This was where he stayed.'

'Ah. Perhaps in time it will become the Scott Room.'

'Not', I said, 'if we can expect any future visits to be like this one.' Virginia laughed.

As we approached the door to the drawing-room my beloved wife gave me the gentlest of pecks on the cheek and whispered, 'Fasten your seat belt.'

'I know, I know,' I said, 'we're in for a bumpy ride.'

When we entered the drawing-room, several pairs of eyes, a majority of them belonging to Rundles, turned towards us. To our left, as we entered, were two enormous windows, displaying the dismal vista of the lawns in a winter rainstorm. The rain was turning to sleet, but the thunder had quieted and there was only the occasional lightning flash far away to the south. The room itself was agreeably warm and its vast expanse of oak parquet reflected the splendid log fire blazing under the huge, hideous Victorian portrait of Sir Josiah Rundle (with its moderately pretentious title, 'The Laird of Sealsay', calligraphed on the brass plate beneath it). To the right of the fireplace stood an enormous Christmas tree – a fine, straight fir, laden with candles, and dressed with hundreds of glass and tin baubles –

a few pine needles scattered about the cloth beneath it. All in all, the drawing-room had as festive an aspect as you could have wished for. A little *joie de vivre* seemed utterly in order. This was not, apparently, Letitia's view, however: for, as we entered, she rose from the desk by the window, where she was writing, and walked grimly straight past us – without a word – out into the hall.

Colin and Iona were nowhere to be seen, and so Alistair, Colin's brother (who had celebrated his first birthday my first summer at Sealsay), took it upon himself to make us welcome. Like most of his family, Alistair had grown so used to his sister that he did not even think to apologise for her. 'Patrick . . . and you must be Virginia. I shan't say Patrick has told me so much about you, but I *do* feel as if I've known you for ages. Let me see, which of us do you two know?'

What was left of Alistair's reddish hair was now well-mixed with grey; but his spare frame seemed impervious to the advances of age. When he beamed at Virginia, it was with the air of one who had broken many a maiden's heart. His genial demeanour, which he'd had from his earliest youth, reminded me of the old Colin: friendly, comfortable, courteous, uncomplicated. And it was all the more striking because they looked so different. Colin's dark colouring, rimmed now with his mop of white hair, and Alistair, balding, with his red-headed Celtic looks.

In Alistair's case the Rundle charm had a professional overlay. He was MP for Kintyre, on the mainland, and the last twenty years of cultivating votes by chucking babies under the chin had given a slightly counterfeit air to his naturally pleasant manner. Alistair was an old-style Tory, inclined towards the politics of *noblesse oblige*, who had learned to appear more hardnosed and to conceal his wetter instincts, as the cool winds of Madam Thatcher's new vision blew across his party. I never knew how much politics really engaged Alistair's interest; he attended to the affairs of his party with an air of remote, if dutiful, obligation. Indeed, the general tone of his rare remarks about policy conveyed the impression that it would be indecent to betray too great an interest in such matters. What was important, his tone suggested, was to do one's duty by Queen and country. To *enjoy* politics, to take it too seriously: *that* would be a sign of depravity.

Alistair's wife, Marie-Hélène, who had been draped elegantly on the sofa to the left of the fireplace when we entered, deposited her sherry glass carefully on the mantelshelf as she rose to greet us. She was, as always, beautifully dressed. She wore an extremely handsome dark blue suit, a necklace of tiny, elegant pearls, and an elegant silk scarf draped over her shoulders. She would not have been out of place at a cocktail party in London; and yet she seemed so utterly relaxed in her clothes that no one could ever have thought she was overdressed.

I remembered the first time I had seen Marie-Hélène, years ago, one summer at Sealsay, when, as a teenager, she had been sent for the holidays to improve her already excellent English. Her father, Charles-André de Souillac, was an acquaintance of Colin's father, Sir Henry Rundle, and the old duke had followed the custom of his class in insisting that his children should learn English *in situ*. Meeting this extremely self-possessed thirteen-year-old, I had asked her politely, in the slow speech that naturally comes upon one when one is addressing foreigners, where she lived. 'Château Souillac, Souillac,' she had replied with a look of mild puzzlement, as if no one could be in serious doubt where a Souillac could come from. 'And you, Mr Scott,' she had continued in virtually unaccented English, 'where do *you* live?' That was a story I had told Virginia, and as Marie-Hélène approached us, my wife turned towards me, facing away from the others in the room, and pantomimed, 'Château Souillac, Souillac, I presume?'

'Hallo, Patrick. Virginia, lovely to meet you at last,' Marie-Hélène said, inviting me to kiss the air in the vicinity of first one and then the other of her elegantly powdered cheeks.

'We should begin with Emma,' Alistair said smoothly. 'Virginia, Emma Gale. Emma, Virginia Scott. Emma edits *Glitz*, a magazine she invented.'

'And Colin pays for it,' Emma added, laughing. 'Hallo.' As she shook my hand, her huge blue eyes gazing candidly into mine, I was almost compelled to take a step backwards, caught, as I was, between admiring her looks and being astonished by the energy she radiated. Emma shook her golden fringe prettily as she reached out to take my hand. As her hair rippled, it was as if it caught the firelight. (The pageboy haircut was, I am sure, designed for this delightful effect.) She was wearing blue jeans and a cream silk blouse, under a rather smart scarlet riding waistcoat, and a necklace of what looked like Chinese porcelain beads. The whole effect, as Jinny suggested to me later, was a sort of chic version of *Country Life*. When she turned her attentions to Jinny, I could see that even my unimpressionable wife was impressed.

Alistair continued with the introductions. It took a good while, and by the time he was finished it was time to go in to lunch.

As we crossed the hall, I was able to tell Alistair briskly I could answer a little legal question he had asked for my help with. If a look of annoyance crossed his face, it was so fleeting that I scarcely caught it. I wondered if he knew already that he could not, as I had discovered, do what he wanted or whether he merely thought discussing business over lunch was bad form. 'Splendid,' he said blandly, 'let's discuss it properly later.'

When we arrived in the dining-room, Colin and Iona were already standing at opposite ends of the long table, and Letitia was seated on Colin's left. 'Patrick,' Iona said brightly, tapping the chair to her right, 'come and keep me company, and Jinny, you sit next to the laird.' Everybody else disposed themselves around the table. I watched the family taking their places, adjusting their established patterns to us, the new arrivals.

One thing I could have predicted: Alistair sat next to Letitia, maintaining her custom of isolating herself from the rest of the world with Rundle men. When I first saw her, she had sat between her father and her brother; now, it was her two brothers – both of them, I reflected, older now than their father had been then. It occurred to me also as I glanced at her occasionally throughout the meal that the tremendous appetite she had displayed the first time I saw her was still very much in evidence. She was surprisingly slender for someone who ate so much.

Letitia's anti-social behaviour was par for the course. But the whole family was edgy. Iona was continuing to ignore Colin. Jessica, their middle daughter, the television actress, smiled a wry smile at me as she sat down, as if there was some secret that we shared. It was the sort of look that makes a chap check that he has his trousers properly done up.

Only Maria, Colin's youngest daughter, seemed relaxed, unaware of the general nervousness. She dumped the infant she was carrying on the chair between herself and Angela Horseman, the tall, black and extremely pregnant Jamaican woman who had been introduced as a friend of Jessica's. 'Just think,' she said cheerfully as the child began to wail gently, 'a year or so from now yours will be just about Oliver's age. Have you thought about names?'

'Well, we t'ought about Sappho and Vita,' Angela said with apparent seriousness; which produced giggles from Gavin and Jessica . . . which produced, in turn, from Maria a look of mild bewilderment.

'What interesting names,' she said blinking as if it would help her to follow what was happening. 'But would they do for a boy?'

'She's a girl,' Angela said, 'we already know dat. But I t'ink I could trus' a man call' Vita, don' you?'

Emma Gale had alighted on my right, and, since Marie-Hélène was next to her, I found myself helping the ladies on both sides of me into their seats. A most enviable position, I thought, between Iona, still a fine-looking woman, and the radiantly beautiful Emma, who couldn't have been more than thirty-five, almost incandescent with what old Josiah Rundle would probably have called 'animal magnetism'.

Conversation with Emma Gale was rather like fencing in a high wind on a tightrope. Not only was there a constant playful thrust and parry, but her pace was breathless and it required a good deal of concentration to keep up with her. 'So, Sir Patrick,' she began as if picking up a conversation started somewhere else a moment ago, the words gushing out at a speed somewhere close to Mach One, 'are you still constantly on the lookout for murder?'

'I'm afraid that once you get involved with one or two of

them, they tend to find you. Solve one and everyone thinks you can solve all the others.'

'And who *was* Jack the Ripper?'

'There you are, you see: one of my early failures.'

'Come on, Sir Patrick, you're not going to get me treating you like an ancient ruin. I saw the way you tackled the task of seating two women at a single bound. Have you ever seen my magazine?'

Since I had thought we were talking about my little sideline as a sleuth, it took me a moment to grasp that Emma might simply have chosen a new topic. Once this possibility occurred to me, I was able to respond with a belated and apologetic, 'I fear not.'

'Well, I'm not altogether surprised, since its market, as my advertisers would say, is rather less A than B with aspirations. Also, though I hate to drag the subject of age up again, we think of our readers as being largely between eighteen and forty. But we do have lots of riveting interviews: last month, for example, we persuaded Sting to interview the Lord Chancellor.'

'I know you are going to think me very ill informed, Miss Gale, but who exactly is—'

'The Lord Chancellor? The chief law officer of the Crown, which is something that you as a QC might be expected to know. Being a rock star, on the other hand, Sting isn't expected to know anything at all.'

'Now that I know who they both are, I am bound to say that I should have thought that it was the Lord Chancellor who needed the most persuasion.'

'I didn't persuade the Lord Chancellor. I persuaded his wife. By covering a ball in our pages.'

'Good thinking. Next time I have some ideas about law reform I shall try the same route.'

'But you cannot offer to cover a charity dance in *Glitz*.'

'I am sure the Lord Chancellor's lady has other needs.'

'None last month as pressing as this one.'

That topic covered, I left it to Emma to pick the next one, and she cheerfully obliged. 'Next month, we're getting Christian Barnard to talk to Benazir Bhutto about . . .'

As Emma began again I turned to smile at Iona, in the hopes of sharing with her the task of amusing the whirlwind to my right, and discovered that Iona's narrowed eyes were focused on Emma in a gaze that was frankly less than friendly. I raised my eyebrows in involuntary query and Iona realised I was looking at her. Her eyes dropped for a moment to her plate, and, as she looked up at me again, her face softened into an embarrassed smile. Emma fell silent as Iona opened her mouth slightly, as if to speak; and then Iona patted my sleeve gently with her delicate hand, all the while gazing over my shoulder distractedly at nothing in particular, and said not a word.

At this moment, Jonathan, Maria's husband, took the opportunity offered by the silence to draw us into his conversation with Joanna, the oldest of the Rundle girls. 'Iona, Joanna and I have decided that you really ought to put a jacuzzi in the conservatory.'

Joanna laughed her loud gleeful laugh and said, 'Mother, I decided no such thing. Jonathan wants every house in the country to end up like a villa in Hampstead, with all mod cons and no character. Trust an architect.'

'That', Emma said, 'is the last thing you should do, isn't it, Maria?' This remark unaccountably caused Colin to glare at Emma.

'I don't know what you mean,' Maria said, blushing. 'I trust Jonathan implicitly.'

'Splendid,' Emma said. And then she turned towards the laird and went on evenly, 'What, after all, is a marriage without trust?' It did not surprise me that Colin was once more nibbling nervously at his lower lip.

Iona rang the bell and Parsons (along with a thin young woman who seemed to be called Trish) cleared the table for the pudding. Iona's hands were shaking visibly, and she was alarmingly pale. 'Would you all excuse me,' she said, her voice quavering. 'I'm afraid that I'm not feeling at all well.' The table fell silent as she hurried out of the room. Colin shot Emma an angry and reproving glance, and scowled as he followed his wife out of the room.

Letitia had been sitting silently between her brothers, exclusively attentive, as always, to her food. Now she spoke for the first time since the meal began: 'Let's see if my brother can sort that one out. Magazines. Hah!'

Everyone resolutely pretended that nothing had been said. I wished I had the vaguest notion of what was going on.

It should not go unremarked that luncheon was irreproachable; the '64 Beychevelle that Colin had brought up from the cellar was a most excellent accompaniment to the steak-and-kidney pie; and the lemon pudding that followed, with its sweet-sour citrus taste, was remarkably complemented by a well-chilled Beaumes-de-Venise. The standards of the house had *not* declined. When Alistair, who had taken charge, offered us seconds, I avoided Jinny's eye, which I am sure was casting sharp darts of disapproval, and volunteered to help avoid waste. Even Emma's enthusiasm for conversation had paled with the departure of both our hosts, and so I did my best to enjoy the rest of this excellent meal without distractions.

Angela announced as the meal came to an end that she was going up 'to give my baby a res'' and Jessica accompanied her out of the room. Joanna rose and grasped the hand of her taciturn husband, Christopher. 'I think Christopher and I are going to walk up Ben Moray.'

Alistair asked Marie-Hélène if she would like to join them. 'Why not? The wever 'as cleared a little.' (Marie-Hélène's French accent reappears from time to time, unprompted by anything obvious. Jinny has a theory that the precipitating factor is stress. If that was so on this occasion, it was the only sign of it. Marie-Hélène remained smoothly poised throughout our rather extraordinary luncheon.)

Christopher and Joanna greeted the news that Uncle Alistair and his wife were to join them with a display of less than unalloyed pleasure. They were in a somewhat unsociable frame of mind. They had sat side by side during lunch, absorbed from the start in conversation with each other, manifestly delighted by each other's company, holding hands under the table and rubbing noses from time to time. (It was an unedifying spectacle and I wondered why Colin and Iona permitted it. This sort of thing is, surely, mildly disturbing in a couple both of whom are approaching forty.)

Alistair, however, was oblivious to the effect of his having invited himself along with them and responded only with,

'Good. By the back door in ten minutes in raincoats and wellingtons,' as he marched his wife to the doorway. There, he waited for Jinny and me to join him and ushered us through, taking the opportunity to suggest to me that we have a meeting at about five, 'after everyone's settled down for tea in the drawing-room.'

Jinny and I walked across the hall back to the drawing-room with Gavin and Emma and we were followed by Jonathan and Maria.

'Let's see,' Gavin said. 'Who haven't you seen yet? Joanna and Christopher have a beastly eight-year-old called Justin, who's with his nanny, Monica, somewhere. The baby, as you will have gathered, is Oliver, and she's got two more, Marietta and Colin, who aren't much older and who come with a Swedish au pair.'

'Marietta is three and Colin's four,' Maria said firmly, 'Justin is *not* beastly and Marit is Norwegian. Really, Virginia, it's best to ignore everything Gavin says.'

'I know,' Jinny replied evenly, 'I've been ignoring everything he says for years.'

As she spoke, I noticed Letitia disappearing from view down the corridor towards the kitchen and the household offices. Being Letitia, she did not announce any intentions or bid any farewells. That was entirely in character. But there was, as it turned out, another reason: she would hardly have wanted me to know that she had plans to make sure she never saw us again.

3

When we arrived at the coffee tray, Maria said, 'I'll be mother' – a remark that was somewhat undercut by the gesture of handing the baby firmly over at the very same moment to his father. 'Coffee, Lady Scott?' And when Jinny nodded, she went on, 'Milk? Sugar? It's decaffeinated, of course, we don't have real coffee in the house ever.' Maria proceeded in this way, repeating mechanically the same formula and occupying several minutes getting cups poured for each of us, except Gavin, who had walked over to the drinks table and poured himself a hefty dose of Laphroaig. That done, he turned around, to mouth the words 'Coffee? Sugar? Tea?' rather unkindly behind Maria's back as she finally offered a cup to Jonathan.

Virginia took me off for a moment, once we both had coffee in hand, guiding me towards the windows nearest the door and furthest from the gathering. My good wife affected to point to something far away beyond the lawns, somewhere between the sodden grass and the brightening horizon. She spoke quietly. 'I'm going to take Gavin off for a walk later and find out what on earth is going on. I want him to myself, so when it comes up, say you're going to do some reading or something.' Then she spoke more loudly, 'Lovely, isn't it, darling; the light on the hillside. I can see why the others wanted to go walking in the hills. I'm so glad that beastly storm has passed.'

We returned to the company and it became clear pretty quickly that Jonathan was engaged in an unreciprocated attempt at flirtation with Emma. Maria hovered with her infant son once more in her arms, interjecting the odd irrelevant remark into their conversation; and Gavin smirked occasionally at Emma from his place on the sofa, behind Jonathan and Maria, browsing through a copy of yesterday's *Times* that had presumably come over on the boat with us.

As we re-entered the group, Jonathan was saying, 'That piece you had on postmodern architecture by Fred Jameson was just terrific.' This was not, I felt, a topic on which I had much to contribute and so I found myself attending to what Desmond Morris and his kind call 'body language'. Jonathan addressed Emma from very close, looking down a couple of inches from his five foot and ten or so inches into her unblinking eyes. Rather than retreating, she managed to indicate by a certain tension in her posture that she did not care for this oppressive closeness. It worked. As she replied, he moved back in a series of small steps, each one prompted by some particular point of emphasis in her reply. Plainly, Emma was the boss.

'Ah, you thought so,' she began sceptically, as if it was an interesting but remote possibility that an intelligent person could hold so ludicrous an opinion. Jonathan took his first tiny step backwards and she continued, 'I have never been able to grasp why Fred thinks everything in the world has to have something to do with late capitalism. What is capitalism late *for*, exactly, do you think?' Step. 'That sort of talk always makes me think of the White Rabbit dashing about with his fob-watch out, desperately trying to find the Mad Hatter's tea-party. You know – "I'm late, I'm late for a very important date."' Emma sang these words in a pleasing voice and forced Jonathan back a further pace. The whole performance was quite riveting. 'Perhaps *that's* what capitalism is late for: tea at the Jamesons'? Do you think?'

'Some people think Jonathan's work is rather postmodern,' Maria observed vaguely. 'But I've never really understood what it meant.'

'Don't worry, love.' Emma chucked baby Oliver under the chin as she addressed his mother. 'I expect we shall have to wait for Oliver to grow up and tell us *all* what it means. And by then, it will be too late, and we shall be beyond postmodernity. Life these days is just one damn post after another.'

Jonathan affected to find this last remark hilarious, until Emma stared him into silence. 'Heigh-ho,' she said finally, after knocking back the dregs of her coffee, 'time, I think, for a siesta.' Miss Gale pantomimed a grand departure as she swept out of the room.

We heard the sound of muffled apologies as she passed out of sight, and it was clear that she had bumped into someone. It was a small dark-haired girl, in her late teens, wearing what looked like overalls. She had two children in tow.

'This', said Jonathan, addressing Virginia and myself, 'is Marit, who looks after our children. The big fellow is Colin – wee Colin we call him up here – and the pretty miss is Marietta. How are you two lovelies?' The children were plainly not up to yet another set of adults, and they rushed to their mother's ample skirts. 'Colin, Marietta, come and say hallo to Sir Patrick and Lady Scott.'

'I'm sure we shall have plenty of time to get to know each other later,' Virginia said when the children continued to hover reluctantly at their mother's side, 'but I think that Gavin is going to show me some of the secrets of the isle. We are planning a less demanding walk than the one up ben and down glen that your kinsfolk have undertaken. Will you come along too, Patrick?'

'I don't think so, my love. I have some reading that I must do. The Landsdowne business, still.' Life is so much easier when you know what you are expected to say.

Gavin followed Virginia and me out into the hall and I waved them on their way. As they set off together I heard him say, 'My dear Jinny, will you ever speak to me again now you have met all my wretched sisters and my strange aunt and tyrannical uncle and all their dreadful hangers-on?'

Jinny was off to pump Gavin, the only Rundle she knew well, about the warning signals being given off by several of our company. But one did not need a particularly sophisticated radar to identify one major source. It was quite obvious, from the hostility I had briefly glanced in Iona's eyes, that Miss Gale of *Glitz* magazine had diverted Colin somewhat from the marital straight and narrow. Perhaps Iona had recently raised her suspicions with her husband. That would account for Colin's frayed nerves and explain Iona's coolness towards him. It would also account, at least in part, for the breathless reassuring to suppose that underneath her steely exterior, Miss (or, as I am sure she would rather I said, Ms) Gale was feeling as anxious as she made the rest of us feel.

But there were many more oddities for Jinny to decipher. Almost everyone was behaving peculiarly. Letitia had been uncharacteristically loquacious in the morning: and her one remark at lunchtime was more than she had ever said at table in my hearing before. Gavin's normal flow of charm was hardly in evidence. Alistair had been less than civil when I brought up the trust business he had asked me to investigate, and then, to top it all off, Iona had suddenly shot off like a frightened rabbit during lunch. It was as if Sealsay House had been invaded by demons; tiresome and childish demons, perhaps, more imps than devils, but certainly troublesome enough to bode ill for our holiday. If there had been a boat to take us back to the mainland, I think we would have made our excuses and run off. But we were stuck for a while. On the whole, a rest away from the

Rundle roller-coaster, in the quiet of our room, seemed the best of my few available options. 'Appropriate enough', I thought, 'that this is the Green Room. Here I can relax and draw strength for when I next step out into the Sealsay drama.'

I removed my jacket and tie, slipped off my shoes, and lay back on the bed. In an access of diligence, I actually had brought along the briefs for the dreaded Landsdowne affair – an entirely unnecessary waste of legal time and talent that could have been resolved in an instant if old Landsdowne had taken legal advice about his testamentary dispositions or the young Landsdownes had discovered that it was possible for brothers to be on speaking terms. The case had been boring our chambers for seven or eight months and I frankly had little stomach for it at the moment. Lunch had started late and it was now a little after three o'clock. I must have fallen asleep almost at once.

Colin and Iona stand solemnly in long white robes, his hair blowing wildly in the high wind. We are at the cliff top. Their children – Maria (carrying her baby), Joanna and Jessica, all three in the same white robes, accompanied by Gavin in a bow tie and white dinner jacket and trousers – are standing behind them. They are chanting something, but I cannot make out the words. Jinny and I are standing side by side, in a vast iron cauldron, over a roaring fire. The water is bubbling, and we should be hot, but I feel nothing physical: I am petrified, not by the prospect of boiling to death, but by the almost religious intensity with which the Rundles are singing. I know that, whatever the words are – Gaelic, perhaps? – they are cursing us. Colin approaches and pours a mixture of herbs into the cauldron, and Maria's voice rises above the weird song: 'Not too much caffeine, we don't allow caffeine in the house.' In the world of the dream this is not absurd. It is terrifying: I know, above all, that Jinny and I are in danger. The Rundles want us dead.

I awoke shivering from this strange dream. I had been asleep for about an hour. The winds had quietened, but they were making enough noise to swamp all the other sounds of the house. I could not shake the aura of danger that the dream had created: I felt a vague sense of threat from the house itself, as if the hostility I had imagined was oozing through the walls. And I was anxious about Jinny, even though I had no real reason to think she was in peril. I got up and looked out of the window, hoping to catch a glimpse of her returning from the hills, but it was too dark to see very much. I went to the bathroom and washed my face. 'You're being ridiculous,' I said to the nervous-looking chap in the mirror. 'Pull yourself together.' But I knew I would not be able to relax fully until Jinny was back and I was sure she was safe. 'Irrational.' I said the word four or five times: it was as soothing as saying a rosary. Gradually, I convinced myself that my anxieties were groundless.

Still, when Jinny had not returned half an hour later I was beginning to worry again. And then I heard urgent steps coming along the corridor towards the room. I knew that they were Jinny's and something about the sound of her tread made me uneasy. I walked swiftly across the room and opened the door to meet her.

When Virginia arrived, the look on her face confirmed my forebodings. She was very pale and had obviously been running, for she was still out of breath. And she had been crying. She hurled herself into my arms and I held her for a moment before either of us spoke. I wondered what on earth could have happened, but I knew I must wait for her to speak. Between sobs, she bgan to describe her walk.

'Oh Patrick. It's so awful.' She sobbed again. 'We were walking on the cliff top. And Letitia.' She could not go on. I gathered her tighter in my arms and kissed her brow. She took a couple of deep breaths and then spoke again quietly. 'She's . . . she's been swept out to sea.' Jinny paused for a moment and then looked up tearfully into my eyes. 'Patrick, she killed herself.'

We sat down together on the bed, Jinny's head on my shoulder, looking bleakly at the darkened window. She was about to begin to explain what had happened when there was a firm knock on the door.

'Come in.'

It was Gavin. 'Patrick.' He paused. 'Jinny, are you all right? I've phoned the coastguard and the police on the mainland. Papa is off to get out the boats. Mother insisted on going along. But it'll take a good half-hour to get from the harbour to the

Moray cliffs. I'm afraid there's not much chance of finding her. The weather's cleared but the seas are still pretty rough.'

From Gavin and Jinny I pieced together what had happened. They had walked uphill in the sunlight after the storm along a path that winds its leisurely way up to a high, blue lake, several hundred feet above the house, and then, around a hill, towards the cliffs that face the Atlantic on the island's other shore. From there they could have walked up to the ruined tower at the peak of Ben Moray. It's a long and beautiful walk. As they reached the cliffs, Gavin thought he saw his aunt a quarter of a mile ahead of them and shouted out her name. But there was still enough of a wind to carry his voice back to him and she did not respond; and so he ran a little ahead of Virginia and shouted again when he got closer. This time she turned and looked towards him and then, without ever replying by word or gesture, turned and launched herself off the cliff.

'She did what?'

'She just jumped over the cliff,' Jinny said hopelessly.

'I saw her body below on the rocks, and then she was washed out to sea.' Gavin's voice was hushed.

'By the time I arrived by Gavin at the cliff's edge, there was no sign of her. It was as if she had never existed.'

We were all still for a moment. Gavin, tense and sombre; Jinny, calmer now, her breath recovered, looking beautiful and sad. Each of us alone with our thoughts. The darkness had descended as we spoke. The wind had died down. The house was eerily quiet.

Gavin coughed edgily and excused himself. As he left, he told us that everyone would be gathering soon in the drawing-room for tea. 'I don't suppose anyone but the children will want to eat,' he said glumly as he closed the door behind him.

Jinny finished her part of the story. She had told Gavin to run back down to the house with the news and sat for a few minutes gazing intently out to sea, scanning, too, the rocks beneath her, for any sign of Letitia. Then, convinced there was nothing more to be done at the cliff's edge, she had come back down, and found herself, as she approached the house, running across the lawn with tears in her eyes.

'It was almost as if she was waiting for someone to watch her go.' Jinny paused for a moment, as if awaiting a response.

When I said nothing, she went on in her stillest, smallest voice. 'Oh Patrick, she was so horrid when we arrived. I'm afraid I rather took against her. But she must have been very troubled, very sad to do what she did. I feel awful for thinking ill of her.'

'Letitia has spent her whole life making people dislike her. You mustn't feel guilty.' I found myself repeating Gavin's formulation, echoing involuntarily his intonation. '*Nobody* liked Letitia.' Sitting there on the bed with my wife in my arms, watching the darkening sky, I was overcome with remorse as well. And also with a great sense of loss. It was, I felt, just terribly, terribly sad that I had understood nothing of this woman I had known almost all my adult life. And, like Jinny, I wondered what had driven her to this desperate leave-taking.

'I think', I said, 'that we should go down and wait for news with the others.'

Contrary to Gavin's prognostications there were no munching children in the drawing-room. 'We've packed all the children off to the nursery,' Maria said, 'with Marit and Monica. It's a great treat for them to have tea in here between Christmas and New Year. It's a custom Granny started . . .' She paused reflectively. 'I suppose it gave the servants a little less to do. I remember being so excited as a child. Uncle Ali, do you remember . . .' She trailed off. The glares of her kinsfolk suggested that, just at *this* moment, they did not totally relish her reminiscences of childhood teas. 'Oh, I say, I'm sorry. It's all so nervous-making.'

It was hard not to agree.

Apart from Colin and Iona, and Jessica's friend, Angela, all the adults in our party were present. Virginia and I sat side by side on – or rather in – the huge sofa that faced the fireplace, sipping tea. Joanna and Christopher had drawn two chairs together in a corner, under the amused surveillance of Emma Gale, who eyed them periodically. She was making notes on a sheaf of what looked to me like proofs, tapping energetically with her long red nails on the table where she sat. Alistair stood by the writing desk, staring imploringly at the phone, as though convinced that it would deliver up his sister's fate if he begged it with sufficient urgency. Gavin, as usual, was nursing a glass of whisky. Plainly, he was getting a start on the Hogmanay season.

A few moments into the silence after Maria's withdrawal from conversation, Marie-Hélène got up from her seat by one of the windows and walked across to her husband, touching him gently on the arm. 'Come on, Ali,' she murmured, 'sit down. It may be a long wait.' Alistair turned distractedly towards his wife, and then drew his left hand through his thinning hair and slumped on to the seat at the writing desk.

Jessica was the next to speak. 'Look here,' she said firmly, 'it's no good our sitting about like this and getting into a great funk. We don't know yet that she didn't simply dive into the water and get swept out to sea. She's always been a strong swimmer. She may just have meant to scare us all. That would be typical of our Aunt Letty.'

'You know very well that she hated that name,' Alistair said. 'I don't think that it is in the best taste to use it now.'

'Really, Uncle Ali.' Gavin's tone was mocking. 'We don't have to pretend we *liked* the old thing.' He turned to Jessica. 'Jess. I was there. She didn't dive, she jumped. And where she jumped, she would have landed on the rocks and *then* been swept out to sea. There isn't the slightest chance that she survived. And, frankly, I don't think there's much chance we'll find the body any time soon. Probably be washed up somewhere north of Oban.' He turned to the drinks tray and refreshed his glass.

'Don't be morbid,' Marie-Hélène said, with more firmness than anger. She did not turn towards us; she was watching her husband's face contorted in grief. If Gavin was right, even Alistair did not like his sister Letitia. I am that rare thing, a Catholic only child, and so I know little of such fraternal feelings. But I suppose you do not have to like a sister to feel her loss. He had, after all, known her literally for the whole of his life.

'She was frightfully generous, Letitia, wasn't she?' Maria said. 'I mean she always gave one such super Christmas presents.'

'You may have liked those books she always gave you, but I

got a pair of black nylon socks, this year,' Gavin said. 'Too small. And I distinctly saw Marie-Hélène shudder when Alistair opened his present.'

Marie-Hélène blushed mildly. 'It is just that I don't 'appen to like Brut.'

'A men's aftershave,' Gavin glossed helpfully.

'Well, she doesn't . . . she didn't know a great deal of the world,' Maria said.

'She was rather like a nun, living in a nunnery all 'er life, not quite sensitive of the changes in the world outside,' Marie-Hélène carried on Maria's theme.

'Which is no doubt why she gave Jessica a book on finding a man,' Gavin remarked, rather tactlessly, I thought.

'Do shut up, Gav.' Jessica was obviously not in the mood for a fraternal dig in the ribs.

'I don't think she was much like a nun, Marie-Hélène.' Emma Gale's voice was louder than the others and it commanded everyone's attention. Jinny had been peering into the fireplace, with a look I know very well (a look that means she is thinking up new adventures for her character, Bella Sharpe). But even she now turned her attention to Emma. 'Your sister-in-law certainly read *Glitz* from cover to cover.'

'Well, she was always very interested in Colin's projects,' Alistair replied.

'Indeed. She was so interested she wrote me long, long letters about how awful the magazine was. And I'd say that the woman who wrote those letters read enough other magazines to know that Brut was not so much the *crème de la crème* as the curdled milk of gentlemen's fragrances.'

'I'm sure she was trying to be kind,' Alistair said loyally. 'Whatever else you say about Letitia, family came first for her.' This comment silenced the others; I doubt it convinced them. There was a small explosion from a log in the grate, and Gavin walked over to investigate, and began poking the fire.

'Well,' Jessica said, 'if there's not likely to be any news soon, I'm going to go up and see how Angela's doing. She's not been feeling too good. Fetch me if there's any news.'

She closed the drawing-room door firmly behind her and the noise roused Joanna and Christopher. 'Isn't there something useful we can do?' Christopher asked the assembled company.

'No, dear Kit, I'm afraid not,' Gavin said drily.

'Perhaps, darling, we should go and talk to Justin now that he's had his tea. Ever since I told him about Letitia, he's been worrying about whether she'll come back to haunt him. I'm afraid the poor dear is terribly upset.'

'Joanna, love,' Gavin continued, 'your son absolutely detested Aunt Letitia. She told him what she thought of him. I should think that for an eight-year-old nothing could be more delightful than the death of a hated great-aunt.'

'He's always been a little bit afraid of the dark. He's only been sleeping alone for the last few months,' Christopher said.

'Guilty conscience, if you ask me.' Gavin tittered.

This last remark finally roused Alistair from his gloomy silence. 'I really do think that you should drink a little less, Gavin. It might help you to keep a civil tongue in your head. The next few hours will be trying enough without family bickering. I'm sorry, Patrick, Virginia, that my family is behaving so badly. But', he went on in the tones of a politician addressing a news conference, 'we have, as you can imagine, been somewhat upset by the news.' I distinctly heard the whispered words 'pompous ass' released from the pursed lips of Lady Scott. I prayed that, since those lovely lips were a mere six inches from my ear and the fire was crackling nicely in the grate, these words were heard – as they were intended to be heard – only by me. It was time for us, too, to make our excuses.

'I'm afraid I rather overslept this afternoon, so I think I ought to get a little fresh air. Virginia, will you keep me company?'

'Of course, darling.'

'We'll forgather here at about a quarter to eight,' Alistair said as we left. 'Marie-Hélène has asked Mary to prepare a very light meal. I don't suppose we shall be dressing for dinner,' he added vaguely.

'I don't suppose we shall be *eating* dinner,' Virginia murmured as we shut the door behind us. 'Why are all politicians so smarmy? Even when they have real feelings, they seem to be unable to keep away from unctuous formality. I'd say Alistair gave new meaning to the idea of extreme unction.'

'I don't think that's terribly fair to Alistair, darling. He's obviously very upset.'

'Odd that,' Virginia went on. 'Gavin was telling me this

afternoon that Alistair absolutely loathes Letitia. Always has. But recently he has really got it in for her. A few weeks ago he discovered that she has been writing a book about the family. She was going to say that her father had . . . oh, what's the right word, "interfered with her" sounds so euphemistic . . . molested her, you know. Not good for lovely Uncle Ali's parliamentary career.'

This rather stunning intelligence stopped me in my tracks. I stood still, looking out of the hall window into the stormy landscape outside; Virginia stopped, too, at my side. I found it difficult to believe either that old Sir Henry would have made advances to his daughter or that she would suddenly have been gripped by the urge to write about it. 'Did Gavin believe Letitia's allegation?' I asked, after a while.

'He seemed to.'

'He didn't really know his grandfather. I wonder if Alistair believed it. Or Colin.'

'Gavin didn't say anything about that, but I rather assume that he would have mentioned it if Alistair thought Letitia was lying. He didn't say that Colin knew about all this. Just Alistair.'

'It's funny,' I went on, 'I'd never have thought of Letitia as a writer.' We set off again down the corridor to fetch our coats, walking in single file because so much of the space was taken up by the library carpet.

'That's the other curious thing he told me. Gavin says that Letitia had quite a writing career. He told me he found out quite by accident a year or so ago when he was in Horace Strachan's office in Edinburgh. He's Gavin's trustee and Letitia's. I gather he inherited the Rundles from his grandfather. Letitia's only trips off the island are . . . were . . . to see Mr Strachan every once in a long while. Gavin claimed to have chanced upon a letter to the tax people on the advocate's desk identifying Daphne Lomond, the pseudonymous author of *Highland Fling* and *The Lass Within his Arms*, as Letitia Rundle.'

'I realise that our opinions of Gavin do not entirely coincide, my love, but the chances of his having found out by accident are not very good. Horace Strachan was presumably instructed to keep this from the family. He'd hardly have left letters strewn about his office.'

'*My* opinion of Gavin is that he is an amusing young man with rather fewer scruples than one would like. *Yours* is that he is an unscrupulous bounder. We disagree only about whether he is amusing. Naturally, I didn't believe his story about how he found out for a minute. But however he found out, you must admit it's rather riveting. I don't suppose there are any of them about.'

'I rather doubt that Colin and Iona would have acquired a book called *Highland Fling*, unless it was a dance manual.'

By now we had reached the coat room and were donning our wellingtons and overcoats. Sealsay sits in the Gulf Stream – there are palm trees in the garden – but at the turn of the year in this season of storms it can be cold, windy and very, very wet. As we stepped out of the front door on to the gravel, a gust of wind lashed at us. But the winds had cleared the clouds and the moon was rising. It was a lovely winter's night.

When we returned about twenty minutes later from a brisk stroll up and down the drive, the house looked warm and welcoming. In the moonlight, the craggy, grey stone shimmered with an almost purple cast. The lights in the drawing-room and the main part of the house twinkled merrily, and there was a single bright light in a window on the west tower over the nursery, a welcoming beacon that would have been visible for miles. As we entered, the grandfather clock in the main hall struck the half-hour. It was six thirty. We set off down the corridor towards the coat room and found Justin – the ill-mannered child I had met on the landing the day before – squatting on the floor, his mop of red hair drooping untidily over a cat. The boy looked up guiltily when we came in and scuttled out towards the kitchen. The animal disappeared under the serried ranks of coats, and when Jinny bent down and spoke to him tenderly, he came out to run his nose against her hand. The fur on the scruff of his neck was stiff with what looked like chewing gum.

'Horrid child,' Jinny said.

*

We were making our way towards the stairs when the telephone rang. We looked at each other and then made instead for the drawing-room. Perhaps there would be some news.

Alistair was on the telephone talking quietly when we entered. He was the centre of a rapt circle of watchers. Marie-Hélène stood behind him, her hands again resting gently on his shoulders. Jessica and Angela had rejoined the company, but Joanna and Christopher were presumably still with their son in the nursery. Gavin was at the fireplace, steadying himself with a hand on the mantelshelf, obviously even less sober than he had been when we left.

Alistair replaced the receiver in its cradle. 'That was Horace Strachan,' he said. 'Colin phoned him to ask whether there was anything we needed to do except notify the police and the coastguard. He's coming over tomorrow on the ferry. It's the last boat of the year: the next one's not till Tuesday. It seems they're taking an extra day off because New Year's Day falls on a Sunday.'

'What about the police? Are they going to send someone?' Emma asked.

'Actually, no.' Alistair summarised the situation briskly. 'There's no suspicion of foul play. It's up to the coastguard to search. And the coroner will come over from Oban in a week or so with a constable to collect evidence for the inquest. I mean, there isn't a body, is there? And when we do find her . . . if we do . . . Paul Crawford is perfectly capable of filling out a death certificate. The cause of death won't take much forensic skill.'

'I don't know, that seems rather odd to me. Don't the police want to make sure that we're telling the truth? I mean for all they know, she could have been pushed over a cliff,' Emma went on.

'Are you making an accusation, Miss Gale?' Gavin's muted tone didn't mask a hysterical undercurrent. As usual, it was difficult to tell whether he was being entirely ironic or totally serious. 'Did I creep up on my beastly aunt with the lovely Lady Scott and push her over the edge? What you have, dear Emma, are the nasty suspicious gutter instincts of a journalist. The laird has told them that his dotty sister committed suicide. Why on earth should they imagine that anything criminal was going on?' His manners were deteriorating with each glass of whisky.

'You know perfectly well that I was suggesting no such thing,' Emma said quietly. Her calm tone was as hostile as Gavin's, but it carried more menace. I wouldn't like to get on the wrong side of Miss Gale.

I thought it might help to weigh in at this point myself, using what Jinny calls my summing-up voice. 'The fact is, if tomorrow's the last boat of the year, no self-respecting Scots constable would take kindly to being sent off to Sealsay for nearly a week to collect two statements from Gavin and Jinny saying they saw Letitia jump off a cliff. It really can wait. No witnesses will be going anywhere. I don't think it's unreasonable, Miss Gale. I shouldn't worry about it.'

'It is so sweet of 'orace to come all this way in the middle of 'is 'olidays,' Marie-Hélène observed. 'I suppose 'is wife will be coming, too. What is 'er name? Linda?'

'He didn't say so,' Alistair replied. 'But I suppose we should ask Parsons to get a double room ready.'

''Orace is quite capable of filling a double room all by himself,' Gavin said, aping Marie-Hélène's accent. His uncle strode angrily over towards him and pushed the electric bell beside the fireplace, his hand passing just to the right of Gavin's left shoulder in a threatening gesture as he did so. I couldn't hear everything he growled in his nephew's ear. But we all heard the final: 'For God's sake, Gavin, pull yourself together.'

Not long after Parsons had left with the information that the Edinburgh advocate would be needing his room tomorrow – the Strachan Room, it was called, because his grandfather had always stayed there – the telephone rang again. This time it was Colin. They had landed back in the harbour, after an uncomfortable trip around the island. There was no sign of Letitia in the sea near the Moray cliffs; no sign of her body on the rocks. News of her fall had spread from the bar of the Sealsay Hotel and a dozen of the men had set off to spend the night scouring the beaches. Colin and Iona were coming home.

Once Alistair rang off, Emma asked if she might use the phone, 'now that Colin's call has come through.'

'Of course,' Alistair said. 'Why don't you use the telephone in the library?'

'Have to call in some changes,' Emma said by way of explanation, waving her galleys. It struck me as extraordinary to keep people in a magazine office on the twenty-ninth of December. I do not think I could recommend Emma Gale as an employer.

It will come as no great surprise that our dinner conversation was more than moderately dull. Nobody ate very much. Colin tried to tell anecdotes about one of his trips up the Amazon or into Sarawak. At one point, I heard him explaining to Jinny how the Amerindians taught their children to fish. At another, he said to the table, 'Extraordinary thing about the Indians is, they live in just a few hundred feet on either side of the river. If you take 'em deeper into the forest than that, they're as lost as the next man. That's why they carry those thumping sticks . . . to bang hollow trees. Means they're lost.' Normally, Colin's tales were sufficient to keep any party lively. This evening they seemed rather less than thrilling. His heart was not in it.

When the ladies retired to the drawing-room, the port circulated without takers, and Colin suggested we join them almost immediately. No one took coffee and within about ten minutes people began to make their good-nights. Virginia and I expressed our sympathy to Colin and Iona as we set off for bed. 'I am *so* sorry, Colin,' Jinny said. And then she hugged Iona gently and added, 'If there's anything we can do . . .' Iona stifled a sob and held on to her for a moment. Then she pulled herself erect. 'We shall pull through. Poor Letitia.' And her face was suddenly very strong and brave.

Virginia took a long luxurious bath in the great Victorian tub of the Green Room, and came out looking sleepy but refreshed. 'I mentioned Justin's cat-loving *jeu d'esprit* to Joanna over dinner, but she wouldn't hear a word against him. She just said he adored the cats and that he couldn't possibly have stuck the stuff in his fur. No wonder he's such a spoiled brat.' I looked up and mumbled agreement distractedly. Jinny has strong views on child-rearing, which I do not controvert.

I had been lying in bed ruminating, making the odd note on the back of a large envelope I had brought from the office. A thought was crystallising in my head. I gazed thoughtfully at my wife. 'Jinny, darling. You look ravishing.'

'Thank you, my sweet.' The kiss she planted on my forehead was soft, so soft, and the aroma of English lavender was mildly distracting. But I had some questions to ask Virginia and I was wondering how to frame them without giving offence.

'Nice boy, Gavin,' I began.

'Rubbish, Patrick. He's not nice at all.'

'Well, interesting.'

'That's better.'

'And certainly very plausible, I should think. Since Colin is financing his forays into art-dealing, he must need that. Very important in his business to be plausible. There he is in that gallery in Kensington Church Street trying to persuade people that those paintings are worth what he's asking. People spending great sums on paintings wouldn't want to deal with someone untrustworthy.'

'Patrick, why don't you say what you're thinking?'

'Was it his idea or yours that you should walk together this afternoon?'

'Actually, I think he suggested it over lunch. He's been very solicitous ever since I arrived . . . which is nice for me, since I barely know the others.'

'Well, my love, I assume that Gavin mentioned the incest business before you came upon Letitia.'

'Yes, of course. We wouldn't have been gossiping about her writing habits *after* she died. Though, come to think of it . . .'

'Let me guess. As you stood there looking out to sea, a thought occurred to young Gavin. Perhaps Aunt Letitia had been driven to her death as she relived the terrible experiences at the hands of her depraved father.'

Virginia said nothing for a moment. Then she went on in a tone I could only describe as prim. 'As it happens, Patrick, what he said was, "She must have suffered terribly." And I just gawped at him, because I didn't know what he meant. So, then, he added, "All these years, living with such a terrible secret."'

'Well, as I said, he's a plausible fellow.'

And my wife said, 'Darling, you have an awfully suspicious mind.'

'It's been a very tiring day. I think we should turn in.'

'Come on, Patrick, you can't leave it at that.'

'Overcome with anguish from a wrong done to her sixty years ago, Letitia leaps over the cliffs, crashes to her death on the rocks, and is whisked out to sea. There's something I don't like about the whole business.'

'Really, Patrick, I don't suppose Letitia enjoyed it much, either.'

'Well,' I said, 'let's just hope the body turns up soon.'

And with that we set about falling asleep. It had been a long and exhausting day and we were both in need of a good night's rest.

It was not to be. When we woke again it was about three in the morning, as I discovered from glancing bleary-eyed at my watch.

'What an earth was that?' Virginia asked. 'It sounded like a child screaming outside our door.'

'It could have been the wind,' I said without much conviction. I went over to the window and opened the curtains. The weather had worsened again in the few hours we had been asleep and the wind was making a frightful racket in the trees and around the house. There were too few clouds for rain, but they were ominously grey and their numbers were growing. They scudded darkly across the moon, casting innumerable mobile shadows. I put on my dressing-gown and went to the door. As I opened it, I caught sight of what I thought was Joanna turning the corner at the end of the corridor that led to the children's bedrooms, next to the nursery in the west wing below the tower. A moment later, Christopher appeared from their bedroom, two doors down from ours.

'I'm frightfully sorry, Patrick, something's disturbed our son.'

'Really?'

'Yes, Justin just came rushing in screaming that he'd seen a ghost. Joanna's gone to settle him back down in Monica's room.'

'It's natural enough', I said, 'for a child to imagine such a thing just after he's heard someone has died.'

'Absolutely. I'm afraid he took the news about Aunt Letitia

very badly. You know, he's really such a sensitive child.' Christopher paused for a moment, reflectively. 'But actually he didn't say anything about her . . . just now, I mean. It wasn't *her* ghost. It was a big man carrying his head under his arm.'

'In short a rather conventional country-house ghost.'

Christopher smiled. 'Exactly.'

'Probably a dream, then.' He nodded. 'Ah, well, good-night,' I said. 'And don't worry about us, we shall have no difficulty getting back to sleep.'

I wasn't sure that was true. A loud storm was gathering. There was plenty of racket to disturb us; certainly more than enough to disturb the sleep of a troubled child. I volunteered to transmit the contents of my conversation to Virginia, but she said she had heard it all. She had also made cotton-wool plugs for our ears. As I lost consciousness for the second time, entirely oblivious to the sounds of the storm, I wondered sleepily whether the ferry bringing Horace Strachan would be able to land.

4

Breakfast was usually available in the dining-room from about half-past eight until ten. Exhausted by the stresses and strains of the previous day, our sleep disturbed by the affair of Justin's ghost in the middle of the night, and our ears insensate from Jinny's cotton-wool, we awoke rather later than is our habit. We washed and dressed hurriedly, and arrived at the breakfast table at half-past nine to find almost everyone else still assembled. The children were in the nursery. Otherwise, only Alistair and Marie-Hélène were missing.

They were an extremely gloomy lot. Iona looked as though she had not slept a wink. The paleness of her always-pale skin was emphasised by the black dress she was wearing. Colin had apparently cut himself a number of times shaving, so that his face was covered with an almost comical patchwork of plasters. He stared ahead down the table towards his wife, brooding. Gavin, perhaps predictably, looked like the man with the nastiest hangover in the world, and sat nursing a cup of coffee with his eyes closed.

'Good morning, all,' I volunteered with more cheer than I felt:

A murmur of response went round the table. 'Kippers, scrambled egg and bacon on the sideboard; toast on the table. And Patricia is on her way back with more coffee and tea.' Iona was trying to sound cheerful, too.

In the circumstances, the ordinary courtesy of enquiring after how we had all slept was out of order, and it did not surprise me that no one asked. The eggs and bacon and the kippers had hardly been touched, and, tempted though I was, a stern look from Jinny reminded me of the path of duty. I collected my allotted slice of toast and – butter being forbidden me and margarine, which I am permitted, being unavailable at this, as at all decent, tables – I spread it with the pleasant marmalade from the Sealsay kitchens. Virginia took only a slice of plain toast. When the maid arrived with the tea, Virginia and I each took a cup.

Chatter at breakfast is never welcome. But on this day, the general air of gloom inside, in combination with the appalling darkness outside, made one long for some rousing entertainment.

'Sleet,' said Maria wearily, gazing out of the window.

'I suppose the boat will be able to land,' her husband responded.

'Oh, I expect so, Jonathan,' Colin said. 'It's dark and wet, but the winds have fallen. It's the wind that stops them dockin' . . . or rather the swell from the wind. Still, it can't be very pleasant out there today. I hope that Horace doesn't have too awful a trip.' Colin took a great gulp of tea and then went on. 'Look. Iona and I feel that we can't really go on with the *ceilidh* tomorrow night. I mean, what with Letitia being . . . gone. On the other hand, we can't really cancel the whole thing. Wouldn't be fair to the islanders. Bad omen for the New Year and so on. So I think it would be best if we just had 'em up here, fed 'em and gave 'em a little to drink, and then sent 'em off as soon as we've seen the New Year in. Alistair and Marie-Hélène have gone down to the 'otel to get the Wrigleys to set up for dancin' tomorrow. Rather dull for you two,' he said, turning to us, 'but I don't see what else . . .'

'Do you think everybody will come?' Joanna said. 'I mean it's not as if they don't know what's happened.'

'I've told Alistair to tell the Wrigleys to put it about that we want 'em all here. After all, I feel I should say something about what's going on.'

While Colin was speaking, Gavin rose gingerly from his chair and made his way out of the room. 'I think I shall lie down for a moment. I'm not really feeling too good.'

'I think it might be wise', Iona said, when he had left, 'if we all tried to keep Gavin away from the whisky as much as possible.' She smiled a sad, wan smile; and then sighed. 'I'm afraid that actually being the one that saw Letitia go has rather upset him.' Iona was rising to follow her son out of the room, when Emma Gale appeared, looking a good deal more robust and energetic than the rest of us. She might even have been described as cheerful.

'Good morning, all,' Emma said as she entered. This seemed to me a perfectly proper thing to say, even if, in our difficult circumstances, it might tactfully have been said with less vim and vigour. And yet the effect of Emma's appearance on Iona was quite extraordinary. She raised her hand to her mouth as if she was about to be sick and then fainted completely away.

It was several minutes before she regained consciousness. We had moved her to the *chaise-longue* that sits in the bay window of the dining-room and she lay there, pale, almost translucent, as fragile a creature as one could imagine, breathing shallowly. Virginia, who has always managed to be able, without a training in the Boy Scouts, to 'be prepared', produced a phial of smelling salts from her handbag, and wafted them gently under her nose. Eventually, Iona coughed and spluttered a little and came to.

Her first words were: 'Too silly. I don't know what came over me. It's all this business with Letitia.'

'Are you all right?' Colin asked, in a tone that struck me as oddly restrained. I wondered if he was simply embarrassed by his wife's weaknesses, and the possibility made me cool considerably towards him.

Gradually, we all settled back around the table, leaving Iona on the *chaise-longue* with Jinny perched next to her. Emma ate a small breakfast, while the rest of us, who had largely finished before her arrival and Iona's fainting spell, sat talking quietly and glancing over from time to time to see how she was. After a while, she asked Virginia to help her upstairs and disappeared saying she was sure she would be better soon.

In the hall, the clock struck ten and Parsons came in a moment later with Patricia, who was anxious to clear the table.

'Ah, Parsons,' Colin said. 'Her ladyship and I have decided that we shall see the New Year in without dancing tomorrow. Would you and Jock please return the carpet to the library?'

'If I may say so, Sir Colin, we'll need a little help. When we took it up, we had Andy and Alex MacIntosh to assist us.'

'Very good, all hands on deck then, chaps. The gentlemen will give you their assistance, Parsons . . . Won't you all?' Colin said. There was a great rumbling of chairs as Colin, Jonathan, Christopher and I rose to the task. 'Really, Patrick, I'm sure that the family will be able to do it, there's no need to trouble yourself,' he continued.

'I should feel quite worthless if I didn't offer what little support I can.'

'Well we can't have you feelin' worthless, old chap. So let's forgather in half an hour for the purpose. That will give Parsons and Patricia time to get the table cleared. Shall we say half-past ten?' As we left the dining-room, Colin drew me off to the side. 'I wonder if I could have a word with you Patrick? In the library?'

'Absolutely.'

I had not yet been in the Sealsay library on this visit, but I remembered it from many a happy evening's browsing over the years. The older books must have been acquired *en masse* from an earlier collection: it was the library of an educated Scottish gentleman of the latter part of the eighteenth century. At the time of my first visit, I had recently been introduced to Hume's ethical writings by the law don at Clare, who was also tutor in moral sciences. And I remember discovering in astonishment that here, in the remotest Isles, I could deepen my study with

Balfour's *A delineation of the nature and obligation of morality: with reflexions upon Mr Hume's book, intitled, An inquiry concerning the principles of morals*, published in Edinburgh in 1753; or that I could read the earliest edition of Locke's *Essay*. But Sir Josiah himself had acquired a vast library of Victorian technological works – books, both popular and specialised, on the engineering of industrial machinery – and, more surprisingly, a large number of books discussing the merits of Darwin's evolutionary theories, published in the decades after *Origin of Species*.

Sir Josiah had not had much learning, himself. He was, he used to say in his broad Lancashire accents (in a remark much quoted by his descendants), 'a practical man, though they do say practice makes perfect'. But he had the greatest respect for scholarship. And if he could not possess it mentally he could buy, like any Victorian self-made man, the appurtenances of scholarship; he could also purchase for his sons and grandsons the best educations the Empire had to offer. Colin and his father had left the collection as a kind of monument to the old man: only in the large block of shelves that stood in between the windows had they added anything. There were works on travel, and maps and charts of one kind and another, acquired by Colin in his researches for his many trips. The vast bulk of the books that were actually read in the house were kept in the various studies and bedrooms.

The room looked strangely bare without the great red Persian carpet that normally filled the floor. As Colin shut the door, I looked around the shelves, reminding myself of the many discoveries I had made among those ancient books. A marvellously lucid exposition of the workings of the steam engine, complete with wonderful drawings; an essay by an obscure Scottish jurist on the advantages of Roman-Dutch law; brilliant drawings of Darwin's Galapagos finches. This was not the place to look for Daphne Lomond's *oeuvre* but I made a mental note to see later if I could find copies of her works in one of the many bookcases scattered about the house.

It struck me as I scanned the room that something else was missing – something other than the carpet I had seen in the corridor – and I realised in a moment that above the mantelshelf, where there had been a fine portrait (was it a Raeburn?), there was now a rather ordinary mirror. There had also, so it seemed to me, once been a rather fine and evocative Canaletto of one of the less grand canals of Venice, on the facing wall, above the grand piano, where now there was only a modern seascape. The fireplace was still as magnificent as ever, with the great carved stone griffins on either side of it, and the Rundle arms above, with its strange motto: *Ferreus.*

As I stared at the coat of arms, Colin followed my gaze. '*Ferreus.*' He laughed an unhumorous laugh. 'Made of iron. Father always said that old Josiah Rundle was proud that he had bought his son the education to have come up with that. Firm, unyieldin', iron. We're supposed to be a tough lot. Letitia certainly was tough . . . at least until the end.' He breathed in deeply. 'Let's sit down, shall we?' This tentativeness was out of character.

We sat on either side of the fireplace, piled high with logs ready for lighting. 'The fact is, Patrick, that I need your advice about a sort of police matter.'

I nodded, urging him to continue.

'It's all rather complicated. Where to begin? Let's see. After we all went up to bed last night, I went through Letitia's room. I mean, I wanted to see if there was any explanation for what she did.'

'You thought she might have left a suicide note.'

'Exactly. Or a diary. Or some such thing.'

'And did you find one?'

'Well, in a manner of speaking. There was a letter to me, on her dressin' table.'

'May I see it?'

He reached into the breast pocket of his jacket and pulled out a single sheet of writing paper. It had the Rundle arms and the words, 'Sealsay House, Sealsay,' printed at the top, with the telephone number – Sealsay 201 – below. And on it, in a large flowing hand, written in purple ink, were the words: 'Ask Alistair.'

'Is that her writing?'

'Oh yes, no doubt of it. She always used that ghastly ink.'

'Do you have the envelope?'

He handed me a matching envelope, with the Rundle arms on the flap. On it was the single letter 'c'.

'Is that how she normally addressed notes to you?'

'Yes. Always. I've had scores of 'em over the years.'
I looked again at the note. 'Did you?'
'Did I what?'
'Did you ask Alistair?'
'Oh yes, of course, at once.'

Haltingly and with a great deal of embarrassment, Colin then began to tell substantially the story I had heard from Virginia the night before. There were, however, a few more details. Letitia, Colin said, had written a book about her childhood, and, in the course of it, had said that her father had molested her. Alistair had been contacted privately by the publishers saying that they were naturally concerned about publishing such an allegation if there was any doubt about its truth. 'Alistair told me he had challenged Letitia, and she told him she was sure of what had happened. But he asked her to reconsider; and she did, indeed, recall the manuscript from the publisher.'

'Where is it now?'

'I don't know. We couldn't find it. Perhaps,' he said hopefully, 'perhaps she destroyed it.'

'Why didn't the publishers contact you?'

Colin thought about that for a moment. 'Well the chap who actually got in touch was an advocate Alistair knows in Edinburgh. Someone who advises the publishers in question. But I suppose they just thought that the story would be more embarrassin' for someone like Alistair, in public life, than for a private person like myself.' (There was something faintly ridiculous in the idea that Colin, who was certainly one of the world's better-known adventurers, was more of a private person than Alistair, but I thought it best to let that pass.)

'And Alistair never mentioned this to you until last night?'

'No. He thought he had dealt with the matter and that I didn't need to be bothered with it.'

'But why did she kill herself *now*?'

'Alistair's theory is that she had dredged it all up in writin' the book and that relivin' it had rather unhinged her.'

'And what do you think?'

'I assume that Letitia told me to ask Alistair because she thought he would emphasise it had somethin' to do with the business with Father.' He paused and breathed a heavy sigh; and then continued in a tone of exasperation. 'But, as you very well know, Patrick, Letitia's never been exactly an ordinary person. It's hard to know why she did most things.'

'Do you think your father actually . . .?'

'No. I don't.' Colin's response was swift and absolute. 'My father was a strong-willed man, difficult, in some ways, but nothin' he, or Letitia, for that matter, ever did or said, suggested he was a . . .' – he paused before spitting out the word – 'pervert. Still, my brother has had more time to think about it and he appears to incline to the view that it's possible. Marie-Hélène read somewhere that it happens more often than we think, and even in good families.'

'Suppose your father is innocent. Why would Letitia have killed herself?'

'Because she *thought* he did it. I mean, damn it all, Patrick, how would I know? She wasn't quite right in the head. And she had a vivid imagination. Always reading. Actually – God, this is all so embarrassin' – it turns out that she'd been *writin'* romances for years, too.' He shook his head sadly. 'I knew that there were things goin' on in her head that she didn't tell us about, but I'd never realised she had a whole secret life.' Colin snorted cheerlessly. 'She used to give her books to Maria as Christmas presents. Maria likes that sort of women's nonsense. And Letitia never once told her that she'd written 'em. Talk about a dark horse.'

We sat in silence as I digested what Colin had told me. 'So what you want to know is whether you need to tell the police about the note and Alistair's hypothesis?'

'Yes. Exactly.'

'My opinion as a lawyer is that you should. You have a legal obligation to do so; concealing evidence from an inquest would be a crime. On the other hand, it's hard to see how they could find out that you had concealed the note if you destroyed it. Who else knows it exists?'

'Iona. Alistair. Marie-Hélène.' He paused.

'None of your children?'

'No.'

'Miss Gale?'

Colin's cheeks reddened somewhat and he looked away like a child caught with his hand in the sweet-jar. 'No, of course not. I haven't spoken to her since we all went up last night.'

'Then, if you four were to agree to say nothing about it, how would the police or the coroner know? They couldn't ask me, because what you have told me is between a lawyer and his client. But, of course, they might find out about the manuscript from the publisher and then the rest would come out anyway. And the coroner may feel that he needs more reason for Letitia's suicide than that she was slightly dotty. Still, as I say, that is a matter for you all to decide.'

He nodded. 'You've been very helpful, Patrick. Actually, just gettin' it off my chest has been a relief.' He looked at his watch. 'And now we're all due in the hall to help move the carpet.'

Jinny was back from settling Iona in her bed and seemed to think she was all right.

'What was that all about, do you think?' I asked quietly.

'Haven't any idea. She just said she suddenly felt faint,' Jinny murmured. Then, raising the volume, she added, 'Come on, Patrick, time to do your man's work for the day.'

'You didn't really roll this thing up very tidily, did you, Parsons?' Colin said genially. It was not meant as a serious reproach. Parsons inclined his head equally casually – acknowledging his fault or simply declining to defend himself, I couldn't tell – and the six of us – Colin and myself, his two sons-in-law, and Parsons and Jock – set about the task of lifting the carpet and taking it into the library. The carpet was indeed heavy. It was also very bulky. We were cheered on by the ladies, who came out of the drawing-room when they heard the noise we were making, and followed us into the library. Jinny, Emma Gale and Jessica moved the furniture out of our way, Emma sneezing occasionally and complaining about the dust. And pregnant Angela leaned against the bookcase watching with a twinkle in her eye. Because the carpet had been there so long – it was probably placed there just after the house was finished – the wood showed clearly the outlines of its normal position. We lined it up at one end and began to unroll it.

Which is how it came about that all of our party – save Iona and Gavin, Alistair and Marie-Hélène, and the children and their nannies – were present when Letitia's body, not damp and sodden and drowned, but certainly quite dead, rolled into view.

If one could judge by the stains on her night-dress – there were few on the carpet – Letitia had died a bloody death some time before being placed in this undignified position. It was a horrible sight, horrible enough to distract me, for a moment or two, from the extreme difficulty of our situation. There was no policeman on the island. The last boat of the year had already left Oban. The weather was worsening. For all we knew, it would be days before a policeman could arrive. And in the mean while we were stuck on the island – probably in the house – with a murderer. I knew that if I was to find out who had done this terrible thing, what I needed to do now above all was to watch the reactions of all those in the room to this shocking development. I tried to muster my powers of concentration.

First, I glanced across to make sure Jinny was all right. She was sinking into a chair and turning her head away. Maria shrieked and then fainted almost immediately afterwards. Emma Gale paled and covered her mouth and stared for a few moments at Letitia before she too turned away. All the colour that had enlivened her face at breakfast had drained away. Angela was sick into the fireplace. Jessica burst into hysterical tears. As for the men, every one of them – Colin, Christopher, Jonathan and the two servants – seemed completely astonished. Colin gave a groan of such physical pain that I wondered for a moment if he had suffered a heart attack. And he was the first to speak. But all he said was, 'Oh God, no!' before falling to his knees beside the body and taking hold of his sister's cold hand. Everyone in that room put on a completely convincing demonstration of utter shock and surprise. If any one of them had known Letitia had gone to her final rest wrapped in a century-old enormous Persian carpet, he – or she – was a highly proficient actor.

'I think, Colin, that it would be best if we left Letitia as she is,' I said mildly. 'Perhaps we could gather the household in the drawing-room and decide what to do next.'

Colin was in an extremely compliant mood. Parsons helped Jonathan carry Maria out and lay her on the sofa in the drawing-room, and the rest of us followed: first, Angela on Jessica's arm, then Maria on Jonathan's, Joanna on Christopher's; then Emma (who seemed rather gruesomely curious about the state of the body, hanging back for a final glance), then Jock, and finally Jinny and me. I closed the door behind us.

'My God, Patrick. How awful she looked.' Jinny was leaning on me, her face pale. As she spoke she squeezed my hand distractedly.

'Are you all right, my sweet?'

'Nothing that won't heal.'

'Good.' I turned to Jock who was standing a few feet away obviously uncertain what he should be doing. 'Do you have a key to this room?' I asked him.

'Nae, Sir Patrick. It'd be with Mr Pairsons.'

'Thank you. Perhaps you would go and collect the rest of the household . . . I believe the children and their nannies are in the nursery. Mr Gavin is in his room upstairs. No need to disturb her ladyship. I should like to speak to them all in the dining-room before they join the others.'

As we entered the drawing-room, Parsons was standing quietly by the window. 'Ah, Parsons,' I said. 'Perhaps you would lock the library and come back in here. I've asked Jock to summon the others.'

Last night I had told Virginia that I hoped the body would turn up soon. But instead of ending our troubles, its arrival compounded them. Now what we had was not an implausible suicide but an inexplicable murder. And given Letitia's disposition, it was likely that practically everyone in the house had a motive.

5

'Well, Patrick, what are we to do?' Colin was beginning to recover, though he looked disoriented and his voice was still weak. As he spoke, he ran his hands through his hair and, when he was finished, stood with his hands lightly on his hips, his shoulders slumped.

'We've taken the first step, which is to get everyone together. Next, I think we should telephone Dr Crawford and get him up here. The sooner he sees Letitia . . .' I realised that it was not the time to discuss the merits of an early forensic analysis. 'Then we must call the police. Is it Oban?'

'Yes, I told them what happened yesterday. Perhaps you would call them?'

'I shall. But I think it would be better if I telephoned from elsewhere. I don't want to cause any further distress.'

'Parsons, would you show Sir Patrick to the estate office? Do use it quite freely to work from, if you need to, Patrick.'

We went back across the hall and along the corridor that led towards the kitchen. I glanced out of a window that looked over the front lawn and saw Justin squatting in his sou'wester. As I peered more closely, I realised that he was once more holding a cat. He appeared to be trying to attach a tin to the animal's tail with a piece of string. I tapped crossly on the window, but he obviously didn't hear.

Parsons looked at me and shrugged slightly. 'Master Justin is not very fond of the cats.'

I tapped more loudly.

He turned and stared at me crossly. As he did so, the animal escaped, running away dragging the can on its tail. I turned into the office from which Colin managed the affairs of the island. 'Prospero's cell,' I said out loud.

The desk was rather untidy, but I cleared a little space for myself after collecting a few sheets of notepaper from the drawer. Parsons stood waiting. 'The numbers, sir, of the doctor and the police, are written on that piece of paper sellotaped to the desk.'

'Thank you, Parsons,' I said, excusing him. 'I shall join you all in the drawing-room as soon as I have telephoned.'

First, I phoned Crawford. All I knew of him was that he was a widower and an alcoholic, who had settled on Sealsay a few years back; and that in return for a cottage near the hotel (which is to say, the bar) and a small stipend, he tended to the minor ailments of the society and made the decision as to whether and when it was time to call for the coastguard helicopter to ferry his patients off to the mainland. I introduced myself to the doctor and told him that Colin would like him to come up to the house at once. 'Is it his sister?' he asked.

'Yes.'

'Is she all right?'

'We were hoping you could come and examine her,' I said, which, while not exactly untruthful, was, I suppose, not the most informative answer I could have given. But if we were to keep the news from spreading, it was best, I thought, to tell him as little as possible until he arrived.

There was only a slight pause. 'I'll come at once.'

Then I called the police and told them such facts as I knew. I thought it best to keep my speculations to myself. When I finished, Inspector MacAlister to whom I eventually ended up giving most of the details, said, 'Well, that was a vairry thorough accounting. Now, here's our problem. The last ferry's left and there's no another till Tuesday. We've a sma' boat of our own, but in this weather we could never land on Sealsay. So I'll have to call out the coastguard and try to send someone over in a helicopter. Though I'm no vairry confident', he continued evenly, 'that they'll want to come over in *this* weather. In the mean time, Sir Patrick, I'm afraid I'm going to have to leave you in charge.' He paused, for a moment. 'I expect you know what you're doing. You're the one that solved that case at Cambridge a while back, aren't you? Where they murthered a laird?'

'Yes, that's right. Though there I had the very capable aid of a police officer.' There was an awkward silence between us. Finally I said, 'Do I have your permission to get the doctor to take a preliminary look at the body?'

'Yes. And ask him if he's got what he needs to do an autopsy.'

'Very good.'

'One more thing. Could you tell them to keep out of Miss Letitia Rundle's room? We might as well see if we can do some forensic work.'

'I'll pass the message on.'

There was a pause for a moment and I assumed that Inspector MacAlister was thinking, as I was, whether there was anything else we should say to each other. Finally he said, 'Before you go, would you mind telling me something?'

'Delighted to.'

'Why in God's name do you think she staged her own suicide in the first place?'

'To tell you the truth, Inspector, I haven't the faintest idea. But I intend to find out.'

'Did she do it by herself?'

'No, that I am sure of. But who else was in on it, I really couldn't say yet.'

'I'll expect you to keep in touch. Oh, and if the phone goes, as it may in the storm, there's a couple o' radios on the island . . . I know there's one at the 'otel. Goodbye. And good luck.'

'Thank you, Inspector. I rather expect we'll need it.'

When I got to the dining-room, Gavin had arrived along with Maria and Jonathan's three infants and Marit, who looked after them. Joanna and Christopher's son Justin was there, too, with his nanny, who was dressed in a starched uniform of a sort I thought had gone the way of the tram. Then there was Mary, the cook, Jock's young wife, Patricia, who had been helping Parsons at table, and two other young women dressed in aprons. 'Marit, would you be so good as to take the children – yes . . . including you, Justin – into the drawing-room and return. Perhaps, Parsons,' I continued, 'you would introduce me to the staff? Mary and Jock, I know, and Patricia has been helping in the dining-room.'

'The two young ladies are Miss Ann Callander and Miss Elizabeth McFee. They come in to help over the holidays.'

'Thank you, Parsons. Miss McFee, Miss Callander, I'm Patrick Scott.' The two young islanders bobbed me a curtsy, as Marit returned alone.

'Sir Colin asked whether you would be coming soon?' she said in a soft Norwegian singsong, reminiscent, as I noticed for the first time, of the Gaelic lilt of the islanders.

'Yes, we shall all be able to go about our business in a few minutes. Thank you all for coming. I shan't take any longer than I have to. As you know, Miss Letitia Rundle was seen falling over the Moray cliffs yesterday. It now appears that her fall was not fatal.' I looked at Gavin. His jaw had dropped.

'Well, where is she then?'

'She is in the library.'

Gavin blanched. 'Thank God.'

'No. I'm afraid that she is not alive.'

'But you just said . . .'

'I said the *fall* did not kill her.'

'What did?'

'Somebody or something else.' Gavin fell silent. 'I have notified the police and they will get here as soon as they can. In the mean while, I think it will be best for everyone to be careful. We don't yet know how Miss Rundle died, but she may well have been murdered. And if she was, there is a killer on the island, perhaps even in the house.' The two young women looked nervously about them. 'I don't think you have anything to worry about. But perhaps you can do the rest of your work around the house today together. Jock, you should keep Mary company. And Marit and Monica, you should stick together with the children. I'm afraid that, in this weather, that'll probably mean entertaining them in the nursery. These precautions are probably quite unnecessary. Miss Rundle was killed for a reason, and whatever it was, it is unlikely to involve any of you. But I do need to ask you to cast your minds back over the period since you heard that Miss Rundle had gone over the cliffs, and tell me of anything strange that has happened since then.'

'Well . . .' Mary began.

'It's best if we talk in private, I think, if you do have anything to tell me. I expect you will be busy, Mary, between now and lunch. Shall we meet in the estate office at, say a quarter past two?'

She nooded her assent, unhappily.

'Unless you feel it is something that should not wait?'

'It'll wait,' she said.

'Will it be a'right fer us to go hame this evening?' Ann Callander asked.

'Good Lord, yes. Perhaps Jock could drive you home, though.' I looked at Parsons and he nodded, accepting the commission to arrange it. 'Well, if anyone else remembers anything, I shall be in the estate office at half-past two, after talking to Mary. And meanwhile, take care.' At this moment I remembered Justin's cat. 'By the way, I think one of the cats needs a tin untying from its tail.' The servants all turned to look at Justin's nanny, who sighed deeply as she left the room.

As the servants left, Gavin appeared set to join them. 'I wonder, Gavin,' I said, 'if you could spare me a moment?'

'I know, I know, I shouldn't have made up the story.'
  'What story?'
  'The one about Letitia being swept out to sea.'
  'Ah, so you *didn't* see that?'
  'Obviously not, or she wouldn't be in the library.'
  'What did you see?'
  'Aunt Letitia jumping over the edge.'
  'And then?'
  'And then I waited for Virginia.'
  'Why didn't you look over the edge? You might have been able to do something. She might still have been alive.'
  'Not me, Patrick.' He hung his head. 'No head for heights. Never have had. If I'd gone any closer to the edge, I'd have been sick. I knew Jinny would go and look.'
  'What would you have done if she had gone and looked and seen Letitia on the rocks below?'
  'She wouldn't have.'
  'Why?'
  'Because other people have leapt off the Moray cliffs. Everybody on the island has heard the stories. You hit the rocks or you hit the water. Either way you're taken away. Either way you're dead. Aunt Letitia knew that. Anyway, if Virginia had seen something, I wouldn't have told her that I'd seen Aunt Letitia being swept out to sea. I waited till she'd had a look over the edge.'
  'The stories must be wrong. If your aunt went over the cliff, she must have escaped death somehow.'
  'How?'
  'I was hoping you could help me with that.'
  Gavin thought for a moment. 'I suppose she could have jumped on to a ledge and then climbed back up when we were gone.'

'But then Virginia would have seen her when she looked over the edge.'

'Not if the ledge had a cave behind it.'

'Are there such places on the Moray cliffs.'

'I'm not the best person to ask, am I? Father or Uncle Ali would know. Or Jessica, our tomboy.'

'And, if that's what happened, how would she have got back up? Your aunt *was* over seventy.'

'Perhaps someone helped her. Took a ladder. I don't know.'

'So when you saw your aunt go over the cliff, you really thought she was dead?'

'Of course I did.' He looked at me, suspicion dawning. 'You don't think *I* helped Aunt Letty plan her disappearance, do you? Why on earth would I do that? Besides, it would amuse her to have as many of us as possible convinced she had snuffed it.'

'Well the amusement didn't last long.'

'Look, I knew that she was under a good deal of strain.'

'Because of the incest business and the book?'

He squinted at me in a frankly hostile manner. 'I see Virginia passed that on to you.'

'And you thought that ancient episode was a reason for your aunt to kill herself?'

'Not a reason, exactly. But she *had* dredged up all that unpleasantness from the past. It was bound to disturb her really. I mean, you know what she was like. She wasn't exactly an ordinary person. It's hard to know why she did most things. Talk about a dark horse.'

As we passed through the hall back towards the drawing-room, I heard the sound of a car drawing up in the driveway. 'Go ahead, Gavin,' I said. 'It's probably the doctor come to look at your poor aunt.'

And so it was. But he was not alone. He had been driven up by Alistair and Marie-Hélène, the latter, I noticed, dressed as elegantly as yesterday, but now in black. Of all the women in the family, only she and Iona were dressed in mourning. I met them at the front door.

'I gather Letitia's here,' Alistair said brusquely. 'Where is she?'

'She's in the library, Alistair,' I said. 'And she's dead.'

'Well, of course she's dead. She fell off a bloody cliff, didn't she?'

'Evidently not, Alistair. In any event, that's not what killed her.'

All three of them looked at me aghast. Alistair turned to his wife and some sort of message passed between them. Marie-Hélène reached for the nearest chair and collapsed elegantly into it, covering her forehead with a graceful hand. The doctor's face revealed his confusion, as he sought to work out what was going on.

'May I see her?' Alistair asked quietly.

'I think it would be best if the doctor was to examine her first.' In a murder investigation it is best to keep as many people as possible in ignorance of the condition of the corpus delicti. When he gave the impression he might insist, I went on, 'The others are in the drawing-room. I think Dr Crawford should perhaps see that everyone's all right. It was rather a shock and Miss Horseman is in the later stages of pregnancy.' He helped Marie-Hélène up and we all made our way to the drawing-room.

We entered the room together and Dr Crawford greeted the family. He had a quick look at Angela, and concluded that she was fine, and then he and I returned with Parsons to the library. Parsons unlocked the door and then stood aside to let us pass. 'There's no need for you to come in here, old chap,' I said, sensing a natural reluctance. 'But don't let anyone else in.'

To begin with Crawford simply stared at the bloody body lying on the carpet. Then he turned around and addressed Parsons. 'I think I shall need a drink.' Paul Crawford's taste in alcohol was apparently known to the butler, because Parsons disappeared wordlessly into the hall.

Finally the doctor set about his business. He offered me a pair of rubber gloves, before putting a pair on himself, and then began carefully to examine Letitia's neck wounds.

Parsons knocked gently on the door a minute or two later and Crawford went over and fetched his whisky. I looked at Paul Crawford, wondering what sort of man would have retired to be the doctor in this remote place. His clothes were conventional enough in a country doctor, from the tweed jacket and gaberdine trousers to the well-worn brogues. He even had a tweed cap poking out of his jacket pocket. Dr Crawford's bearing was extremely upright, and the general correctness of his dress and demeanour was sharply at odds with his ruddy, drunkard's face.

'So, what do you think?'

'After a cursory examination, I'd say she died early this morning from stab wounds on the right-hand side of the neck.'

I knelt beside him, looking at Letitia's thin, sad face. Her features were oddly calm. And then I noticed something about her eyes. I reached across gingerly with my forefinger and pulled down one of her eyelids. It was covered in tiny brown pin-points, where the capillaries had burst. 'Tardieu's spots. Wouldn't that suggest she was suffocated?'

Paul Crawford glanced at me and then at the body. 'How the hell do you know about Tardieu's spots?'

'Once before I had to deal with a murder where the victim was buried alive.' I shuddered involuntarily, remembering the terrible look on the face of that poor young man. Letitia's face was beatific by comparison.

'Well, Tardieu's spots they certainly are. Tiny pin-point haemorrhages in the eyelids and the conjunctivae.'

'If she was asphyxiated, why the stab wounds? It doesn't make much sense, does it?'

'I can't tell you without looking inside her. But, come to think of it, there's not much blood around: so I'd say there's a good chance she was stabbed after she died.' He paused. 'Look, I'd really like to do an autopsy. And if we're not going to do one soon, I think she should be put in cold storage somewhere. There's no morgue on the island, but there's a big empty freezer in my surgery.'

'Do you have everything you need to do an autopsy here on the island?'

'Absolutely. And in my opinion if we're to find the bugger who did this, the sooner the better.'

'I'll tell the inspector you'll be doing an autopsy, then. And, in the mean time, I think it would be best if you kept even your preliminary findings to yourself.'

I went to make my second call to Inspector MacAlister. I told him that Crawford had volunteered to do an autopsy.

'Guid. I've asked about him. He's done an awfu' lot of autopsies in his time. He should do fine.'

'There's another thing I'd thought of,' I said. 'When the boat returns to Oban today, there'll probably be no one on it. Most of the traffic this time of year's this way. But you might want to see who gets off . . .'

'Well now, there we're way ahead of you, Sir Patrick,' the inspector replied, his voice crackling on the old black Bakelite handset. 'But d'you think this business is likely to involve anyone outside Sealsay House?'

'Probably not. But I suppose you never can be too careful.'

'Before you go,' I said to Crawford, as we made plans in the library, 'I've a question for you.'

'Let me guess. You want to know whether I told Alistair and Marie-Hélène that you had said Letitia was alive?'

I smiled. 'I didn't say she was alive, actually, but, as a matter of fact, that is roughly what I wanted to know.'

'After your call, I went over to the bar. They were there, making arrangements of some sort with the Wrigleys. "They've found Letitia, she's up at the house," was all I said. And Marie-Hélène said, "Dead or alive?" Then Alistair said, "Well, dead, presumably, darling. You wouldn't survive a fall off the Moray cliffs." And she said, "Of course." Well . . .' He paused. 'By that stage I was rather confused, since you had rather given the impression that she might be alive. But I said nothing.' He chuckled grimly. 'Make of it what you will.'

Crawford set off with Jock in the Range Rover, the body wrapped in a sheet in the back. 'I'll telephone you when I'm done,' he shouted as the car drew away. 'And don't worry, I shan't tell anyone else what I find.'

Jock's instructions were to drop off Crawford and the body and then go on to meet the ferry to collect Horace Strachan. 'I think it might be best if we kept Letitia's condition to ourselves,' I told him. 'Best not to reveal it to the islanders yet.' As I returned to the drawing-room, Colin was announcing that lunch would be at a quarter past one. I wondered if anyone would feel like eating. I passed on MacAlister's message about leaving Letitia's room alone.

'I don't think anyone but Iona and me would be likely to go in there. Oh . . . and, of course, the servants. I'll get Parsons to tell the girls not to go in there.'

A sudden wave of exhaustion came over me. I suggested to Virginia that we should go up to the Green Room to rest.

As usual, it was helpful to try and organise what I had found out for Virginia. I told her what Dr Crawford had said was the probable cause of death. 'So that means stabbed from in front by a left-hander or from the rear by a right-hander,' she said.

'Probably.'

'Gavin's left-handed at tennis.'

'I know.'

'Anyone else?'

'Not Colin. We played tennis at Cambridge. I don't know about the others. It won't be hard to make a list.'

'What did Alistair say when you told him Letitia was dead in the library?'

'He said, "Of course, she's dead. She fell off a bloody cliff." But, somehow, it didn't seem genuine.'

We lay on the bed, side by side, in silence for a few moments.

'Whoever killed her,' I said after a pause, 'I don't think anyone could have put her in the carpet on their own. Would have taken at least two people.'

Jinny nodded in agreement. 'So that means we're looking for confederates. That should help.'

'Well, the plot on the cliffs involved confederates, too, probably.'

Another silence.

The rain was pouring down noisily, beating on the windows. 'I hope poor Mr Strachan can land,' Jinny said.

'There'll be plenty of islanders home for the holiday who'll be very sorry not to land, too. And *everyone* will be sorry if the provisions aren't landed. If the last Hogmanay I was here was anything to go by, there'll be twenty or thirty cases of whisky due for consumption in the next few days.'

'What I can't understand is what really happened up there on the cliffs.' Virginia returned to the puzzle at hand.

'Maybe you should go over again exactly what you saw on the cliff top.'

'Why don't you just tell me what you think I saw, and I'll correct you?'

'Righty-oh. You and Gavin walk up by the tarn and over towards the Moray cliffs.'

Jinny assented.

'You see someone who looks like Letitia—'

'We see Letitia,' Jinny interrupted, 'you really are awful, Patrick. Why can't you just let some things be as they seem?'

'Someone who looks like Letitia standing on the cliff's edge about, what, a couple of hundred yards away?'

I paused. Jinny said nothing. I waited.

'Go on,' she said eventually, 'ask me.'

'Could it have been someone else?'

'I suppose so. But Gavin went up close. And though she said nothing to him, he was only a few feet away when she jumped. And she turned to face him before she made her leap. So if it had been somebody else, he would have known. She was wearing a scarf, but her face wasn't covered.'

'Ah yes, Gavin. Plausible Gavin. How close to the cliff's edge was he when you arrived?'

'A few feet, maybe a dozen.'

'So he wasn't actually looking over the edge?'

'No. Why?'

'Because he's just told me he never looked over the edge. It seems he's afraid of heights.'

'But why would Gavin lie about it?'

'To cover up the fact that he was too scared to look over, he says.'

'But you don't believe him?'

'It wasn't one of his more plausible moments, it must be said. Look, if you were far enough away to be fooled about *who* it was, then you might have been fooled about *what* really happened. So let's go on. You went to the spot where whoever it was jumped from.'

'Yes.'

'Are you sure?'

'What do you mean?'

'Well, could Gavin have misdirected you? Could you have been a little distance from where she actually jumped?'

Virginia paused, then she went on thoughtfully, 'I had to pass out of view behind a small mound on the way up to meet him. That's when I thought he looked over the edge. But if he'd moved a bit while I was out of sight . . . But Patrick, how can you be sure?'

'I'm not. I do know that Gavin has already lied once about what happened. But I don't know if it was Letitia or not. And if whoever it was jumped at a point where there was a ledge with a cave behind it – something Gavin suggested was possible – I don't know why they would have put on such a stunt. After all, it was bound to be extremely upsetting for the whole family until Letitia reappeared. Not, I suppose, that Letitia herself ever minded upsetting people.'

Jinny developed the look she gets when she is thinking strange thoughts. 'Suppose', she said slowly, 'they were all in on it.' Her conviction evaporated immediately. 'I don't know. At breakfast everybody except Emma Gale seemed really genuinely grief-stricken.' I looked sceptical. 'And Alistair didn't look as though he was feigning grief yesterday.' I continued to look sceptical and Virginia went on less certainly. 'And Iona's grief last night seemed genuine, too.' The last remark ended on a rising tone, more question than statement.

'Iona had been weeping on and off all day, before the news about Letitia; and frankly the brave and suffering heroine performance last night was entirely out of character. As for Alistair, his performance struck you at the time as smarmy and unctuous, if I recall aright. No, the really interesting question is why Letitia would agree to stage her own death.'

'Who says she agreed?'

'If it was her up there on the cliffs, she agreed. If it wasn't, she may not have. But then, where was she in the interim?'

'Come to think of it, Patrick, if it *was* her up there, where was she between the time she climbed back off the ledge and the time somebody bundled her up in the carpet?'

'Not very likely that even as spritely a seventy-year-old as Letitia was up to jumping on to ledges. Couldn't it have been somebody else?'

'But who?' We looked at each other, knowing very well that we had no idea. 'Well, she must have hidden somewhere in the house while all this was going on. And then . . .' Jinny paused. 'And then somebody killed her.'

'Whoever put her in the carpet presumably was waiting for a suitable time to get her out and dispose of the body. Which probably means they were in a hurry. So far, I'm afraid, we have too many unanswered questions.'

'Is there anyone we can rule out?'

'The children. Probably the two maids. They don't live in the house, apparently. Anybody else *could* have done it. Still, it seems unlikely that the Norwegian girl or Justin's rather sour nanny would have had much of a motive. Though the way Letitia treated people, who knows.'

'So what's the next step?'

'I think, perhaps, that after lunch we should walk up to the cliffs. We can look for Gavin's ledges and caves. Until we can work out what Letitia did yesterday afternoon – and why – we probably won't be able to find out who killed her.'

6

Something like nine out of ten homicides are solved within twelve hours, my friends at the Yard tell me. The boyfriend has disappeared, he's apprehended at his mother's, there's a blood-stained shirt in the laundry hamper, and his alibi is paper thin. A robber goes on a spending spree with the credit cards of the man he stabbed in the alley. Most murders are easy. But if you don't bring a villain to justice in the first day or so, the odds of ever finding the guilty party diminish dramatically. Unless it was purely random, the murder was probably performed with care or cunning. And those performed with deliberation demand a particular approach. The trick to solving crimes of this kind is rational reconstruction. Your job is to piece together what scraps of evidence you can and then to work through what happened in imagination, with those bits and pieces as props. The problem, of course, is that the imagination is always too eager to fill in the gaps, always too easily satisfied with its own inventions. Over the years, in the dozen or so killings I have found myself trying to understand, I have learned, to my cost, that my own imagination is more easily satisifed than most. As a result, I was restraining myself, as much as was possible, from imagining Letitia's last few hours. But as I sat at the writing-desk in our room, making notes of the proceedings of the last few hours, I was drawn, willy-nilly, to that task.

Could it really have been Letitia up there?

In my mind's eye, she waits at the cliff top: tall, slender, wrapped in black. Who is she waiting for? Gavin had planned the walk with Jinny over lunch, sitting across from her. Had she heard their plans? Or did she know beforehand that Gavin would be bringing Jinny, because they had planned it that way all along? Or did she expect to be seen by Alistair and Marie-Hélène, Christopher and Joanna as they came down from Ben Moray? At all events, once Jinny and Gavin come into view, she faces them as Gavin runs towards her. They speak. What do they say to each other?

'Here we go, Aunt Letitia,' Gavin says. 'Jump now, while Virginia's still a fair distance away. She'll have to pass out of view of this point to get here. And when she does, I'll move further down.'

Letitia replies, 'You were always a wicked child, Gavin. You're enjoying this much too much.' And then she jumps on to the ledge and moves back into the small cave for her period of waiting.

She waits ten, twenty minutes longer, in the cold and the damp, knowing that Jinny may come back to the edge, look out to sea, searching for a sign of hope. Then she drags the ladder out of the cave, sets it against the cliff face and climbs up carefully. No one sees her. It is getting dark. She walks down the route the others have taken in the gathering darkness as the weather worsens.

It didn't seem right. It simply couldn't have been Letitia up there. To jump down at her age would be to risk broken bones. And then the long wait in the darkness. Why should she subject herself to that? But if it wasn't Letitia up there, where was she?

She waits in her room. She has written the note to Colin, her brother, smiling to herself at the shock in store for him. 'Ask Alistair.'

No. Not her room. They will come there when they hear she has gone over the cliff's edge.

After lunch, she goes to her room only to drop off the note on her dressing table. Then she makes her way to one of the many deserted rooms of the vast old house.

Perhaps in one of the towers? With a little burst of excitement, I realised that I had discovered something. 'Jinny,' I said, 'you remember when we came back from our walk last night, before dinner? There was a light in the west tower above the nursery.'

'Was there, darling?'

'Yes. And then Justin said he saw a ghost in his room at the base of that tower in the middle of the night.'

Jinny's eyebrows travelled elegantly up her forehead. 'So now we know where Letitia was last night.'

We were interrupted by the gong for lunch.

'Perhaps. But I think we might make a quick tour of the nursery wing and the tower later.'

As we arrived in the hall, the family was making its way from the drawing-room into the dining-room. Colin appeared last with Horace Strachan, with whom he was deep in conversation. I had met the lawyer once on the island, very many years ago – sometime, I think, in the mid-sixties. He must have been about thirty at the time, and he was already a very large young man. But in the intervening years, he had become enormous. I scarcely recognised him. His vast girth was enveloped in a rather loud tweed suit, dusted here and there with ash and the occasional leaf of tobacco. From his waistcoat pocket protruded the bowl of his pipe; but it wasn't needed at the moment, as he was busily drawing on a cigarette, puffing smoke all around him as he made his stately progress. His upper lip, which had sported years ago the thinnest, so far as I could recall, of moustaches, was now encrusted with a vast growth of hair; if this was a handle-bar moustache, these were the handle-bars of a particularly vast bicycle. His cheeks were crosshatched with tiny red lines, like a crude etching. He looked really quite unhealthy. Ordinary locomotion was not easy for him, and his breath, even as he waddled slowly into the hall, came in shallow pants.

Strachan must have arrived off the boat while Virginia and I were upstairs. 'Ah, Patrick, have you ever met Horace Strachan?'

'Indeed I have, years ago. How do you do, Mr Strachan? But I don't think you've ever met Virginia, my wife?'

'Lady Scott,' Strachan said, bowing ever so slightly, perhaps in the vain hope that he might once more glimpse his long-lost feet.

'How was your trip over, Mr Strachan?' Jimmy asked. 'Was it as rough out there as it looked?'

'It's not the worst voyage over to Sealsay I've ever had. But there was some worry about whether we'd be able to dock. In the end, the swell was not as high – does one say high? – as it might have been. But the wind was coming back up again by the time we left, so it may be that we were lucky to get in.' This long speech exhausted him and he settled happily into a seat at the table.

Iona, who kept tugging anxiously at her necklace, organised us all into our places. She kept me beside her and Jinny stayed on Colin's right; most of the family sat where they had sat the day before, though Joanna, I noticed, moved into Letitia's place: as if, as the eldest daughter of the next generation, she had inherited this seat at Letitia's passing. Opposite us, on Iona's left, sat Horace Strachan, whose girth kept him farther from the table than I suspect he would ideally have desired. Once more, Angela was absent, 'laid low', I heard Gavin say, in his facetious way, to Jinny, 'by the bairn in her belly.'

'It's a bad business,' Horace Strachan said, over the soup, looking across at me for a moment, and then turning his melancholy gaze down to his bowl. The sight of the steaming leek and potato soup cheered him up a little, and he set noisily about the task of consuming it. It did not take him long. As Parsons appeared discreetly at his shoulder to refill the bowl, he sighed. 'Poor Letitia. Sir Colin tells me that you have been empowered by the police to investigate until they are able to come. An awesome responsibility.' Iona's head fell, as if she had blacked out for an instant, and as she raised it back up, she breathed out heavily.

'Indeed,' I said as I watched Iona. I decided I should suggest to Colin that she should see Paul Crawford as soon as possible. It was possible that her symptoms were simply those of the stress of Letitia's death, following on her discovery of her husband's infidelity. But her fainting spell this morning already had me worried. 'A murder investigation is a particularly unpleasant duty among friends. Colin was telling me earlier', I continued, 'that Letitia had a secret life as an author.' I wanted to turn the subject away from Letitia's death, which appeared to be distressing Iona, but it was appropriate enough, I thought, to speak of her life.

Horace Strachan's face displayed a mixture of acute embarrassment and professional decorum. 'It was very difficult for me to keep that from the rest of the family; but she insisted, and I know my duty. I'm afraid she even used me as a pretext for visits to her publisher.' He sighed heavily and then returned to the consolation of his soup.

'Very extraordinary, the whole thing,' Colin said from the other end of the table. 'Once every couple of years, she would go off to Edinburgh, supposedly to see Horace. Iona and I couldn't understand why she didn't just talk to you on the telephone or when you came here; but she insisted, and in the end, I thought she must just enjoy the trips. She never went anywhere else. I don't think she's been off the island more than a couple of dozen times since Iona and I were married. And then never for more than a day or two.'

'When was the last time she came to visit you?' I asked Strachan.

'In the summer, I can't remember the exact date. It was about the time of the Edinburgh festival, I think. Yes, that's right. I think Letitia met up with Jessica . . . isn't that right?' Strachan turned affably towards Jessica, who was seated to his left.

'Yes, it was rather sweet. She'd never been to a professional production before, she said. She was thrilled. I introduced her to the cast. Of course, she didn't *say* anything to them.'

'But she enjoyed herself?' Jinny asked.

'Oh yes. Of course, she had some criticisms of the production. I think she said I would have been better suited to ads on the telly, come to think of it. Very exacting, Aunt Letty was. Still, she did say she thought the play was on the whole rather well written, of its kind.'

'And what was the play?'

There was a brief pause. And then Strachan said, '*Macbeth*.'

Jessica looked mildly sheepish. 'It's a sort of actors' superstition that you don't actually say the name.'

'I know. For the true thespian, it is just "the Scottish play".' I turned to Strachan. 'And did she visit her publisher on this trip?'

'No,' he said firmly. 'At least not so far as I know.' And as he looked away I wondered why I was absolutely sure there was something Horace Strachan was not telling me.

Parsons and Patricia served the main course, but no one save Horace Strachan took more than a very modest helping. He struggled manfully with the dual task of being both the only serious eater at the table and the only person inclined to conversation. In between periods devoted solidly to his food, he chattered breathily about the trip over and the weather and the state of the trains between Edinburgh and Oban.

During a lull in his monologue, I noticed that Strachan, having put away a fairly hefty helping of lunch, was gazing hopefully over to the sideboard. Iona caught his glance and turned to Parsons, inclining her head ever so slightly. Parsons duly set off to refill his plate. It was an established routine.

'Did you read her books, Mr Strachan?' I asked, as Parsons reloaded his trencher.

'I fear not. But somebody read them in great quantities. She made a pretty good income from them. I rather admired her for it.'

'Maria's read them all, haven't you, Maria?' Iona called discreetly down the table.

'Haven't I what, Mummy?' Maria was preoccupied with keeping Oliver happy.

'Haven't you read all of Aunt Letitia's books?'

'Absolutely. She gave them all to me, every one, over the years. I loved them. When I read the first, when I was about fifteen, I told her I loved it. After that, it was a sort of thing between us. *A Tender Magic*, it was called. And do you know, Sir Patrick, she absolutely never told me that she had written them. When Gav told me yesterday I was flabbergasted. Too bizarre.'

'Do you have them here?'

'Oh, yes. This is where I keep them. Any Christmas, if a Daphne Lomond had come out during the year, I knew I would get it from Aunt Letitia. This year I got *Love Vanishes*, but I haven't had a chance to start reading it yet. Would you like to have a look at them, Sir Patrick?'

'You know, I believe I would.'

As we were leaving the dining-room after lunch, it was nearing a quarter past two, and the time of my tryst with Mary, the cook. But I mentioned to Strachan that it would help me a great deal if he could explain a few things about Letitia's situation to me.

'Of course,' he said, 'though there are, of course, certain professional confidences . . .'

'I understand completely; perhaps you might want to ask Sir Colin to consent to your discussing family matters with me. There's no great hurry. We can talk later on this evening.'

Strachan gave a friendly nod. 'Frightfully good food one always gets here . . . though I suppose that the family is not at its most appreciative.' His eye followed the retreating rump of Emma Gale, which cheered him up enormously. Then he smiled cheerily at me. 'Still, even at the saddest of times, Sir Patrick, one must attend to the physical man.' He pulled a pipe meditatively out of his pocket and rolled off after Emma, beaming.

I watched him go, cheered by his zest for life. I found myself chuckling quietly as I made my way to the estate office to meet Mary.

She and Jock were both waiting outside the room. 'Come along, then,' I said, 'let's go on in.'

'It's locked,' said Jock dispassionately.

'Perhaps you could ask Parsons to let us in.'

'Vairry guid, sir. I'll no be long.'

A couple of minutes later we were all settled comfortably in the office to which I had asked Parsons to give me a key.

'Well, Mary, what was it you wanted to tell me?'

'It's a sma' thing, Sir Patrick. Perhaps, it's nothing at a'. But there was a guid deal of coming and going in the kitchen, las' night. When I came in in the morning, there was a fair amount of food just gone. Cold chicken, bread, milk, that sort of thing.'

'I seem to remember coming down with Sir Colin to the kitchen in the middle of the night for snacks when we were young. Was it any more than usual?'

Mary laughed shyly. 'Och, yes. This was much more than usual; much more.'

'Was there any dirty crockery or cutlery . . . plates, knives and forks?'

'Och, yes.'

'How many?'

Mary thought for a moment, counting out on her fingers. 'There was three plates, three forks, two knives, a bread-knife . . . That's all, I think.'

'I expect you washed them up at once.'

Mary smiled modestly as she nodded. 'Och, yes, Sir Patrick. I don't like a mess in ma kitchen.'

'Of course not, Mary. Was there anything else?'

'Well, I don't know if it matters, but there is one more thing. Miss Letitia's thermos flax is missing.'

Normally, after dinner, Mary told me, she would make up a flask of coffee for Letitia to take up to her room when she went to bed. Letitia was in the habit of retiring fairly soon after dinner. Mary, believing that Letitia had been swept out to sea, had not made up the flask last night. But it had been gone from its place in the cupboard in the morning.

'Thank you so much, Mary, you've been very helpful.' I smiled at Mary and her husband, both of whom seemed somewhat relieved now that Mary had unburdened herself. 'I know it's rather a lot to ask, but I wonder if you could just keep this business of the midnight feasting to yourselves. It's all a little embarrassing.' Jock and Mary did not catch my drift. 'I mean, obviously some members of the family felt they couldn't eat too much at dinner on the evening Miss Letitia was supposed to have been drowned, but then hunger overtook them in the middle of the night. Naturally, they wouldn't want it to get out.'

'Och, I see,' Jock said. 'We'll keep it tae oursel's.'

'Splendid. Thank you so much.'

As they left, I looked at my wrist-watch. It was about twenty to three. I had promised to be available to the others, if necessary, at half-past two. But no one was outside. I decided to wait a little longer. And, in the mean time, it seemed as good an idea as any to call Inspector MacAlister.

As I picked up the telephone, I heard a scratching noise at the door. I went over and looked up and down the corridor in both directions. There was no one visible. I took a further step and tripped over a piece of fishing line that had been attached across the doorway a few inches off the ground. Fortunately I was able to steady myself. At my age the bones break more easily and heal more slowly than one might like, as I learned in the aftermath of the Pelham affair. I muttered 'Damnation', and, as my voice carried down the corridor, I distinctly heard the sound of an eight-year-old boy giggling in the coat room, two doors away. A moment later Justin, unmistakable with his tangle of red hair, ran out and through the main hall, presumably on his way back up to the nursery. I undid the filament – which was fastened between two drawing pins – and returned to the business of calling MacAlister.

I brought him quickly up to date, admitting frankly that I was not much further forward. The late-night meal in the kitchen could have had the innocent explanation I had suggested to Jock and Mary. But one of the midnight feasters might well have been Letitia, who had, after all, missed dinner. And since she probably had accomplices, they might have eaten with her. Anyone, after all, who knew she was not dead would need to feed an undiminished appetite. 'I've two or three chances to find really helpful information this afternoon, Inspector. From the doctor, from a trip to the cliff top – if the weather permits – and from Letitia's lawyer.'

'I better give you ma home number,' MacAlister said. 'Call any time. *Any* time. Ma wife's used to it.'

There was no more knocking on the door while I was on the telephone. But when I came out of the office, I found Alistair hovering about in the hall. As I locked the door, with the key Parsons had given me, he said, 'Virginia tells me you're off to see Crawford. I wondered if I might come along?'

'I'd rather you didn't, Alistair. It's easier to discuss these things without family around. And she won't be in . . . Well, I mean, it's an autopsy.'

'Quite.'

As he turned to go, I remembered that, in all the confusion around Letitia's 'suicide', we had forgotten the meeting we arranged for last evening. 'I don't suppose you'll want to discuss business now, Alistair,' I said. 'But we were going to talk last night about that trust matter you asked me to investigate a few months ago. Actually, I'm afraid the news is not good. So far as I've been able to discover, a trust of the sort you described set up in Scotland would be pretty unbreakable. If it's not indiscreet to ask, is there a reason why you didn't ask Strachan about it?'

'He's my trustee,' Alistair said. 'He set the thing up for my father. He'd hardly want me tinkering around trying to get out of it.' He laughed sardonically. 'Very firm ideas my old father had about not spending capital.'

'Ah well, sorry I couldn't come up with anything.'

'No matter. It was only a small amount anyway, and Strachan, not being one for letting the grass grow, tells me that Letitia's left me a rather hefty sum, actually. She never spent any money, you know. I suppose it amused her to leave me the income from those awful books. She heard me disparaging them to Maria. So . . .' His voice drifted off. We walked, side by side, into the hall, and across it into the drawing-room. Colin sat brooding at the writing-desk, and Virginia was reading by the fire. There was no sign either of Justin or of his parents.

'I wonder, Colin,' I said, 'if I could borrow a car? I need to go down to see Dr Crawford.'

'Absolutely. Jock'll take you in the Range Rover. Would you ring for Parsons, Ali?'

'Don't you think it might be better if we had our walk first, darling?' Virginia said, smiling brightly, in a manner that suggested this was not a suggestion to be denied. 'It'll be quite dark in a couple of hours, and I should like to get out.'

'Absolutely beastly weather,' Colin opined.

'Ghastly,' said Alistair. 'It'll be even worse if you get up over the hills. If you do go, wrap up.'

'We will.'

'I'll tell Jock you'll want drivin' down later,' Colin said.

'We'll be back about tea-time, wouldn't you think?' Virginia said.

'Yes, if you'll excuse me from tea here, I'll go down about then.'

'Shall I come too, darling?' Virginia asked. (This was what my classics master, old Griffin, would have called a question expecting the answer yes; an effect Jinny achieves by combining a certain intonation with a firm stare. So much more effective than the crude Latin '*nonne*'.)

'If you'd like to,' I said, uncertain as to whether Jinny really wanted to hear Crawford's account of Letitia's autopsy, or whether she just wanted to keep away from the house.

'Then I think I shall.' And she smiled brightly again. 'But first we must have our walk.'

7

The path that Gavin and Jinny had followed the day before runs up out of the fields to the west of Sealsay House. So we turned right outside the great front porch, marched a hundred or so yards across the lawn, and entered the clump of rhododendrons that separates the garden from the fields. The day was dark, and the westerly winds lashed at our faces, buffeting us back as we made our way into the hills. I had brought a walking-stick for poking around at the cliff top, and Jinny had her shooting-stick, and we needed them now as we slipped about on the sodden earth of the pathway. A quarter of a mile later we were high enough up to be able to look back over the gardens to the house. Jinny rested for a moment on the shooting-stick, scanning the house and the grounds.

Each wing of the house is long and thin, to take advantage of the fact that in these climes, in the summer season, the sun shines much of the day from the north. The drawing-room and library are in the east wing, to the left of the main hallway. Each of these rooms is entered from a long corridor, lit by a score of tall windows, that passes along the northern side of the wing.

The east tower sits over the end of the east wing, above the drawing-room; and beyond it, at the end of the wing, is the vast area of glass of the conservatory. Above these rooms are most of the family bedrooms, Colin and Iona's, Alistair and Marie-Hélène's, at the front, and the rooms of the next generation where Maria and Jonathan (and their infant) and Jessica and Angela slept, to the rear. In the east wing, too, is the Strachan Room, where Horace was ensconced to the rear, and Emma's room (called, after some mysterious early visitor, the Smith Room) which looks over the front of the house.

The west wing is by and large the business end of the house. Here are the kitchen and the pantries and the laundry and the offices, and, at the end, on the ground floor, a suite of rooms that had been turned into a flat for Jock and Mary. In this wing, too, on the first floor, are the nursery and the bedrooms for the children and the nannies, Letitia's room, and Christopher and Joanna's, and five spare bedrooms, of which the Green Room, facing the front of the house, was the first.

The whole building is constructed of stone from Sealsay's quarries. The battlements on the towers and the crenellations that run the length of the façade produce an effect of military severity, contradicted by the humour of the great stone animals and the vast expanse of window glass, made possible by the installation of an elaborate system of central heating. Sealsay House must have been the first building on the island whose fireplaces were decorative.

As we looked down, we saw that the lights were on in the hall and the drawing-room; and there were lights too in the west wing, probably in the nursery, and in the kitchen below it and to the left.

'Not the prettiest house,' Jinny said, as we stood gazing down at it. 'But it looks awfully warm and tempting in this weather.'

'We don't have to go, if you're not up to it,' I said. 'I can go up with Gavin in the morning.'

Virginia's response to this faint-hearted proposal was to stride off again up the pathway, waving me on. It was a minute or two before she let me catch up with her. We strode on in silence for a while and then she stopped again and pointed her shooting-stick the way we were going. 'Don't look now, Patrick, but I think we're being followed.'

'Who is it?' I said, walking on to a small stone outcrop and sitting down on it as if for a rest.

'Alistair, I think.'

I turned my head slowly, scanning the horizon, but by the time I looked back the way we had come there was no one in sight.

'There's no doubt where we're going,' I said. 'This route only takes you up to the cliff top. So I can't see what he could find out by following us.' But at this moment, Alistair reappeared out of a dip in the path and waved at us. We waited the few minutes it took him to reach us.

'Thought I'd join you, if you don't mind,' he said puffing a good deal from the exertion of catching up.

'Of course,' I said. 'We were making our way up to the spot where Jinny saw Letitia yesterday.'

'I imagined you might be. I think I can show you what must have happened.'

As we approached the top the winds grew stronger, and though the rain was still holding off, the air was full of cold salt spray, sharp on the cheeks and on the lips.

'This is where we were when we first caught sight of her.' Virginia had to shout to be heard above the rising gale. 'Gavin ran ahead, disappearing around that mound there and reappearing not long after with . . . Letitia. Then she jumped and I rushed up round the mound and found Gavin alone.' Three minutes later we were at the spot. 'I can't remember what the first thing was that we said to each other, but I remember I ran over there to the edge. But I could see nothing, so I came back to Gavin and he said he was going to run down to the house for help.'

'What was the weather like up here yesterday?' I asked.

'We went out in the spell of sunlight when the storm subsided yesterday afternoon. By the time we got up here it was a little windier, but there were breaks in the clouds, and there was no rain. She'd have had much more control over where she landed up yesterday than you would today.'

The three of us stood a foot or two from the cliff top in the howling wind, staring out into the wild darkness of the Atlantic. 'Nothing between here and Canada,' Alistair shouted. There were black clouds all the way to the horizon, blacker and darker than the clouds now obscuring the sun. We were in for more rain. Gingerly I peered over, looking for the ledge on to which Letitia could have vaulted.

'I don't think she can have done it here.' Alistair's voice was raised over the roar of the wind. Best, I thought, not to mention yet that it was very unlikely to have been Letitia who had made the leap. 'The nearest spot where there's a ledge she might have caught on is a little up that way.' He led us twenty or thirty feet further along the cliff and then stopped and peered over. 'This is it.' Then he turned around and walked back beckoning us to follow. Behind a rocky boulder was an opening in the mountainside. 'The secrets of the isle,' Alistair said, pulling back an imaginary curtain. 'I brought torches.'

We followed him down into the dark cave, using our walking-sticks to stop us from slipping on the wet rock. We went in single file, Virginia between the two of us, each of us shining an electric torch on the ground ahead. Fifteen feet in, we were at the top of a stairway with a rusting metal handrail. Here, out of the wind and the rain, the storm seemed very far away. Alistair no longer had to shout. 'The monks carved these steps out. You can go right down to the base of the cliffs. Grandfather found the place amusing, so he had this rail put in. Used to go all the way down and look at the pounding ocean.' He paused, for a moment, to catch his breath. 'Don't worry. We don't have to go down all two hundred and eighty-three steps.' We had reached a sort of landing, with an entrance off it; a little light filtered through. '*Suivez-moi*, as Marie-Hélène would say.'

We followed him for twenty or thirty feet back in the direction we had come, the rock path rising steeply as we went. From the moment we entered the tunnel, we could feel the strong, wet wind blowing at us. We were obviously approaching an opening in the cliff facing directly into the westerly gale that had buffeted us at the surface. And when we reached the end, Alistair stood aside to let us peer out. 'There's no doubt about it,' Alistair said. 'This is where Letitia landed.'

For a brief moment, as we stood in the entrance to the cave, I saw Alistair's face. The still firmness of it sent a shiver down my spine. There was not a hint of sadness or of compassion. For just that moment I wondered if he had come here intending to send us to the fate Letitia had imagined for herself. But he stepped back into the darkness, out of reach – ready, I suppose, for the journey back to the house – and I dismissed the thought as absurd.

I was not yet quite ready to leave. I made to look out on the ledge but Virginia caught my arm. 'It's not safe, Patrick, in this weather.'

'She's right,' Alistair said out of the darkness of the cave.

'Are you sure you can jump down from the cliff on to this ledge?'

'Done it many times,' Alistair said, moving back to where we were standing. 'Of course, I was rather younger then.'

'How big a drop is it?'

'Can't be more than ten feet.'

'When do you suppose the last time was that Letitia jumped down?' Virginia asked, unable to conceal her scepticism.

'Before yesterday? You never know with Letitia. I wouldn't have suspected she still had it in her. It's a good trick for a lady of seventy. That's why it didn't occur to me that she might have been putting on a stunt until she turned up this morning.'

'Who knows about this place?'

'Most of the islanders.'

'It's funny I've never heard of it in all the years I've been coming here.' It did seem odd.

'Father forbade anyone to come here. There was an accident years ago. Gavin's generation has never been allowed in here, though they may have heard talk, I suppose. They may have come for all I know. They just weren't supposed to.'

'So that's one question answered,' I said. In the light of the opening we could all see each other fairly clearly. I looked directly into Alistair's eyes. From his embarrassed expression I inferred that he was trying to decide whether or not to apologise for having waited to tell us about this place.

'I know you must think it odd that Colin or I didn't just tell you about this place yesterday. But the fact is that Gavin was so certain that he had seen Letitia swept away. It didn't occur to any of us to doubt him. And you didn't say you were coming up here when you left just now,' he went on lamely. 'When Gavin told us Letitia had jumped we made sure that he described the spot pretty precisely. He was certain that she couldn't have landed on the ledge. I don't know why he was so far off.'

'Have you ever seen Gavin up here on the cliffs?'

'Of course.'

'Near the edge?'

'Of course. Colin used to take him climbing on these cliffs when he was a few years younger.'

'So you'd be surprised if I told you that Gavin had no head for heights . . . that he was prone to vertigo.'

Alistair guffawed; and then, as Virginia stared in amazement, he looked mildly penitent. 'Is that what he told you?' Alistair chuckled again, this time with more restraint. 'Not one for the strict letter of the truth, our Gavin, is he? No, my bet is that he was in on it with Letitia. Hmmm. I wonder. What a prank, eh?'

Virginia shivered as a particularly icy gust of wind lifted the hems of our overcoats. The clouds overhead now were darker and more menacing. A thin rain had begun, but it was the kind of stormy drizzle that promises a real wetting. I looked at my watch. It was a little after four.

'If we set off now we'll be back at the house by tea-time,' I said. 'And Jock will be waiting to take us to see Dr Crawford.'

We hurried back towards the house with very little conversation. By the time we reached the plateau from which we had watched the house an hour and a half earlier, it was almost dark. The weather had worsened throughout our walk, so that now the lights that had almost kept us from departing drew us more irresistibly back. The house looked so warm and welcoming that it was hard to remember that less than a day ago in that house someone had murdered Letitia Rundle.

'Last night,' I said to Alistair, as we entered the house, 'when Virginia and I came back from our walk at half-past six, there was a light in the west tower. Just now, when I looked, there was not. Do you think that it's possible that that's where Letitia spent last night?'

'I suppose it's possible,' Alistair said. 'Perhaps we should go up and have a look?'

It did not surprise me much that there was no obvious sign in the tower of Letitia's stay. As we walked through the rooms, I looked out of their windows trying to work out which one we had seen the light in. The most likely candidate was a room with a bed and a cupboard, and a few other items of furniture. The bed was made, which was odd for an unused room in a neglected tower, but it did not look as if it had been slept in. Odder still, there was a rather hard pillow lying on it, which felt as though it was stuffed with something other than the down which filled the pillows we were sleeping on. I picked it up absent-mindedly as I stared about the room. Jinny took it from me. She pulled back the bedspread on the bed and put the pillow under it.

'Can't resist tidying up, eh?'

Jinny did not take this remark kindly. She glared at me stonily for a moment and then said, 'Have you finished?'

'Just a little longer.' I knelt down (something that is accomplished these days with a little less ease than in the past) and ran my hand across the wooden floor. It was not very clean, and it had certainly not been polished recently. And then I noticed that there were tracks in the dust on the floor, leading to the cupboard. It had been moved recently from its place against another wall. I was about to enquire of Alistair about this, when I thought better of it. Officially, he knew nothing of Letitia's movements. I did not want him yet to think that I doubted him.

I raised myself (with equal difficulty) and looked about me again. There were sheets over the few items of furniture. But as I looked under each sheet, I found no evidence that anyone had sat on the chairs or written at the desk at any time recently. And there was nothing in the cupboard.

As we came down the stairs, I asked if there was any other way up into the tower. 'Another staircase? No. I suppose you could climb up the drainpipe?'

When we reached the nursery floor, I asked Alistair where Justin slept. 'In the room on the left,' he said. 'Actually, I used to sleep there when I was a boy.'

I stepped into the room for a moment. It was empty. But it had doors on both walls. 'Where do those doors go?' I asked.

'One goes to a bathroom that this bedroom shares with Letitia's room. The other goes into the nursery.'

Jinny cast me a furtive look. I wondered if we had been having the same thought.

On the way back down the corridor, Alistair identified the occupants of each room for me. Justin's nanny, Monica, and Marit – Maria and Jonathan's au pair – had rooms opposite the nursery and Justin's room, respectively. And next to Marit was the room Maria's two youngest children shared. 'The baby sleeps with Maria and Jonathan.'

We stopped off together in our room on the way back down. 'I'll tell Jock you'll be down in a moment,' Alistair said.

As the door closed, Virginia said excitedly, 'Out of the tower, through the nursery, through Justin's room and the bathroom, into her own room. No wonder Justin saw a ghost.'

'If she came down the stairs and into the nursery she would never have had to come round down the corridor in full view of anyone standing outside our room, or Christopher and Joanna's.'

'But she could still have been seen by Monica or the Norwegian girl, because they have rooms opposite the nursery. And if she made a noise and wakened the children in the night either of them might well have woken up.'

'It was only to be for a few days. All the children and nannies are off next week back to London. Once they've gone, it's the perfect arrangement.'

'Didn't Christopher claim Justin's ghost was a man?' Virginia asked.

'I don't suppose one should put too much weight on that fact. But if Gavin was in on Letitia's plan, he might have made his way through from Letitia's room to the tower. Or it might have been Colin.'

'Why Colin?'

'I knew Colin was involved as soon as I was sure Gavin was.'

'Oh?' Jinny said. 'How?'

'When I asked them to explain Letitia's actions. They both passed on the incest story, even though Colin didn't much like it. And they both said, "It's hard to say why Letitia did most things" and "She's a bit of a dark horse". They'd agreed to tell the same story.'

'So Letitia could get back and forth to her room and Colin and Gavin – and anybody else – could visit her in the tower. If Colin was seen going into Letitia's room, he could say he was dealing with her papers. As you say, the perfect arrangement.'

'*If* she was in on it. Remember that if it wasn't Letitia up there on the cliffs, we can't be sure that she was in on the plot. She might have been locked in the tower against her will. Either way, it was a perfect way for Letitia to seem to die without actually dying.'

'But she did die,' Jinny said. 'So now we must go and find out from Dr Crawford *how* she died.'

8

The road from Sealsay House to the dock runs along the eastern side of the island. Sealsay House itself, the home farm, the hotel, the port offices – most, in fact, of the buildings on the island – lie in the shelter of the hills that reach their peak at Ben Moray. Protected from the worst of the westerly winds that whip in off the Atlantic, they also lie in shadow as the sun sinks behind those hills. In summer, a drive over to the western coast in the mid-evening will let you watch the sun set a second time. The stormy weather that had circled the house last night would not have been the worst weather on the island. That would have been on the largely uninhabited western shoreline. But now, as we drove down to the hotel, and the doctor's house beside it, the weather on our side was as bad as I had seen it, the rain falling in great sheets, the trees whiplashed by the howling gusts. I wondered, for a moment, how safe we were in the Range Rover.

Horace Strachan was right. They were lucky to have landed when they did. In this gale the ferry would have had to turn back and lie in the island's lee waiting for the wind and the swell to fall. No police boat was going to land this afternoon. And no helicopter would be safe in the raging tempest over the island. At the best of times, December the thirtieth was not in the height of the island's finest season.

But even now, in the worst of times, seen through the blur of windscreen wipers, the island had its charms. To begin with, the road is open on both sides to the meadows that slope down to the shore to the east and the pastures that rise to the hills to the west. In those rising pastures, where the sheep graze on the sparse grass of winter, there are copses of oak and of chestnut, interspersed in many places with pines for winter wind cover. The sheep here are all from the home farm, they are the laird's sheep, but their care is in the hands of David Sealsay. Further on, Colin's father had planted mile upon mile of firs west of the road for most of the eight-mile drive to the dock. As the day drew to its close, the firs – silhouetted against those dark skies – evoked the northern woods of the Norse sagas. Anachronistic as it was, I imagined the first monks of Sealsay, the men who built the abbey whose ruins stand on the plateau to the north of Sealsay House. In my mind's eye, I saw them arrive in the bay where the dock now sits, stare up into those woods, thinking of wood as shelter from the wind, as fuel, as the boards of their new homes. I imagined them landing on that stony shore in their dark robes and kneeling on this earth and thanking God for a safe journey.

Virginia and I sat silent the whole way. We were in the back seat, huddled together, for warmth and for comfort, heads together, staring over Jock's shoulder through the watery glass of the windscreen. Engrossed as I was in my reverie, if a wild Viking horseman with a horned helmet had risen up in the lights of the headlamps, cape riding the wind, I think I would have shown little surprise.

Jock drove slowly, and it was a good quarter of an hour before we arrived at the doctor's house, by the hotel. 'Why don't you wait in the hotel, Jock,' I said. 'We'll be over when we're done with the doctor. Oh . . . and remember, not a word about Miss Rundle's body.'

Paul Crawford greeted us warmly. He offered us each a glass of whisky (which I, under Jinny's unspoken command, reluctantly declined) and then, when he saw we could not be persuaded, set off to make some tea. 'Now you just settle down in front of the fire there, and I'll be back in a moment.'

When he returned, he had poured himself the whisky we had rejected. He also had a notepad. 'It'll no be long. Ha! I'm beginning to talk like these people. What I meant to say was: Your tea will soon be ready. That's better.'

'So, Dr Crawford . . .'

'Would you mind awfully calling me Paul? "Dr Crawford" sounds like a fellow on active duty, soberly walking the wards.'

'Of course, Paul. What did you find?'

'Gets right to the point, your husband, doesn't he, Lady Scott? No messing about. Well, here's the story so far. You sure you want to hear all this?' he said to Virginia. 'It's a wee bit gruesome, I'm afraid.'

'No, go on. I'll be all right.'

Letitia had indeed been stabbed in the neck, a little above her collar bone, in a spot directly below her right ear. The weapon had entered seven, perhaps eight times. Whatever it was was shaped something like a skewer: a blade perhaps six or seven inches long – not particularly sharp and nowhere more than a quarter of an inch wide. It had hit her carotid and so blood should have come pulsing out as she died. 'So, at first, I thought, wherever she was killed, there was an awful mess to clean up. That was before I looked in her stomach. About a couple of hours before she died, our Letitia had a good meal.'

'When did she die, roughly?' I asked.

'Patience, Sir Patrick, patience. All in good time.' He took another sip of his whisky and the kettle started whistling in the kitchen. 'Hang on a moment. I'll be back in a sec' with your tea.'

As he left the room I asked Jinny, who looked slightly peaky, if she wanted to go on listening. 'Of course, I do, Patrick. Don't be silly. It's absolutely fascinating.' I suppose I must have looked questioning, because she went on, 'Oh really, Patrick, it's not as if I knew her.'

Crawford was back almost immediately with a tea-tray. 'There's some digestive biscuits, too, if you're in the mood.' He eyed us professionally. 'No, I can see that you're not up to that. Now, where was I?'

'The meal.'

'Ah yes, the meal. A good meal. Letitia liked her food. But that wasn't what caught my attention. You see, the contents of her stomach were less well digested than I would have expected. Either she'd eaten just before going to meet her maker or she'd eaten at the normal time – eight or nine say – and something had slowed her digestion. So I did a blood test. She was full of phenobarbitone. There was oodles of the stuff. And with that much phenobarbitone in her, Letitia was definitely asleep, unconscious, dead to the world, when that nasty skewer severed her carotid. As a matter of fact, she was not just unconscious, she was dead.'

We sat for a moment, all three of us staring silently into the fire. Nobody asked the questions that must have been going through all of our minds: Why would anyone poison a woman and then stab her when she was already doomed to die? Why would they stab her once she was dead? The storm raged outside, as it had raged last night, and I had a vision of Letitia's body, caught in a lightning flash. I imagined a hand raised with a stiletto coming down over and over again, piercing her neck. And the blood oozing, not spurting, because there was no heartbeat, because she was already gone. But try as I might I could not imagine the face behind that hand. I tried imagining Colin, or Iona, Alistair or Marie-Hélène, or Gavin or his sisters or brothers-in-law or Emma Gale. None of the faces fitted. I have seen enough murders to know that that means nothing. But so far, with no motives and scarcely any other clues, no one looked especially plausible as a killer.

'If you don't mind my asking, why did you look for phenobarbitone?' I asked finally, breaking the silence.

'Good question. And the answer is, it's good to have the family doctor around when you do an autopsy. You see, glaucoma runs in the Rundle family. Colin has a touch, so does Jessica, Gavin's too young to be sure about yet. They say old Sir Henry had it too. And Letitia's had it for years. I knew that if she'd taken an overdose it would have slowed her digestion.'

'But she wouldn't take phenobarbitone for glaucoma. It's a barbiturate. Knocks you out.'

'Indeed, Sir Patrick. And you don't take it for insomnia either, these days, do you?'

'If you say so.'

'Unless, that is, you're predisposed to glaucoma.' Paul Crawford beamed triumphantly at me. 'I knew that house was swimming with phenobarbitone because Letitia and Jessica both have a great deal of difficulty getting to sleep. Letitia's been taking it for years now to help her sleep. I only know about Jessica because she forgot to bring hers once and she asked me for some. And, of course, I've always got it for Letitia.'

'So you were just checking to see whether Letitia had planned to sleep last night?'

'No. I was checking because her digestion seemed rather slowed up . . . and because there were no signs of struggle, no scratches, no tissue under the fingernails. So she was unconscious when she died. And since she was dead when she was stabbed, there was no mess to clean up. The blood on the rug leaked out slowly. Whoever did this, did a beautiful job.'

There was a long silence. At least, I thought, Letitia did not suffer. It was not much consolation. And the way she had died left little doubt that we were dealing with a cold-blooded murder.

'How many pills do you reckon she'd had?' I asked Paul.

'Thirty, perhaps more.'

'And how many would she have taken normally, just to get to sleep.'

'Normally you'd take a couple. But once you've been taking the stuff as long as Letitia had, you need more. She probably took five if she wanted to sleep. She could have taken more. But she knew she couldn't take thirty. And Letitia wasn't suicidal, or I wouldn't have let her have them.'

'But if she was used to taking big doses, wouldn't it have taken more than the usual amount to kill her?'

'That's the trouble with phenobarbitone. Your dose keeps creeping up, but the lethal dosage stays much the same.'

'It doesn't make a great deal of sense, does it?' Virginia said suddenly. 'If you've poisoned her, why stab her?'

'Don't know. Don't know. Beyond my medical competence,' Paul Crawford said. 'But I can tell you one more thing. I would say that Letitia died at between three and four this morning. Judging by the condition of her stomach contents, she probably ate that last meal sometime not too long after two, perhaps a little earlier. There was a lot of coffee in her stomach. That's a good way to disguise phenobarbitone: in a cup of strong black coffee. If she didn't simply fall asleep, she would probably have lost consciousness about half an hour after she took the stuff.' He stopped and thought for a second: 'Probably nearer to an hour in her case, since she's so used to it.'

'So between three and four she dies. Then sometime later she's stabbed.'

'Paul, can you tell us anything about the murderer?' I asked.

'That's the brilliant thing, Sir Patrick.' Crawford laughed. 'Almost nothing. Normally, you'd say: "Blow to the right side of the neck from in front and above: assault by a tall left-hander from in front, which probably means someone strong enough to overpower Letitia." But she was unconscious. Anyone could have laid her on the floor and stuck the skewer in a few times. It was done pretty forcefully, actually. Presumably to make it look like an attack on a live victim. But anyone in the house – except, perhaps, the children – could have done it.'

'One thing's sure,' Virginia said. 'Whoever did this was in the house last night. Nobody else would have had a chance to feed her coffee laced with drugs. She'd hardly have taken it from a stranger.' There was a long pause. 'So she died from the phenobarbitone,' Virginia added matter-of-factly.

'Well, that's what you would think, wouldn't you?' Crawford paused. 'I've left the strangest thing till last. Actually, she died of suffocation. Your husband pointed out to me that there were signs of asphyxia around her eyes. So I looked at her lungs. All the signs were there. If you want the technical language she had slight acute emphysema and oedema of the lungs, with scattered areas of petechiae. In laymen's terms, her lungs were swollen with fluid in some places and collapsed in others, and there were little haemorrhages all over the place. Oh, and on the insides of her cheeks there were tears in the mucous membrane caused by someone pressing down, probably on a pillow, and forcing her cheeks against her teeth. One odd thing, by the way: the pillow that was used. Wasn't stuffed with down. Normally, even if she was unconscious, there'd be fragments of down in the nasal mucosa and the trachea.' He looked at Virginia, who had grown pale as she clutched her teacup to her. 'Are you sure you're all right, Lady Scott? If it's any consolation, it would have been very easy. She wouldn't have known about it. The phenobarbitone would have seen to that. And she wouldn't have resisted at all. As I say, whoever stabbed Letitia Rundle was stabbing a corpse.'

'You've done a marvellous job, Paul,' I said, suppressing my irritation at the rather theatrical way he had chosen to present his conclusions. 'Amazingly good. And now I think that you ought to talk to a friend of mine.'

I dialled Inspector MacAlister's number.

MacAlister was impressed. But he also had some news for us. 'The boat's back, though they had a hell of a ride. Only three passengers. We asked 'em all routine questions. One was a young woman whose mother works in the hotel on the island, off to spend the New Year with a boyfriend. We called the hotel and the boyfriend. They confirmed everything. Then there was a young black man, an American professor, looking rather sickly, who'd been out to Sealsay because he'd heard that one of St Columba's monks was an African. Said he wanted to "know what the brother went through". He'd one of them very American names: Skip, I think. Obviously he had nothing to do with it. But the third passenger, now he was a much more interesting person.'

The police had started routine questioning of a tall, slender young man with long hair. What was he doing on the island? Tourism. Where did he stay? The hotel. (That was confirmed.) What did he do on the island? Walk. Did he, by any chance, walk up on the cliffs on the western side of the island in the middle of the afternoon yesterday? Absolutely not.

What was his profession? He was an actor.

At that point something about the young man's manner suggested to Inspector MacAlister that he ought to ask if he would accompany him to the station. When the young man refused, MacAlister arrested him on suspicion of conspiracy with person or persons unknown to commit fraud by simulating the death of Letitia Rundle. This inspired speculation struck home, and the young man's bravado collapsed. And then he clammed up, asked for a lawyer and refused to say another word. When they searched him, they found a black dress and a grey wig in his knapsack, along with £1,000 in crisp twenty-pound notes. His driver's licence was in the name of Joseph Wells.

'What are you going to do with Mr Wells?'

'He doesn't yet know that Miss Rundle is dead. I think once he knows that the issue isn't fraud but murther, we'll get something out of him. But we'll leave him overnight in the cells to think about it.'

It was close to half-past six when we got off the phone with MacAlister. Paul Crawford suggested we go across to the bar for a drink. 'I will not pretend that I care much myself for the notion that there is a late evening hour at which tippling becomes appropriate. But I realise others make such distinctions.'

The cold rain was turning to sleet and the high winds, which roared round the walls as we came out of the shelter of the house, stung my face. Virginia turned her back into the wind and walked backwards between us towards the hotel and the bar. The stuccoed walls of the Sealsay Hotel, a great cube of a building, were taking a severe beating. We aimed for the side door to the large bar, next to the small dining-room, through the window of which we could see half a dozen empty tables.

Even from a dozen yards away you could hear, over the noise of the wind, the cheery sounds of a festive crowd of drinkers. When we opened the door and stepped in, the crowd fell silent for a moment. Into the warm and smoke-filled silence, Paul Crawford said, 'Ladies and gentlemen of Sealsay, these are my friends Sir Patrick and Lady Scott, who are here on Sealsay for the New Year.'

There was a chorus of welcome. 'Actually, Paul,' I said, 'I recognise a few of these people. Isn't that David Sealsay over there?'

'Indeed it is. I'd forgotten that you've been coming here for many a long year.'

We walked through the crowd to a small table on the back wall of the bar. Over to our left sat Jock at a table of older men, nursing a pint. He nodded as I caught his eye. The rest of the gathering consisted largely of young men in jeans and jerseys. Their coats hung dripping from pegs just inside the door. By and large they had long hair and beards, and cigarettes hanging from their lips. It was early in the evening, but their faces were already ruddy, as much from the wind as from the whisky. We smiled and greeted each group as we passed, and I acknowledged the occasional, mostly older, faces I thought I recognised.

'Sir Patrick,' David Sealsay said, rising to greet us. 'You'll remember Fiona, ma wife.'

'Of course, I do, David; and this is *my* wife, Virginia.'

'Virginia, David and Fiona Sealsay . . . or should I say Macintosh?'

'It's a pleasure to meet you.' Fiona Sealsay spoke gently, her soft voice shy and friendly.

'And this is ma boy, Niall,' David clapped his arm round the shoulder of the handsome young man beside him, with his dark Celtic looks and blue eyes, 'who you'll nae doubt see havering around the kitchen at the great house, waiting for that Annie Callander though not, I should think, in this weather.'

Niall blushed and smiled and looked away. I had met the boy, who was David's grandson, before, when he was a child. His parents had died in a car accident in his teens and David and Fiona had raised him.

'Well, this is all very cosy,' Paul Crawford said. 'But what we now need is a drink. What can I get for you?'

It was a pleasant enough interlude from the grim business up at Sealsay House. I had always liked David Sealsay. He had a kind of solid dignity, the sort of person it would seem merely patronising to call 'one of nature's gentlemen', since his manners were the result not of nature but of the nurture of careful parents. He was humorous, too, in a mildly ironical way, as if living here on the island, dependent on the whims of the sheep and the weather, had made him sceptical of human pretensions. But Letitia's death – which he presumably still thought of as a suicide – brought out his mildness and his compassion.

'So you found her,' he said as we settled down with our drinks.

'Indeed,' I said.

'It's a terrible thing that has happened to her,' David Sealsay said. 'Of course, we never saw her but once a year at Hogmanay. But I dinna think she had a vairry pleasant life. Mind you, she was a different pairson before her mother fell. You wouldna know it was the same lass. And then to die in the vairry spot where her mother died.' He saw at once, from the looks on our faces, that we did not know what he was talking about, and fell, for a moment, into a puzzled silence. 'Now why would they want to keep that from you?'

'I was here the summer after she died,' I said. 'They said it was an accident. Of course, no one felt much like talking about it and I didn't ask.'

'Still, it's a long while ago, now,' David Sealsay said. 'And to my mind, there's no shame to the living when a pairson takes their own life. It's the killing of others that is shameful.'

'What happened?' Virginia asked.

'She jumped from the edge up yonder; from the Moray cliffs. There's steps in the rock, up there, carved by the old monks. You can climb out to a cave mouth and look at the sea. The old laird went there often. They say she went down there and fell from the ledge. Her body came back on to the beach at Kilfadden, but they found a scrap of her dress on the ledge up there.'

It was the second time David had said 'they' said something. 'Are *you* sure it was an accident, David? You don't sound convinced.'

'It's best not to delve too deep in the past.'

'Och, but she was always a sad woman,' Fiona said. 'We were newly married and I was a stranger here, from Kintyre. She was vairry kind. Always coming down to the farm to see how I was settling. And then, one day, she was gone.'

'After that the laird told us all to keep away from the stairs there. Though I doubt that kept the boys away.'

'Have you ever been down there, Niall?' Paul asked.

'Och, aye. I have. I was there yesterday.'

It was his grandfather's turn to look surprised.

'Well, I knew the story of the old laird's wife. I thought, mebbe Miss Letitia might have fallen on the ledge there. So when you sent me up with Gary and Alex last night to have a look, I just climbed down the steps to the ledge there. But there was no sign of her. She definitely went over the edge.'

'What time was that?' I asked.

'Och, now. It must have been about seven. It was long after dark.'

I felt awkward not telling David Sealsay and his family the truth. But the news that Letitia had been murdered was still confined to the residents of the house. Still, if the Callander girl was Niall's girlfriend, it was not likely to stay a secret much longer. Quietly I told them that Letitia had not died on the cliff. I told them I'd be grateful if they kept the news to themselves. 'When Annie Callander tells you about it this evening, you might try and persuade her to keep it to herself, too,' I added to Niall. He was still too shocked to do anything but nod in dumb assent.

As we left, David Sealsay muttered, 'It's a terrible thing . . .'

Paul Crawford came with us towards the door, and we waited there for Jock, who was saying goodbye to his drinking companions. We had both rather taken to Paul, with his courtly melancholia. So that when Virginia suggested, in parting, that he might come up in the morning around ten and go for a walk with us, I was rather pleased. It would be nice to see him, and we could ask him any medical questions we thought up in the watches of the night.

9

We reached Sealsay House at about a quarter to eight, unwrapped ourselves from our overcoats and changed out of our wellingtons, and made our way towards the drawing-room. In the hall, we met Justin, in his green-striped flannel pyjamas, making his way up, in the company of his father, to bed. 'Hallo, Justin,' I said. 'I gather you saw a ghost last night?' Christopher looked at me with mild disapproval. I winked at him. 'I can promise you he won't come again tonight,' I went on. 'I'm going to keep watch all night.'

'I'm not afraid of him, anyway,' Justin said. 'He hasn't even got a head.'

'Well, what did he look like?' Jinny prompted.

'Like a man.'

'Are you sure it wasn't a lady?'

'Women wear dresses, silly.'

Christopher gave me an apologetic, if indulgent, look but I had to be sure that Justin was not making a mistake. 'A lady could wear trousers,' I said.

'He was a man ghost,' Justin said emphatically, 'a man. He went through the wall,' he added triumphantly, 'and a lady couldn't do that.' Justin stuck his tongue out at us and marched on up the stairs.

Christopher ran after his son, catching his hand. 'He's really a very nice chap normally,' he explained, as Justin dragged him away, 'it's the emotional strain of the last couple of days. I'll be down in a minute.'

'Not the most prepossessing child,' Jinny said as they disappeared. I had been thinking much the same thought.

The whole party, save Christopher, the nannies and the children, was gathered in the drawing-room. Even Angela was up, leaning back in an armchair, her belly uncomfortably vast.

It was clear that they had all been speculating about the news we would be bringing back from Paul Crawford. But there was something else in the atmosphere, something not at all pleasant: a slight tension, as if we had interrupted them plotting behind our backs.

Maria, whose mood had seemed less gloomy than everyone else's yesterday, looked positively weighed down with cares. Otherwise, everyone was determined to look pleasant, including Emma Gale, who was, as usual, both beautifully attired and just plain beautiful.

'Welcome back,' Iona said. 'Do come over to the fireplace and dry out. I've asked Mary to do a cold buffet and some hot soup at about eight, and we shan't be dressing.'

'Thank you,' Jinny said and we took her up on her offer of a place by the fire.

'Any news?' Gavin asked tentatively. He did not look at all as though he had recovered from last night's excesses, but I noticed that he was drinking fruit juice. 'About Aunt Letitia, I mean.'

'Not much, I'm afraid,' I lied. 'As you know, she was stabbed several times. Dr Crawford has still to work out, insofar as he can, when she died. But it was probably sometime in the early morning. We shall know much more when he has done some tests.'

If anyone in the room knew anything about autopsies, they were unlikely to believe me. But until we knew more, it was probably not a good idea to reveal the ghastly sequence of abuses to which Letitia had been subjected. If anyone asked me about it later, I could say I was trying to spare the sensibilities of the ladies.

Ever since Inspector MacAlister had told me about the young man on the boat with the £1,000, something had been tickling the back of my cerebellum. Horace Strachan was settled in a comfortable chair in a corner, puffing away at his pipe, and nursing a large undiluted whisky. Jessica was standing next to him and they had been talking quietly. Seeing them together I realised suddenly that between them they had given me the solution to one of our mysteries. I went over to join them, and they both greeted me politely, Strachan with his normal *bonhomie*, Jessica somewhat more restrainedly.

'Did you know that a friend of yours was visiting the island?'

'Really?' Jessica said. 'Who was that?'

'A young man by the name of Joseph Wells. I believe you two were acting together in Edinburgh last festival.'

Jessica Rundle was not a star of stage and screen for nothing. For only the briefest of brief moments did she seem disturbed by this news; if I had not been watching her closely I would not have seen the flicker of anxiety that crossed her fair and famous features. 'Really?' she said again. 'How odd that he didn't get in touch. Perhaps next time.'

'Whom did he play in *Macbeth* last year?'

'Didn't he tell you?'

'I've never spoken to him,' I said.

She had forborne from asking me how I knew that he was on the island; just as I had forborne from asking her how she knew he was no longer here. But now *not* asking would seem suspicious, and so she smiled at me, a dazzling smile, and said, 'Then how clever of you to know. Do tell me. How *do* you know we acted together?'

'Begin with the fact that your Aunt Letitia did not jump over the cliff yesterday.' By now the whole room was silent, as everybody waited for me to continue. 'I suppose she might just have jumped down to the ledge that Alistair showed me today, but it would have been enormously risky at her age. She might have slipped, or broken an ankle. I thought it very unlikely. If that was right, then Gavin had not been entirely truthful when he told Virginia that he had seen Letitia at the cliff's edge. It had to be someone else.' I paused and cast a glance in Gavin's direction. He looked distinctly uncomfortable. 'Until not very long ago I had assumed that it must have been a member of the family or one of the islanders. If Letitia – who has hardly ever left this island and knows almost nobody elsewhere – wished to stage her own disappearance, who else could she ask? But at lunchtime, you, Jessica, and Mr Strachan told me that Aunt Letitia had seen you in a production at last year's Edinburgh festival and that she had met the cast. When the police arrested a young actor off the boat today with a good deal too much money in new banknotes, it occurred to me that there was a third possibility. The rest was guesswork.'

'Bravo, Sir Patrick,' Angela Horseman said drily. 'An' so we come to the close of anod'er episode of "Patrick Scott, detective".'

'I'm afraid, Miss Horseman, that we have hardly begun. You see, I cannot for the life of me think why Letitia would want to do so cruel a thing as convince us all that she was dead.'

'But if it wasn't here on the cliff top,' Horace Strachan said ruminatively, 'how do you know she *did* want to do that?'

'Why else would she have stayed hidden away in the west tower last night?'

'Perhaps she was kept there against her will.'

'She was free to come and go, I believe. She walked through Justin's bedroom, on the way through their shared bathroom to her own bedroom, I imagine.'

'Justin saw a headless man with his head under his arm,' Maria said.

'I know,' I said. 'That was somebody else visiting Letitia; probably a man carrying something to her.'

'I suppose the reason you're telling us all this is to point out we haven't been entirely truthful throughout this business,' Gavin said.

'Speak for yourself, Gav,' Jessica said quietly.

I sighed heavily and massaged my temples with my right hand. I had not really meant to pick this moment to set the cat quite so firmly among the pigeons. 'I realise that there's a reason to cover up private family matters when somebody kills herself. But what you don't seem to understand is that we're now dealing with murder. Somebody – I regret to have to say, probably somebody in this room – murdered Letitia. And it is presumably in the interest of everybody else in this room to find out who it was.'

'Why must it be one of us?' Alistair's voice rose in pitch. He coughed and started again in a deeper baritone. 'There are other people on this island.'

'They had little opportunity and no motive,' I told him.

'Gavin,' Colin said gravely, 'Patrick's right. Tell him what really happened at the cliff's edge.'

'It was Aunt Letitia's idea,' he began. 'Sometime in November, she got Jessica to offer that actor a large sum of money if he would come over here, pretend to be her, and jump on to the ledge on the Moray cliffs.'

'I thought it was just one of her pranks,' Jessica said. 'She didn't volunteer an explanation. But it seemed harmless enough and I didn't see why I should deprive Joe of £1,000.'

'Why did she pick him?'

'He was playing one of the witches in the Scottish play. A tall, thin elderly woman dressed in black. I think Letitia thought he looked pretty much like her from a distance. He was to do the leap in his witch's costume, just before the New Year.'

'It's so typical of Letitia to pick a time that was guaranteed to ruin everybody's fun,' Joanna said. Colin and Alistair glared fiercely at her in the silence that followed; but she went on, with a quiet firmness, 'Well, it's true.'

Gavin continued. 'Jessica's actor arrived a couple of days ago and Letitia told me to take him up there and show him the ropes. His job was to wait till he saw me coming up with somebody and turn towards us. I ran ahead to him, guided him to the spot where the ledge was and told him when to jump. Letitia gave me the money. I left it inside the cave, behind the ledge on Thursday. He was to wait half an hour then change back into his own clothes and go back down to the hotel and catch the ferry back this evening.' Gavin looked at me earnestly and then turned to his father. 'That's the truth.'

'Of course, once we found Letitia this morning, Gavin passed all this on to me. He was to have told you after dinner,' Colin said. 'I suppose I should have got him to tell you at once. But once Letitia was dead, the details of her scheme seemed unimportant.'

'Didn't either of you ask her *why* she wanted to do this strange thing? I mean, if only you three knew, you were causing a great deal of unhappiness to the rest of your family.'

Iona had been standing very still throughout these exchanges, looking increasingly perplexed. Suddenly, she turned to her husband with a look of hatred and rage. 'You all knew, didn't you?' she hissed. 'You let me suffer. My husband, my children, you all conspired against me with that horrid woman. Maybe God will forgive you – I can't.' And she ran from the room sobbing hysterically.

For what must have been a minute there was stunned silence. Then Maria said, 'You didn't! You bloody didn't! You bastards!' and ran out after her mother.

I waited for a moment to see if anyone else would join the exodus of the non-conspirators. 'Am I to understand that everyone still in this room save, of course, my wife and myself, was in on Letitia's plot?'

'Of course not,' Horace Strachan said. 'I wasn't even here.'

'Nor me,' Emma Gale said. 'But I suppose it was kept in the family.'

'Miss Horseman?'

'I knew.'

'Shock's not good for babies,' Jessica said. 'I couldn't risk it.'

Colin had been standing staring out of the window since Iona left, tense and silent. 'What I don't understand is why Iona's convinced I was in on the plan.' Somehow, I suspected that Iona was right. Colin didn't want me to know that he had been in on Letitia's plan. That meant he thought that once I did know, I would be closer to working out *her* motives. 'Jessica and Gavin really shouldn't have let Letitia talk them into this,' Colin went on. But there was something rather unconvincing about the rebuke.

The gong went in the hall, announcing dinner. As the party began to move slowly out of the drawing-room, Christopher came back in. 'Gosh, you do all look glum.'

'Kit, darling,' Joanna said, 'I think I'd better bring you up to date.'

10

'Delicious ham,' Strachan said, helping himself for the third time. 'Absolutely delicious.'

He was certainly right. We had not had much in the way of lunch and our exertions in climbing up to the Moray cliffs had left me with a substantial appetite. But the circumstances of our meal did not allow me to savour the victuals. I soon found myself pushing a plate of half-eaten food aside. Virginia had taken very little and eaten it very slowly. I confess that Nanny had not prepared me for this most difficult of crises of manners. How should one behave at a table occupied by people who had so thoroughly breached the most elementary canons of hospitality?

'If you don't mind, Virginia and I will go off to the estate office. We must make a couple of telephone calls. We really ought to phone Sebastian, our son, and then I must report in to the police. And then, Mr Strachan, if you would be so good, I should like to take up some matters with you. Shall we say in an hour?'

'Delighted,' Strachan said, I assume because this gave him sufficient time to attend to the trifle.

Virginia and I walked in silence down the corridor to the estate office. I unlocked the door with the key Parsons had given me. We entered and I closed it behind us. And I took Virginia in my arms.

'I've never felt so . . . so violated,' she said. 'I mean Gavin just used me for this plot of his aunt's and he didn't even have the grace to ask why.'

'I know,' I said. 'I know. Let's call Seb and tell him what's going on.'

'Darling, do be careful what you say to him. He'll only worry.'

'You talk to him, my sweet. I just want to be sure that the house is all right.'

This harmless remark produced from my wife a lecture on

the virtues of trusting one's children. The gist of it was that we shouldn't have allowed Sebastian to have a party of his medical friends at our house at Ampney for the weekend of the New Year if we were going to worry about what harm they could wreak. I particularly recall Jinny's use of the word 'wreak' because it put me in mind of 'havoc' and made the phone call seem even more urgent. It was a great relief to discover a few minutes later that my son and his wife had no troubles to report.

Jinny chatted to the scion of the Scotts for a little while, confirming that their house party was going rather better than ours, and that Hermione was safely asleep in her cot. Then she passed Sebastian on to me, and we had one of our conversations.

'Hello, Father, I gather you've stumbled on yet another corpse.'

'*I* don't kill them, you know.'

'Well, take care of yourself . . . and of Mama.' My son adopted a mildly censorious tone, which rather undercut the spirit of his good wishes. 'And a happy New Year to you when the time comes.' He rang off. Another intimate exchange between the Scotts, *père et fils*. I had not had time to tell him, as I had meant to, that we should certainly try and phone them at the turn of the year.

'We should telephone MacAlister,' I said distractedly. While Jinny had been busy with Seb, I had been thinking. 'You know, darling, if it makes you feel any better, I wouldn't assume that they really were all in on it. Colin may have told the rest of them and got them to close ranks when the plot began to unravel. And I wouldn't assume that the conspirators don't know what Letitia's motives were, either.'

'But Gavin . . .' Jinny said. I was about to respond, 'Ah yes, plausible Gavin,' when I caught a certain look in Virginia's eye. 'And if you say anything at all about his plausibility,' my dear wife added, 'I shall fill you with phenobarbitone, suffocate you and stab you with a skewer.'

'There's nae doubt they're a weird lot,' MacAlister said, after listening patiently to my account of the evening's happenings.

'And I see you found out Mr Wells's story by yourself. I've taken a statement from him and sent him on his way. They didna tell him very much. He says he's only met Jessica and Gavin, really, though he remembers shaking the old lady's hand last summer backstage. He didn't mention that he was playing one of our weird Scots witches!' MacAlister chuckled. 'The things they get up to in Edinburgh.'

'Well, I think that's all we've got for now.'

'It's a start . . . Are you sure you feel safe? I mean, it's an awkward situation. For all we know, if several of them were in on the first plot, they may also have been in on the murther.'

'So far I think we're all right. We'll move to the hotel if we feel in any danger, don't worry.'

'We'll look at the weather and see if we can get somebody in in the morning. But the forecast isn't encouraging. They reckon the soonest we can get on to the island is Sunday.'

'Well, no one's going to get away before that,' I said.

'True enough. True enough. So now you're going to see what you can get out of Mr Horace Strachan, advocate of Edinburgh, eh?'

'Exactly.'

We said our farewells.

'Nice fella, is he?' Jinny said.

'Charming.'

'Does he have any notion about why Letitia might have set up this whole business?'

'None that he's vouchsafed to me. But maybe we can do a little better. Why would anyone stage their own suicide?'

'Because she wanted someone to think she was dead.'

'And why would Letitia have wanted *us* to think she was dead?'

We both thought for a while about this, without coming up with anything much. Virginia said, 'Well, it wouldn't be a prank. Surely it's too elaborate and bizarre, even for Letitia.'

'No. But perhaps she wanted someone else, someone who would believe *us*, to think she was dead.'

'Of course, she might only have needed to be dead for a bit.'

'I don't think I buy that. If Gavin knew why she did it, Colin must have known, too. Neither of them would go along with a crack-pot scheme like this for no good reason. And if they knew, why shouldn't Alistair have known? Still, you're right, she might have been planning a miraculous return from the dead.'

'That would be quite a shock. For someone with a weak heart it might be enough to . . .' We looked at each other for a moment, 'two souls with but a single thought'.

'It's a possibility. But I don't know why she'd want to kill Horace, who's the only person in the party who'd be susceptible to that sort of thing.' I started again. 'Let's try another tack. Letitia hardly ever goes anywhere. Most of the islanders only see her once a year. Even David Sealsay, who lives on the home farm at the end of the drive, hardly ever sees her. It wouldn't be hard for her to go on living here, as she did before. So suppose she wanted to be legally dead. Most people would have to give up their old life to do that. But Letitia could go on almost as before.'

'Okay.' Virginia provided one of her fine summaries of the situation: 'It's not a prank. But it might have been meant to make someone do something, something they would only do if Letitia was dead. Or it might have been to do with her will, or insurance or something of that sort.'

'Well, we can follow up that line of thought once Strachan tells us about her will and her finances. It's all very mysterious.'

I smiled at Virginia, a tired smile, and she patted me on the knee. I looked around the room. The bookcases were piled high with papers of one sort and another and odd, old books on farming and land tenure and Scottish history. Above the fireplace, on the bare wall, was a large square patch of lighter surface where a painting had obviously stopped the soot from gathering. The sight of it triggered my memory.

'Jinny, I've just had a thought.' I looked at my watch. 'It's only half-past nine. Strachan won't be here for a quarter of an hour or so. I think I'll call Jim FitzGibbon.' Jinny gave her assent when I explained why.

James FitzGibbon is a junior in my chambers. I suppose it's fair to say he's a nice enough chap, and he works very, very hard. But I would barter most of his hours of labour in a flash for a few moments of intellectual clarity. Still, over the years, Smedley, our clerk, has carved out a nice little practice for him, and, while he is not my ideal as an advocate, he is, as I say, a nice enough chap. Because I have occasionally helped him understand the odd legal issue, he is rather embarrassingly convinced of the powers of my ageing grey matter. He is also willing, as a result, to undertake the odd chore. No one else, I suspected, would be grateful for an interruption at half-past nine in the evening the night before New Year's Eve. I imagined him sitting in his little mews house in Fulham, a great pile of papers on his desk, fretting gently about how little of it he understood, longing to be interrupted.

'Hallo, Jim,' I said.

The noise in the background did not suggest that I had caught him in a quiet reflective moment. 'Hallo,' he shouted. 'Hallo. Look, you'll have to speak up – it's awfully noisy here.'

'It's Patrick,' I said. 'Patrick Scott.'

'Oh hallo, Patrick.' His voice perked up reassuringly as he said my name. 'Sorry about the noise. I've got a few people here. How nice to hear from you. How's Solway?'

'It's Sealsay, actually, Jim. And it's . . . well it's rather hard to explain actually. But the thing is, I've the most tremendous favour to ask of you.'

'You haven't got involved in a murder again, have you, Patrick?'

'I can assure that I have not killed anyone.'

'Oh, Patrick, you have. How exciting. Anybody I know?'

'I should very much doubt it, Jim. Hardly anybody knew the person in question. A very private person.'

'Well, go on then, fire away. How can I help?'

'Do you still see that young woman who writes about the art trade? Was her name . . . Elizabeth Hamilton?'

'Well . . . it all depends what you mean by "see".'

'I'm sorry Jim, I'm not trying to pry into your private life, but I need to know something that I think she might be able to find out.'

'Well I *could* telephone her, I suppose.' The prospect seemed both to delight and terrify him.

'Tonight?'

'Ah, tonight,' he said doubtfully. 'Well, I suppose so. What exactly is it that you need to know?'

When I told him, he developed a tone of mild scepticism. 'What on earth has this got to do with the murder of a very private person?'

'Jim,' I said, 'I promise, absolutely promise, that you will get the complete story when I get back to London.'

'All right then, I'll telephone back when I've got the answer.'

'No, James. I don't think that's a good idea. I'm not often near the phone up here. May I call you back in an hour or so?'

'Doesn't give me very long to butter up Liz, does it?'

'Two hours?'

'Done.'

'I'll phone a little after half-past eleven.'

When Horace Strachan rolled in a few minutes later, Virginia excused herself. 'I'm terribly tired, Mr Strachan, so if you'll forgive me, I shall leave you men to your business. Good-night. À bientôt, Paddy.'

'A very handsome woman, your good wife, if you don't mind my saying so, Sir Patrick.'

'Not at all. It's an opinion I share.'

Horace Strachan laughed heartily. 'Very good.' And then, almost immediately, he was serious again. 'I must say it's very odd, very odd indeed, to treat a guest the way you and Lady Scott have been treated by Miss Rundle. And entirely out of character for the family, if I may say so. My family has been looking after the legal affairs of the Rundles, at least insofar as they appertain to Scotland, for three generations. And I don't believe that in all that time, there has been quite such an extraordinary breach of . . . good form.' He sucked noisily at his pipe and then set about cleaning and refilling it.

'I've been coming here on and off for nearly fifty years myself, Mr Strachan, and I'm bound to say it doesn't fit with my sense of the family either.'

Horace Strachan beamed at me. 'Then we are of one mind.' He lit his pipe and began puffing again.

'And that suggests', I went on, 'that she did this extraordinary thing because something extremely important to her was at stake.'

'Aha! But what could that be?'

'Well, perhaps you can help me there, by telling me something. Do you know the contents of Letitia's will.'

'I do. I've a copy with me.'

'And may I know . . .'

'Sir Colin, as executor, has instructed me to provide you with any information you need.'

'May I see the document?'

'It's in my briefcase upstairs.' Strachan made it obvious, by shrugging slightly, and struggling with the arms of his chair, that so long a journey would involve enormous effort.

'Well, in that case, I think the outlines will do for the moment.'

'I should say to begin with that the most significant consequences of her death flow not from the will but from the trusts of which she is . . . or, rather, was . . . the sole beneficiary. But outlines, as you say, outlines.'

11

The outlines were simple enough. Letitia was, during her lifetime, the sole beneficiary of two trusts set up by her father and grandfather. Each was set up in roughly the same terms. In each case half the income each year was to be reinvested to build the capital value of the trust, and she was to have the other half to do with as she wished. She could not, under any circumstances, get access to the capital. If they discovered she had borrowed against future income, the trustees – who were now her brother and Mr Strachan himself – were to reduce the payments to her by the amount of her borrowing. At her death, her brother became the sole beneficiary, provided he was still Laird of Sealsay, and he was free to use the whole capital sum as he wished.

'I've kept the best bit for last,' Strachan said. 'The current capital value of the two trusts is about £4,000,000.'

'So the income is about £200,000? Half of which would have been reinvested. So last year Letitia earned £100,000?'

'Exactly. And the year before she earned a similar amount; and she has earned such amounts now for nearly forty years.'

'Well, what has she done with it?'

'After Her Majesty's Commissioners of Inland Revenue have taken a hefty chunk, she has given most of it to pay for expenses here on the island. Upkeep of the house. Wages. And she has usually given a good deal to her younger brother since he has been in Parliament. The rest she simply saved.'

'Alistair mentioned that she had left the income from her publishing to him.'

'Not just the income. Over the years, she simply deposited all the money from her publishing in a royalty account. She rarely drew on it; but I suppose, since Colin, as her trustee, kept an eye on her other finances, she could have used it to pay for things she didn't want him to know about. She kept her whole publishing career a secret from the family. Alistair will come into about £120,000. And royalties still trickle in to the tune of several thousand pounds a year.'

'Do you know about the finances of the rest of the family?'

'Sir Colin told me that I was at liberty to describe his situation in a general way.'

'I assume that if Letitia got that much, her brothers were also well provided for.'

'Sir Colin got the island and the London house and an estate in Lancashire. Like Letitia he was deeded money in trust by his grandfather, in fact he was deeded considerably more; but unlike her he gained control of that sum on his twenty-fifth birthday. And on his father's death he received about five times what Letitia got. Alistair was not born when Sir Josiah died. He received only a legacy from his mother.'

'Isn't that rather odd? Didn't Sir Henry leave him anything?'

'Sir Henry settled most of his money on his first-born son and on Letitia. I assume that his treatment of Alistair reflected a normal English belief in primogeniture: here in Scotland, as you know, we take a different view. I doubt he would have settled more than a modest sum on Letitia if he had thought that she was likely to marry. After all, she was not in a position to *earn* a living.' He pulled himself up short. 'That would have been her father's view, anyway. Actually, she made a rather good living, didn't she? But from Sir Henry's point of view, he had either to give her an income or to cast her on her elder brother's mercies.'

I nodded. 'I gather you are also Gavin's trustee.'

'Yes. Sir Henry's grandchildren each came into a significant sum when they reached the age of twenty-five. During their minority and until the age of twenty-five, I was empowered as trustee to make income from their trusts available for their aducation and other expenses. But that is coming to an end. Gavin will be twenty-five next year and he will be the last. Letitia told me that was why she was not going to leave them any of the money she had saved over the years from trust income.'

'How much is that?'

'Another quarter of a million pounds.'

I was unable to contain a little show of astonishment. 'Good Lord!' Strachan smiled, pleased that he had surprised me. I pushed ahead. 'Who'd she bequeath it to?'

'To Sir Colin, if he stopped supporting *Glitz*; to Lady Rundle if he didn't.'

Strachan's remark had been phrased and pronounced casually. It had the effect I presume he intended. It stopped me dead in my tracks. 'Well,' I said eventually, '. . . well, well.' Strachan knew how to spin a yarn, and this one had risen in an elegant crescendo. He smiled again, a Cheshire-cat grin of self-satisfaction that took up his whole face.

'Indeed. A message from the grave, you might say.'

'Will the Scottish courts carry out that wish?'

'The way I drafted it, they will. Sir Colin must cease to be publisher of the magazine *Glitz* within a year of Letitia's death, and he must covenant not to support its publication in future by subvention, or subscription; he must pay nothing to any member of the editorial staff; and he must not fund or publish any magazine of which the current editor of *Glitz* is editor or publisher.'

'Does Sir Colin know about this?'

'I told him on the telephone yesterday. Letitia had asked me not to mention it to him while she was alive. I wouldn't say he sounded surprised.'

'When did Letitia make this codicil?'

'On her trip to Edinburgh last summer. Actually, it's not a

codicil. She had the whole will redrafted and then went off to see a psychiatrist who affirmed that she was completely *compos mentis* and acted as a witness to her signature. But, with the exception of the business about the magazine, the substance of the will has not changed for many years.'

'Did you ask her why she made this condition?'

'Letitia Rundle was, as you know, a woman of few words. I made some enquiries after her visit which satisfied me that she was attempting to save her brother's marriage. I must say I admired her for that.'

'You realise it's just as likely to destroy the marriage?'

'I don't think so. I doubt that Lady Rundle would leave, even if she had a quarter of a million pounds; and I have formed the impression that Miss Gale will not stay long after the money runs out.'

'Inspector MacAlister will think that the will gives Colin and Alistair and, arguably, Iona, motives for murdering Letitia.'

'Maybe. But remember, she hardly ever spent money on herself. And she's been giving both her brothers large sums of money for years.'

'Do you have any notion as to why she would have set up that elaborate charade yesterday?'

'She must have wished the consequences I've just described to occur.'

'But why?'

'I've been thinking about that all afternoon. Can't come up with a thing. If she wanted to give Alistair the publishing money, she could have done so at any time. If she wanted to offer Colin or Iona a quarter of a million pounds, she was free to. The only thing she couldn't do was free up the £4,000,000 or so in the trust funds. But Sir Colin was to get all that eventually; and I can't think what he would need it for now.'

For the hour or so we had been talking, Strachan's pipe had been pumping smoke into the room. The smell was pleasant enough but I realised that my eyes were watering. I blinked a few times and then looked down at my watch. 'Good Lord, how late it is! You know, I think I'll just pop out for a breath of fresh air before retiring. Care to come with me?'

Horace Strachan did not exactly radiate the impression of a man keen on fresh air and he looked at me unblinking as if searching for evidence of sincerity. Eventually he decided that I really expected him to consider the proposition. So he took a reflective puff and then sighed deeply, before he said, 'I think that I shall return to the drawing-room for a wee dram.'

I locked the estate office behind us and followed the vast floating bulk of Horace Strachan down the corridor to the hall. 'Good-night,' he said, all geniality, a slight urgency quickening his step at the thought of the Oban malt.

'Good-night . . . and thank you. That was very, very helpful.'

I stepped out through the porch to decide whether I needed an overcoat. Despite Inspector MacAlister's gloomy forecast, the storm was beginning to work itself out. The rain had stopped and the wind had dropped a good deal. Occasionally there were breaks in the clouds through which I could see the moon. Maybe he would be able to get a policeman on to the island the next day.

I heard a step on the gravel over to my right by the kitchens and saw a figure walking towards me, as I stood in the light from the porch. It was Niall, David Sealsay's grandson.

'Hallo there,' he said sheepishly, 'I was just coming to take Annie home, but they tell me that Jock took her and Elizabeth home a while ago.'

'It's very late,' I said. 'Does she normally stay here this late?'

'Och, no. Not when she starts about six in the morning most days. But tomorra's the holiday: there's more than usual to get ready. And she won't come till the afternoon tomorra, so she does nae fa' asleep later.'

'The storm seems to be fading.'

'It'll be back,' he said with the certainty of one who had lived his whole life on the island. 'But maybe we'll have a clear night for the New Year.'

'That would be nice.'

'Aye, it would.'

'Well, I must go back in. I was just taking in a breath of fresh air. Good-night.'

'Good-night, Sir Patrick.'

I went in and walked across to the drawing-room. Then I decided it was ridiculous to bid good-night to a party of people who had behaved towards us as they had done. And then I thought again that I needed to keep talking to them. As I hemmed and hawed I started first for the drawing-room and then for the stairs and then back to the drawing-room again. I heard Virginia's laughter from the top of the stairs, and so I looked up to where she was watching me over the banisters. 'Come up and talk to me, darling,' she said, 'you can talk to the others again in the morning.'

'I have to telephone James at about half-past eleven.'

'Then you've long enough to come up and get ready for bed and talk to me before you phone him.'

I am glad that they have revised the liturgy of the marriage service. All those wives promising obedience over the years, when everybody knows what really happens. Those vows were an unnecessary occasion of sin. Meekly I climbed the stairs.

'Look what Maria's given me,' Jinny said, when we arrived back in our bedroom. On the bedside table was a pile of half a dozen paperback books. I picked one up. *Love Vanishes* was the title and the cover showed a tall handsome Scotsman (or so I inferred from his tam-o'-shanter and kilt), a sort of clean-shaven Rob Roy, standing outlined against a moonlit sky, with a ruined tower on the cliffs behind him and a sylph-like creature in a long white ball-gown in his arms. I was reading through the highly favourable excerpts from reviews in the national press – 'Miss Lomond triumphs again!' said the *Glasgow Herald* – when Virginia removed the work gently from my hands. 'First, the news from Horace Strachan.'

'Well, as our transatlantic cousins would say, the bottom line is this: Alistair gets something over £100,000. Colin gets £4,000,000 from various trusts and . . . this is the best bit . . . another quarter of a million if he stops supporting Emma Gale's magazine. If not, Iona gets it.'

'Well, that's pretty direct.'

'As you saw, when Letitia did say anything she was nothing if not direct.'

'Anything else?'

'Well, it's rather odd, given that Letitia was so well provided for, that Alistair's only inheritance was something from his mother. I mean, why did both her grandfather and her father leave her so much and Alistair nothing?'

'What did they leave Colin?'

'Oh, a very great deal. All the property and a good deal more money than Letitia. But it wasn't tied up, as hers was. *She* couldn't spend any capital at all.' With Virginia, I went through the notes of my conversation with Strachan. 'There's one other odd thing,' I said finally. 'About six months ago Alistair telephoned me with a question about getting money out of a trust. He said it was a Scottish trust, set up by his father, of which he was the beneficiary and he set out some of the terms. He asked if he could get at the capital. The answer, so far as I could see, was no.'

Virginia looked at me expectantly. 'So far I'd say that wasn't odd at all.'

'It's odd because, as I just said, Alistair didn't inherit any money from his father.' I'm afraid I rather snapped at Jinny; she doesn't usually need these things explaining to her.

'It's a jolly good thing their family crest says *"ferreus"* and not *"veritas"*.' Virginia kindly ignored my snappishness. 'They all seem congenitally incapable of telling the truth.'

'Except Letitia, who more than made up for the others.'

Virginia sighed and opened the book she had taken from me. 'I've been reading *Highland Fling*. It's deliciously purple. So's this one. Listen.

'Maria's heart cried out to her. With each beat, she felt the powerful pulse of her longing. Alexander was there, waiting for her under the tower, under the moon – waiting at the cliff top, his own heart beating fiercely as the waves beat on the rocks below. He was strong and gentle for her, strong and gentle in his love for her, gentle and strong as he clasped her to him. She had only to go to him and he would be hers. Hers as he had been hers yesterday, but now for tomorrow and for ever.

'And yet she could not go. Here in the great house at Kilarran, whose battlements had withstood the sieges of centuries, Alexander had come without weapons and laid siege to her heart. And he had won her because there was no man within these walls, no man in the stone-built rooms and the gallant towers, who could love her as Alexander would love her. She longed to go to him. But there was her son. And she could not leave him. She could not leave him in this loveless place.'

Virginia reads extremely well. She is much in demand to read from her own novels, and each time one appears she makes the grand tour of English book shops reading to polite audiences who drink wine out of plastic cups and wait to shake her hand. She read Letitia's prose gently and reverently, without mocking, and as she read it I felt a terrible sadness for Letitia, who had written so much of love and seen so little of it.

'Knowing Letitia, it's rather sad, isn't it?' Jinny said.

I opened *Love Vanishes*. It was dedicated: 'To My Mother, "a lady, both lovely and bright".' I scanned the first page.

Lorna Stuart of Gleniver stood at the cliff's edge, staring out from the isle's edge to the farthest horizon. Her eyes – blue eyes, blue as the clear, sun-swept sky and the reflecting deep – were troubled and her cheeks showed the tracks of dried tears. She had wept long and hard on this day – had come here to weep, where her salt tears would be lost in the mighty waters and the sound of her sobbing would fade before the ocean's roar.

'Much the same sort of thing,' I said. 'But this one's dedicated to her mother, "a lady, both lovely and bright".'

'So's this one,' Virginia said. Each of us reached at the same moment for the pile at the bedside. Virginia picked up the next book – *A Tender Magic*.

'That's the one Maria said was the first?' I said.

'Yes, it came out in 1974.' She turned over the copyright page, with the date, and scanned the page that followed. 'Epistle Dedicatory,' Jinny read. *'To my mother. Words to excuse my silences.* Rather touching. She must have been very fond of her. Perhaps her mother's death unhinged her a little.'

We looked through all the others. All had a dedication 'to my mother', but only in the first, *A Tender Magic,* and the last, *Love Vanishes*, was the dedication followed by an additional, rather obscure, phrase.

'Where does that come from: "a lady, both lovely and bright"?' I asked.

'I have a vague memory of one of those pieces of Scottish folklore collected by Walter Scott:

> 'Oh hush thee my baby, thy sire was a knight,
> Thy mother's a lady, both lovely and bright.'

I am always delighted to be reminded that I married an encyclopedia. I set about getting ready for bed cheerfully, and, my ablutions complete, returned to the bedroom in my pyjamas and dressing-gown to wait the remaining twenty minutes until I was due to call James. Virginia and I lay side by side on the bed engrossed in the world of Letitia's Scottish romances. Lorna, Lady Stuart, appeared to have fallen in love with a handsome crofter rather younger than herself and devised an elaborate mode of escape from her moody and unloving husband. (Moody, unloving husbands were a theme of the Lomond *oeuvre*.) It involved . . . it involved faking her own suicide on the cliffs of the remote island where she was trapped with the unloving and moody spouse aforesaid. The details were rather different, but the idea was obviously one that she had had a long time ago. I assumed, if Jinny's experience was anything to go by, that the gap between conception, execution and publication was bound to have been at least a year.

'If she expected to get away with it, you'd have thought she'd have left rather fewer clues,' Virginia said after I had read a few of the choicest passages.

'She wasn't planning to conceal it from the family, and nobody except Horace and her publisher knew she was Daphne Lomond.'

'True. Still, it's as if she was deliberately leaving a trail.'

'What's happening in yours?'

'Maria, Lady Duncan of Loch Finch, is having this glorious affair with a young crofter to escape the boredom of her marriage to the cruel and unloving Lord Duncan. Lord Duncan seems to be about to find out that his youngest son is not the fruit of his own loins. It's terribly steamy. I wonder if they're all the same.'

'Well, I hate to miss the next instalment, but I fear I must go down and talk to James.'

12

The house was quiet as I came down the staircase into the hall. There was a light on in the corridor leading to the estate office, which gave me enough illumination to make my way. I set about unlocking the door to the office but found it was open, and when I came in, I saw Colin was sitting there, poring over some papers.

'Hallo, Patrick.' He glanced at me for a mere moment and then returned to the papers before he looked up finally, again, and said, 'I expect you need the telephone.'

'Yes, I said I would call a colleague of mine in London.'

'Go ahead, I was just setting off for bed.' He paused. 'I'm very sorry about all this, Patrick. If there's anything I can do to help . . .'

'Well, frankly, it would help if you could persuade your family just to tell the plain unvarnished truth.'

'I really am sorry that Gavin didn't tell you about Letitia's plot at once.'

'He's deliberately set out to mislead us all along. First he said he had seen Letitia on the rocks; then that she had jumped but he hadn't looked because he was afraid of heights; then he admitted it wasn't her at all. Keeping things like that secret is simply idiotic, now that there's been a murder: it puts us all in danger and it wastes police time. I might have asked the police to try to find out who had most to lose from the publication of a book that never existed. We can't find out who murdered Letitia, if we can't find out what she was really up to.' My voice had risen a good deal as I spoke. The more I thought about it, the more infuriating it was that the Rundles did not seem inclined to be helpful. 'I'm sorry, Colin, but you must admit I'm entitled to be a little bad-tempered.'

'Of course. I quite understand. And really, Patrick, it's we who owe you an apology.'

I decided to see if the air of penitence was genuine. 'Have you still no idea why Letitia plotted her scheme?'

He shook his head decisively. No sign of penitence, there. But I thought I might try a couple of other questions. 'It would help me very much if I could ask one or two rather embarrassing questions.'

'Fire away.'

'How long have you been having an affair with Emma Gale?'

Colin reddened again, as he had when I had asked him about her earlier. He bit into his lower lip so hard I thought he might draw blood, before saying sheepishly, 'I really don't see—'

'You can tell me now before we find out who killed Letitia, and then we can keep the business of your adultery separate from the business of her murder. Or we can wait for the police to do their work. They'll collect evidence. They'll snoop around her office, interrogate her staff, ask the islanders, ask Iona and your children. They'll—'

'You've made your point, Patrick. I've known Emma . . . well . . . for about three years.'

'How long had Letitia known about your relationship?'

'I don't know.'

'Did she ever say anything to you about it?'

'I gather she adverted to it when I left lunch to comfort Iona yesterday.'

'Did Emma tell you that?'

'Yes, actually.'

'When was the first time you realised Letitia knew?'

'About a year ago.'

'Did she make it plain she disapproved?'

'What do *you* think? Letitia never kept her disapproval to herself.'

'Did she tell you about the business of the will?'

'I suppose Horace told you that.'

'You *told* him to tell me about the will. And it would have come out eventually when the will was probated.'

'I only learned about it when Horace told me on the telephone yesterday.'

'Since she was planning to be alive after the will was read, she knew she would have to face you. Why don't you think she told you before?'

He snorted a little, as if reprimanding himself. 'All right, she told me not long after she did it. She told me that if I got rid of

Emma she'd change her will and leave the money to the children.'

'But you couldn't.'

'I *didn't*. Damn it, Patrick, I *love* Emma. You can't just throw something like that away on the whim of a dotty sister.'

'When did you tell Emma that Letitia's will left a quarter of a million pounds to you on condition that you stopped financing her?'

'I haven't actually told her yet.' It was what I expected him to say, though I had been hoping against hope. And if he was lying still, it meant he still had something important to hide. I listened with half an ear as he went on inventing excuses: 'I was going to tell her when all this' – he gestured vaguely about him as if he meant the house, the island – 'business is settled.'

The hall clock chimed a quarter to midnight. 'I really ought to telephone my colleague, Colin. But may I ask you one more question?' He nodded. 'How long could you have gone on supporting Emma without Letitia's money?'

'What do you mean?'

'Letitia spent much of her income on the upkeep of the island, didn't she?'

He nodded again.

'If she had just decided not to, would you have had the money spare to spend on *Glitz*?'

'She wouldn't have done that. This is her home, too.'

'Would you have thrown her off the island?'

'She owns a cottage up beyond Kilfadden. She wouldn't have left.'

'Would you have thrown her out of the house?'

'She would have told Iona why I was doing it.'

'You haven't answered my question.'

'Of course I would have gone on supporting the magazine. You must remember, Patrick, I am a very rich man.'

We bade each other good-night; but as Colin was leaving I remembered that I had meant to suggest he ask Paul to have a look at Iona. 'Oh, by the way, Colin,' I said. 'One other thing. Don't you think that Paul ought to take a look at Iona? She's not looked at all well since Letitia first "disappeared".'

Colin stared at me for a moment before answering. I realised he was wondering whether my solicitude for Iona was real, or whether I was just feeling him out. Finally, he looked away and said, 'You're probably right,' and moved off, shoulders sagging, down the corridor towards the main hall.

James FitzGibbon was extremely pleased with himself. 'Clever girl, Liz,' he began. 'I told her what you wanted and she had the answer in five minutes in her files. Your friend, Sir Colin Rundle, has been offloading paintings like crazy. All through his son, Gavin, who's an art dealer. Young Rundle seems to be getting pretty good prices, too. But Liz says that some of the paintings are pretty fabulous. The Raeburn you mentioned was a portrait of someone called Sir Ian Hamilton of Loch Mallen. A real beauty. Apparently he was something of a philosopher, in the circle of Hume. But not worth much: only £20,000 for that. Then there was a Canaletto, a Rembrandt drawing, a couple of Dutch landscapes. Gavin Rundle insisted on private sales but not so hush-hush that it didn't improve his own position as a dealer.'

'Did Elizabeth have any prices?'

'All here.' He read me a list that I jotted down on a piece of paper on the desk. 'I've already added it up. It comes to just over £800,000 – £814,000, she guessed.'

'All in the last year?'

'No, the Canaletto went first, seven years ago. That one went to a Swiss collector. It's disappeared from view. But then last July the Raeburn was bought for the Scottish National Gallery by an anonymous donor. The other sales were mostly in between those two; including a rather splendid Rembrandt drawing that's probably been kept in a drawer. The last sale was a Dutch landscape by a fellow called Ruysdael going to an American museum in October.'

'How did Liz get the prices from the private sales?'

'I gather a lot of people want it known what they paid for paintings . . . and if they don't, the dealer does. She's pretty well-connected. Actually, I got the impression that Gavin Rundle might have been boasting a bit about the prices.'

'Splendid, James, as usual you've come up trumps.'

'Oh, I say, I *am* pleased. Just one thing more . . . Liz did say that she hoped you would pass the news on to her if there was anything fishy about the sales. I mean she *is* a salesroom correspondent for an important newspaper. Sort of quid pro quo.'

'I'll tell her anything that isn't confidential just as soon as this investigation's complete. In fact' – I looked at the calendar on the desk – 'why don't you two come to dinner on Wednesday the week after next, the eleventh?' I hoped I would not regret my spontaneous generosity. An evening with James at home is not necessarily a riveting affair. Still, Elizabeth Hamilton was another matter. And besides, James had given me just what I needed.

'I say, that is kind of you, Patrick. Actually, I felt she'd rather come round to me again.'

'That's splendid, James. Oh, and, happy New Year, when it comes.'

On the two most important questions I had asked him, Colin was still lying to me. I didn't believe that Colin hadn't told Emma about Letitia's will. And I didn't believe that, without Letitia's money, he was still a rich man. With what James FitzGibbon had told me, I could now prove that he had lied about his finances. Establishing that he had lied about what he had told Emma was probably going to be much harder.

I wandered into the drawing-room to pour myself a little bedtime brandy. As I swirled the heavenly liquid around in the snifter and peered meditatively through the fire screen into the dying embers of the fire, Emma swept into the room, swathed in a dressing-gown of cream silk, and holding a notepad, on which she was scribbling frantically. 'Ah, Patrick, we meet again. Alone at last.' She smelled, frankly, delectable. 'Shall we run off together now, or do we wait until the New Year? What are the omens?'

'The omens, which I see clearly from the lees in my glass, are unmistakable. I should return to my bedroom and my wife.'

'And I should telephone my pals in the office in London.'

'It's the middle of the night on the penultimate day of the year and you've got people in the office?'

'I always have someone who can take dictation. All day, every day of the year. I can't type. And anyway there isn't a fax machine in this house. I wouldn't want to lose my precious thoughts – they come so rarely.'

It was a pretty and uncharacteristic moment of modesty.

'Good-night, Miss Gale,' I said. 'I admire your devotion to your craft.'

'Good-night, sweet Sir P. À demain.'

'Indeed.'

I left the elegant editor to commune with the drawing-room telephone.

My normal late-night conversation with Jinny did not move me any further forward. But, once we had covered the latest disclosures, I made sure to organise my notes and write up some of the new questions. By now the lack of a police investigation was beginning to hold me up. The police would have searched the house looking for bloodstains, trying to pinpoint the spot where Letitia was killed. They could have questioned the islanders. Perhaps none of this would have helped. But I rather suspected it would have.

The list of what I knew was less than satisfying.

Letitia began to plan her counterfeit suicide as long ago as last autumn. She conspired with Jessica to recruit Joseph Wells and with Gavin to make sure Virginia saw the 'fall'. (Since we had agreed to come to Sealsay for the New Year only in November, she couldn't have planned that part before then. Perhaps she had simply decided that any guest would do.) She arranged that Colin and Alistair and Gavin would circulate the story of the incest and the book so as to provide her with a motive. (Colin had only reluctantly gone along with this part and the result was his falling back on the notion that Letitia was simply dotty and unpredictable.) Perhaps the rest of the family, save Iona, who had seemed genuinely perplexed by the explanation of the plot, were all told in advance. Given the nature of Emma Gale's relationship with Colin, it was unlikely that she didn't know.

The scheme had gone to plan. Mr Wells had jumped on to the ledge in full view of Jinny and Letitia had hidden in the west tower.

No one had supplied me with a reason why Letitia should

have planned her disappearance. But that I was now pretty sure of. What I knew almost nothing about was the next part. The part where Letitia's plan began to unravel. I decided it was time, once more, to let my imagination loose, hoping, as usual, to discipline it with such facts as I had and to restrain my own credulity.

Letitia sits in the tower room. She is excited. It is as if one of her romances has come to life and she is the heroine. She looks from the window across to where the sun is falling behind the hills, waiting for Gavin to appear running down the path with the news that she has leaped from the cliffs. She savours the thought of Colin, her stuffy brother, having to tell me the story of her rape at the hands of their father. She savours it because it was her mother that she loved, her mother who died so long ago, unloved by her father who lived on. She smiles to herself when she thinks of Colin showing me the note, 'Ask Alistair,' knowing how hard it will be for him to tell the story she has prepared.

Ah, there he is, Gavin, her wayward nephew, running down the hill to the house. She hears vaguely the commotion as he arrives in the drawing-room and tells them the sad news. Jessica already knows. Colin and Alistair know: but the others, how will they react? Maria, sweet, stupid Maria will react naturally. She will be pained, she will weep, she will recover. She will wonder why her dotty aunt would have done such a thing. And she will be right. Letitia laughs at the thought that this stupid child will be right. She will be right to wonder because her aunt is not dead at all, but waiting in the tower for the guests to go, so she can resume her life. She ate a large lunch. It will be many hours till she can slip down to the kitchen for an evening meal. Colin or Alistair will come, her brothers, and tell her how her plan is going.

But it will work. It will work as it worked in Love Vanishes *for Lady Lorna. And then Colin will have all the money he needs to keep the house and the island. In return he will send away that awful girl, Emma, who has reduced her once-proud brother to skulking shamefully about his own house for their adulterous love-making. And then* Glitz, *that rag which would not exist but for Colin's money, will cease to exist, and Emma, who needs Colin only for his cheques, will leave them, and Colin will remember that Iona is his wife.*

This much seemed right. Her motive. It was a motive all of

them could share. It might even seem honourable to them to take money that belonged after all to the family and use it to save the house for the Rundles.

Later on, at about two, one of her brothers comes up to her, passing through her bedroom and the bathroom and Justin's bedroom, disturbing the child, so that he runs shouting to his parents that he has seen a ghost. Under his arm is a thermos of coffee, laced with phenobarbitone, which the child has mistaken for the ghost's severed head.

Or perhaps he only comes to talk and perhaps he goes away and perhaps she gets the coffee later.

Letitia looks at her watch. It is two, now, time to go down to the kitchen to eat. She makes her way quietly down the stairs and slips into Justin's bedroom and travels through the bathroom to her own room. From her doorway she can reach the top of the stairs in a few seconds and slip down along through the hall and the corridor to the kitchen. When she arrives someone is already there, preparing her meal for her, telling her how everything has gone. That person has made Letitia a pot of strong black coffee. As they talk she sips it. It tastes good. She drinks more.

Then she goes back up to the tower to sleep. And an hour later she is so fast asleep that nothing will wake her: not even the pressure of the pillow on her face that will end her life.

But whose hand is on the pillow? I sat up bolt upright realising that I had been missing the most obvious fact in the case.

Virginia knows that if I wake her in the night there will be a good reason. She will grant me the benefit of the doubt.

'It's so obvious. I don't know why we didn't see it. The person who smothered Letitia didn't know that she was already poisoned.'

'I don't know why you say "we" didn't see it. I saw it at once.'

'Well, why didn't you say so?'

'When we were discussing it, I assumed you were aiming to keep Paul Crawford in the dark.'

'But then the person who stabbed her may not have known she was dead either.'

'On the other hand, it may have been done to divert attention from the phenobarbitone and the suffocation. Who could have foretold that Paul Crawford would actually be a good forensic pathologist?' Virginia kissed me, and then she turned over and sighed deeply. 'I think, Patrick, that what you need is a good night's sleep.'

'What I need', I said stiffly, 'is a little more evidence.'

I awoke early and sat at the desk of the Green Room writing while Virginia got up. I was not in a pleasant mood. 'We still don't have any real motives,' I grumbled, as she returned from her morning ablutions. 'If Letitia's plan had worked, Colin and Alistair would have come into their money. Killing her doesn't make any difference to that. And the will with Letitia's stipulations about Emma's magazine would have been made public either way. That gives Emma a motive, I suppose. Letitia probably made it a condition of the whole thing that Colin got rid of her. With Letitia still around, it would have been harder for Colin to go back on his word to her. Of course, they all say that Emma didn't know that Letitia was still alive. But I can't believe that Colin would have kept something like that from the woman he loves. So, at the moment, Emma looks like the next one to pursue. And if it was here, then she could have summoned Colin's assistance in hiding the body . . . but then he wouldn't have led us in the unwrapping of the rug. I simply don't believe he would have done that if he'd known Letitia was in there. I don't know. It's all very puzzling. Still, I suppose', I said gloomily, 'I should talk to Emma after breakfast.'

'Well, don't forget Paul Crawford's coming up for a walk at about ten.'

I had not forgotten. But MacAlister's forecast had been entirely correct and the weather was once more cold and wet. Another walk in this weather was not a particularly appealing prospect.

'The weather's absolutely filthy. Why don't we phone the good doctor and arrange to meet him mid-morning for coffee?'

'*We* can have coffee,' Jinny said. 'I rather doubt *he* will.'

'Right, I'll phone him now.'

*

I used the phone in the estate office, as usual. The little light that filtered through the window reflected from the dust that filled the air. Each time I entered the place – with the dusty curtains, the piles of ageing papers, the battered furniture – I felt like an explorer entering a pyramid, the first visitor for thousands of years. I dialled Crawford's number. After half a dozen rings, he picked up the phone and mumbled, 'Hallo.'

'Paul, it's Patrick, Patrick Scott.'

'What time is it? Half-past eight. Good God, man, don't you know better than to call a drunk before midday?'

'I'm sorry. We were going to meet at ten, I thought.'

I must have sounded genuinely penitent because he bellowed into the phone, 'Don't sound so upset, I was only teasing. I'll be right as rain once I've just topped up. God, it looks awful out. Don't suppose you want to go for a walk in this?'

'Virginia and I wondered if we could meet for coffee somewhere?'

'I'm afraid the island isn't well endowed in the coffee-shop department. But look, I was planning to go over later to see David Sealsay up at the home farm for a chat. He's usually done with farm chores by half-past ten in the morning on a day like this. Why don't we meet there?'

13

Much of the party was already established at the breakfast table when I joined Jinny in the dining-room. Horace Strachan's face was the one cheery sight in a sea of gloom. Even Emma Gale, who had managed to keep her spirits up since Letitia had first disappeared, was now less frolicsome. Emma's outfit today, however, was somewhat more frankly provocative than the clothes she had been wearing for the past two days. She was wearing an extremly short black skirt, dark, rather old-fashioned lace stockings and a dark red silk blouse that was tied rather than buttoned, in a way that gave her a very revealing *décolletage*. Over it all she wore a long cardigan of black wool, open in the front, which hung much lower than the hem of her skirt. She had tied her golden hair back with a large black ribbon: the effect of this schoolgirl hair-do in combination with the clothes of a woman of easy virtue was disconcerting at this hour.

My appetite had recovered somewhat. I felt that I was making some progress towards discovering the various hands that had poisoned, suffocated and then stabbed Letitia. Enough, at least, to warrant thinking that, in the end, we would know. Since Emma looked like the best bet at the moment as a source of further illumination, I took my kippers and scrambled eggs and sat down at the empty place to her left. Horace Strachan had settled himself opposite her, in order to take advantage of the pleasurable combination of a fine breakfast and the vision of a fair lady.

'So, Sir Patrick. How are you getting on?' (I have noticed that tact is rarely one of the virtues of those with vast appetites.)

'Not very well, I fear,' I answered.

Over the next half-hour the whole household found its way to the breakfast table. Maria and Iona were particularly subdued. Jonathan, I noticed, while trying to cheer up his wife, was also glancing surreptitiously from time to time at Emma.

'Since we're all now here,' I said, 'I was going to suggest that everyone should write down, to the best of their recollections, where they were between about midnight and six yesterday morning.' I was getting what I really wanted from my conversations, but I didn't want anyone to think yet that I had ruled them out. This way I could concentrate on the few crucial participants without letting them know that that was what I was doing. 'I shall need to pass the information on to Inspector MacAlister when I talk to him in the middle of the day.' It wasn't the best excuse, I suppose, but I thought it would do.

'Wasn't everybody in bed?' Emma said. 'I certainly was.'

'No, I don't think so,' I replied. 'I, for example, was woken at about three by a noise outside my room. When I looked outside the door I saw Joanna disappearing round the corner towards the nursery and Christopher standing outside their room.'

'Justin said he saw a ghost with its head under its arm,' Christopher added helpfully.

'Which means that somebody probably walked through his bedroom on their way to see Letitia in the tower.' I smiled at

Christopher. 'Then again, two or three people had meals either in or from the kitchen that night. One of them was probably Letitia. Who were the others?'

'My, what a busy lot you all were,' Emma said as she sliced into her kipper. Then she looked up and glanced at Colin. 'Some of us just stayed in bed all night.'

'Well, that simplifies matters a good deal, in your case. But, as I say, not everybody has such a straightforward story. So it would help to have everybody's contributions fairly soon.'

'Right-oh, Patrick, we'll all see what we remember and hand it over at lunchtime.' Colin was speaking for his family.

A rather desultory conversation began around the table centring largely on the weather and the fact that the Hogmanay party was due tonight. Out of the windows spattered with wind-driven rain we could see the rhododendrons, between the house and the beach, quaking from the winds.

'I wonder if we could have a word or two after breakfast, Miss Gale,' I said quietly. 'Perhaps in the estate office down the corridor.'

'As long as it's okay with your wife,' she said with a straight face.

'At the heart of a sound marriage, there is usually a good deal of trust.'

'That's what husbands always say when they're about to be unfaithful. Now what wives say – believe me, we've run articles on this – is that at the heart of a good marriage there's a good deal of tolerance for masculine indiscretions.'

'I am the beneficiary of just such tolerance,' I said, 'which is why I would never abuse it.'

'Then let's go and test your resolve.' The rest of the table had fallen silent. Colin was clearly mildly discomfited by Emma's games. Iona was watching Colin with an air of vengeful amusement. I rose from my place and helped Emma out of hers. Then I went round the table and kissed Virginia firmly on the forehead. The effect was more dutiful, more perfunctory, than I had intended.

When we entered the estate office, Emma cleared a space on the edge of the desk and sat on it, with her legs crossed, her feet balanced on an upright wooden chair. I had planned to sit myself down at the desk, in the position from which I had been making my telephone calls and taking my notes, but from this position, I should now be facing her back. I moved around the table and sat in the armchair by the window.

Emma removed a silver cigarette case from the little black bag she was carrying and took out a gold-tipped, black cigarette. 'You don't smoke, do you? Filthy habit. But if you're orally fixated, what can you do?' She sneezed. 'All this bloody dust – it's everywhere.'

'You have known, of course, for some time that Letitia left Colin a quarter of a million pounds on condition he stopped underwriting your magazine.' I waited a few seconds for some acknowledgement, but when none came I continued. 'You have known, too, since I talked to Horace Strachan, that I know this. And so you will, I am sure, have realised that I know you had a motive for killing Letitia.'

'Shall I confess now, or do you want me to wait until you have me stretched out on the rack?'

'You don't have to tell me anything, of course. You can wait for the police. It's not that I suspect *you*,' I went on, 'but if I don't find out who killed Letitia before too long, somebody else may die.'

'Not very likely, is it, Sir Patrick? I mean, the motive for killing Letitia was obviously money. She's dead. Her money will come to Colin and Alistair. Why should anyone kill anyone else?'

'Colin and Alistair would have got their money if Letitia had remained alive.'

'How so?'

'That was the point of the fake suicide. So why should they have bothered to kill her?' I asked.

'I didn't say that *they* killed her, Sir Patrick.'

'Why should *anyone* have killed her in order to get the money for Colin and Alistair, if they were going to get it anyway?'

'Letitia's plan would never have worked. Someone would have seen her eventually. Then they'd all have ended up in jug for fraud.'

'And now someone's going to end up in jug for murder. Anyhow, I don't think it's obvious that it couldn't have worked.

Letitia has been a recluse for nearly half a century. In any case, if they had thought it wasn't going to work, they wouldn't have gone along with the plan in the first place.'

She considered the proposition, while blowing a series of smoke rings into the air. Eventually she said, 'Maybe.'

'Her death, on the other hand, has made a difference to you.'

'I don't see that.'

'If Letitia were alive, she could insist that Colin stop funding your paper.'

'She's pretty much got him to agree to stop now she's dead.'

'Maybe. But he could still turn down her money. It's only a quarter of a million pounds. He'll be getting another £4,000,000 anyway. And even if he turns down the money it doesn't leave the family, it just goes to his wife.'

'Who can then leave him.'

'That might suit you.'

'It wouldn't suit him.'

'We were discussing *your* motives.'

'If I had killed her, I can assure you I wouldn't have made such a mess. And I wouldn't have left her in a carpet a few feet from the main hall of the bloody house. Whoever did *that* was not very thoughtful.'

'You couldn't have put her in the carpet, I agree. Not by yourself. I helped lift it. Nobody could have done it on their own.'

'Are you suggesting Colin helped me?'

'I'm not suggesting anything.'

'Okay, so I have a motive. As does everybody else in this house. She wasn't exactly Mother Theresa.'

'I am told that Mother Theresa is actually a rather irritating person.' I realised at once that this remark was a mistake. It told Emma that I was bad-tempered and gave her the chance to go on the offensive.

She took it. She stood up and walked towards me, a cold unfriendly smile playing about her bright red lips. 'Frustrating, isn't it? Here you are with your fabulous reputation, confronting an old-fashioned, not to say clichéd, country-house murder that Miss Marples would have solved over tea and crumpets, and you're making rather a dog's breakfast of it. All very vexing, isn't it? The sort of thing that makes a man start to doubt himself.' Emma Gale settled her black-swathed bottom on the arm of my chair. 'No wonder you're looking so tense.' The fragrance that enveloped me was something I have smelled on occasion in the vicinity of an expensive woman at the Royal Opera.

'Miss Gale, Emma . . .' I was not having the easiest time concentrating. 'The police will also regard you with suspicion because you are having an affair with Colin.'

'Will they disapprove of the nasty adulteress, then?'

'No. The point is they will assume that he told you about Letitia's plan in advance. It obviously had consequences for both of you. Until Colin heard about Letitia's stipulation, he had every reason to think he would now be out of his financial difficulties and able to continue supporting your magazine.'

Emma drew away abruptly and began to look interested. 'Why do you think Colin is short of money?'

'Didn't he tell you?'

'I asked first, Sir Patrick.'

'Why else would he have agreed to Letitia's plan?'

'Yes, he told me. He told me about a year ago. That he wasn't sure he could go on supporting *Glitz*.'

'Why were you surprised that I knew he was short of money?'

'Because he's taken a great deal of trouble to hide the fact. He's a proud man, Sir Patrick, a very proud man.'

I knew that wasn't quite it. Emma was startled because she thought Colin might have told me that his finances were in a poor state. And that would have meant that he had told me something without consulting her.

I pointed at the bare wall over the fireplace. 'There used to be a picture in this room, over the fireplace. There was a portrait in the library by Raeburn; a Canaletto. If they'd been stolen, somebody would have mentioned it.'

'Very good, Sir P. Top marks.'

'Do you know what he got for them?'

'About half a million pounds in all.'

Her voice was bored, and she scanned the shelves of the office as she spoke; and so she did not see the momentary look of puzzlement that crossed my face. At least I had learned something from this conversation.

'Well, Miss Gale, it has been a great pleasure talking to you. And now I must go and see my wife.'

Emma Gale smiled down at me. 'Are you absolutely sure you want to leave now?'

I mopped a bead of perspiration from my brow. 'I hope you will not think me ungallant if I say that I have never been more certain of anything in my life.'

'Lucky old Virginia. An untemptable rock of a husband.' She laughed a pretty, false laugh as she stood up, and adjusted her blouse. One thing was certain. Emma Gale certainly wasn't behaving like someone who had just committed a cold-blooded murder. As I left the room she picked up the telephone and waggled her fingers at me in farewell.

When I found Jinny in the drawing-room, she was reading *A Tender Magic*; as I entered she was turning a page, swiftly, as eager a reader as a book could hope to have. She looked at me with a strange glint in her eye, but I could tell that she was trying to conceal her excitement from the others. As I walked over to her, she turned back a few pages, and raised the book towards me. I took it. Jinny stood and pointed to a passage. Once I had read it, we walked together unspeaking out into the hall. I knew what we must do next.

'Last night David said we shouldn't delve in the past. Maybe this will change his mind.'

'Let's go now,' Virginia said. 'Get it done. We don't need to wait for Paul.'

14

More than fifteen hundred years ago, St Columba's monks stopped on Sealsay on their way to convert the Scottish mainland, and dug the first stone slabs from Ben Moray. The monastery they built, whose ruins lie at the island's southern tip, is the oldest remaining building on Sealsay. It was a centre of learning and of prayer until the Norsemen came and sacked it in the ninth century. When the Duke of Kintyre built what is now the home farm at Sealsay as a house for a son born to a woman who was not his wife, it was the first large building on the island in nearly a thousand years. Josiah Rundle, arriving a century later, having acquired the island lock, stock and barrel from the Duke's grandson, required a house more appropriate to the grandeur of his new money. And so Sealsay House was erected, with its two wings and its towers and its enormous public rooms. But the building that he made into the farm house is far from modest.

It is simple in shape and its lines seem especially pure after the fancifulness of Sealsay House. The rectangular front, with its central door with four large windows on each of the first two floors, and a set of two smaller windows above them, looking out of the attic rooms, looks more than anything else like a child's drawing of a house: a square, with the roof a wide inverted V, and the front door a large rectangle set symmetrically in the middle, with a small terrace above the porch also accessible from a single, symmetrical door.

Just before half-past ten, Virginia and I wrapped up in overcoats and wellingtons, and struggled through the raging storm to this farmhouse. It was only a couple of minutes' walk, down the drive and through the little copse that hides the farm from the view of the inhabitants of Sealsay House, but by the time we got there, the damp and the chill had reached our bones. Fiona was only mildly surprised that we had come early and certainly made us welcome. Her ruddy cheeks and frizzy hair suggested she had already been out in the wet wind. She invited us back through the kitchen, to a large parlour with a roaring fire, and David breezed in a moment later with more logs.

'Paul will be here soon, I'm sure,' David said, brushing bits of bark from his Arran jersey. 'But he'll no' be on time – he never is.'

While we waited, Fiona made us all tea and offered us slices of a delicious fruit cake. David was extremely friendly, though somewhat preoccupied. We had seen each other off and on now for all the years since my first visit to Sealsay at the beginning of the war. We had talked occasionally, when we met out walking, or in the bar at the hotel, but I suppose we were not so much old friends as old acquaintances – appropriate enough, then, that we were sitting together on New Year's Eve, when 'auld acquaintance' should not be forgot.

David Sealsay was as much a part of my memories of the island as the peak of Ben Moray or the first view of the port from the ferry. I felt I could trust him utterly, that he was solid. The contrast with Colin, someone I had thought of until yesterday as one of my oldest friends, jarred somewhat. I no longer felt I could trust Colin. Ruminations of this generally melancholy character floated about in my mind as we chatted comfortably. After a time, there was a lull in the conversation, which had passed from observations about the weather to our admiration for the house.

Into this break, which was filled with the sounds of the weather knocking on the windows, David finally asked the question his good manners had kept him from asking at once: 'Well, have you made any progress with the depressing business with Miss Rundle?'

'Not enough, I'm afraid.' I told David and Fiona Sealsay that we now knew why Letitia had staged her 'suicide' and we knew that she had been poisoned and suffocated.

'Annie told Niall this morning that she'd been stabbed.'

'She had been . . . but that was after she died.'

Fiona gasped, screwing up her face and shivering. 'Horrible.'

'And there aren't any obvious motives,' I said.

'But we think you might be able to help us. Let me read you something,' Virginia said, her voice tense with excitement. *'When Joy woke she was sitting upright against the cave wall. The sound that had woken her was her father's voice, angry and loud. It came from somewhere towards the cave's mouth, rising over the pounding of the waves.*

'"Who is the boy's father?" her father shouted. "Who is he? You are my wife, Leonora, and you will tell me the truth."

'Joy could not hear the words of her mother's reply. But what she did hear was her mother's fear, her sadness, her pain. And Joy knew in that moment, with all the certainty of her young spirit, that her mother would never betray the love of her heart. For beneath the fear and the sadness, there was also tenderness, and an echo of the bliss a woman feels in being beloved.

'She did not want to listen any longer, did not want to be here. But when she tried to rise, she found her legs were too weak to bear her up. Joy shivered and drew her cloak tighter about her. Her body trembled with an unaccountable dread. She tried to steady herself. Her shaking hands pressed against the damp wall of the cave, the sharp angles cutting into the soft skin of her palms. And then she heard it. The sound that changed her life for ever.

'It was her mother's scream. And the words she screamed were "Harry, no!" – words that etched themselves deep in Joy's soul. As the scream faded, Joy knew that her father, in his rage, had thrown his wife from the ledge at the cliff's face. And after all else, there was always and ever the roar of the waves.

'What gripped her now was not grief or sorrow; not anger, but terror – a fear as deep as any fear she could ever have imagined. Now she must move deeper into the recess where she was hiding. She must move there and stay still. She must bury herself out of the way and keep silence. Because if she did not, the man – she had ceased to think of him as her father – the man would kill her too.'

As Jinny stopped, David seemed to be struggling to answer. 'Joy in Latin is *Laetitia*,' I said. 'Leonora is Lorna; Harry is Henry. It *can't* be a coincidence.'

Eventually David Sealsay began to speak. 'I've no' said a word about it for forty-nine years. But I've thought about it every day. I've never told a single soul but Fiona what happened. You're right, Sir Patrick, it's all there in her book, more or less. But before I can tell you, there's one telephone call that I have to make.'

It was twenty minutes before David returned. And when he did, he told us what had happened the day Lorna Rundle, Colin and Alistair and Letitia's mother, wife of Sir Henry Rundle, died.

David Sealsay had been out near the cliffs of Moray on the day Lorna Rundle died. He had been moving a herd of sheep down from the high pastures towards evening. 'In those days, Letitia used to run about up there a good deal. She was twenty-one, tall, a wee bit wild, but very pleasant and easy to talk to. Not at all like the woman you met the next summer.'

Letitia was 'walking out', David said, with young Jamie

MacInnis, now and then, though, naturally, she did not want her father to know about it. Sir Henry would never have stood for a liaison – let alone a marriage – with a crofter's son. David had seen them going into the caves at the top of the monks' stair a few times, and so he thought nothing of it when he saw them going in this time. He smiled to himself, in fact, thinking of his own young love – he and Fiona had been wed less than a year. But he was sad, too; he knew *their* affair would come to nothing.

What did surprise him was when Jamie MacInnis appeared a few minutes later alone. David dawdled a bit with his sheep and so Jamie caught up with him and they spoke. 'Is she all right?' David asked.

At first, Jamie MacInnis pretended he didn't know what David was talking about. Then, when he saw that David was not going to tell anyone, he said that Letitia was fine. 'She didna want me down there, just now,' Jamie had said. And he had explained that as he and Letitia had descended the first flight of steps – down which Alistair had led us the day before – they had heard Lady Lorna's voice asking, 'Who is that?'

Jinny and I glanced at each other, spellbound by David's narration. There was something doom-laden in his voice, and his tone disturbed the cosiness of the parlour, with its blazing fire, our talisman against the raging storm outside.

David continued. 'She sounded, Jamie said, as if she was afraid.' Letitia had called back to her, "Mother, it's me," and then kissed Jamie quietly and shooed him away, whispering, "I'll see you by the gate in an hour." He knew which gate she meant; it led from the home farm into the fields between it and the sea. It was their trysting place.

That evening David and Fiona heard that Lady Rundle had fallen from the ledge at the mouth of that cave. The next day, early in the morning, Jamie had come to see David, asking him to promise him that he would never tell anyone that Letitia and he had been there that evening. David's suspicions were aroused. He couldn't, he said, keep a thing like that from the police, if they asked. Again Jamie begged him not to speak of it. Finally, when he could see that his entreaties were getting him nowhere, Jamie said, 'If you swear to me that you will tell no one what I tell you now, I will tell you what happened in that cave.'

'I broke ma word to him only once, when I told Fiona. I couldna keep it from ma wife.'

'Was it him you telephoned just now?' Virginia asked gently.

'Yes. He lives at Carradale these days, in Kintyre. He's worked on a farm there for more than forty years; and he stayed there after he retired. Never married. It took a wee while. I had to tell him what had happened to Letitia. I've never borne such terrible news.' David sighed and looked at Virginia and then at me. 'He told me I could tell you the whole story.'

When Jamie left the two of them, Letitia and her mother walked together to the mouth of the cave, a place they both loved, and looked out to sea together. Letitia had told Jamie that it was as good a conversation as they had ever had; that her mother was warmer and freer than she had ever known her. As it got dark, her mother sent her back, saying she wanted to be alone for a while, that she would wait there for the sunset. It was a lovely Sealsay summer evening; it would certainly be light enough to see her way back down to the house. But as Letitia made her way back through the dark cave, she heard someone coming. Some instinct made her slink back into the shadows and she watched in alarm as her father strode through the cave shouting angrily, 'Where are you, Lorna? Damn it, I know you're in here.'

Terrified, Letitia listened to them shouting at each other, guilty at eavesdropping but fascinated all the same to realise that her father and mother, whose relations in the house had always been cool and civil, were having a heated argument. And what she heard stunned her. For her father was asking her mother to tell him who her lover was. At first she denied it. Then she told him that he was cruel and their marriage loveless. That she was sorry she had fallen but that he had driven her to it. Again, he asked for the name. Again, she refused. And then he hit her. Letitia heard her mother's cry, but she feared her father too much to step forward. And then her mother said, 'I'll never tell you the name of Alistair's father.' Letitia had told Jamie that for a while Sir Henry had said nothing. Then, she had heard her mother scream, 'No, Henry!' And finally there was a scuffle and the fading sound of her mother's scream as she fell over the edge of the cliff.

When Letitia did not appear at the gate an hour later, Jamie rushed up to the cave and found her cowering, a trembling wraith, in a dark corner. Slowly he calmed her; slowly she told her story. And then he walked with her down the hill in the half-light of a summer's night towards the house. She told him he could tell no one. And when he tried to take her in his arms in the rhododendrons by the house, she pushed him away. 'He'll kill you,' she said. And she never spoke to him again.

'Of course, everyone else thought she was dumbstruck by her mother's death. But we knew, the three of us, that it was more than that.'

'*A Tender Magic*,' Jinny said. 'She put it all into her books.'

'David,' I spoke softly. David's story had left us all in a sombre mood. 'Letitia may well have been poisoned to keep this story from being told. If whoever poisoned Letitia finds out you know, he – or she – may try to kill you, too. You mustn't tell anyone this tale again until we have found the murderer. And we must not let anyone – not even Paul – know you told us.'

We sat in silence, warmed outside by the blazing fire and inside by Fiona's excellent tea. I took another slice of cake, absent-mindedly ignoring, I fear, a deterrent glance from my wife. There was a great deal to think about.

The old electric bell rang and Fiona went out and brought Paul back into the parlour to join us. He was red-faced, wet through, and extremely cheerful.

'What a gloomy lot you are. Thank you, Fiona, my dear, you know my views about tea. Poisonous. David?'

David fetched him a glass of whisky, shaking his head as he handed it to him. 'And you a doctor.'

'Don't be so Presbyterian, David. And cheer up, Sir Patrick, I've got some good news.'

'And what, pray, is that?' I asked.

'I have worked out what happened to Letitia.' Once he had captured our attention, Paul was delighted to perform.

Letitia, he told us, had first been poisoned by one person.

She had returned to bed, fallen asleep and then been suffocated by someone else. 'Finally . . .'

'Finally,' Virginia said, '. . . let me guess . . . finally, a third person stabs her, not realising she's dead.'

'Ah ha! You would never make a detective. No. The first person comes back, expecting that by now she will have died. She has. And then he stabs her and puts her in the carpet to make everyone think she has been stabbed to death, planting evidence to incriminate somebody else. But the first murderer aforesaid has not taken account of the presence on the remote island of the brilliant pathologist, Dr Paul Crawford, who sees through the nonsense at once.'

'If the first person wanted to conceal what he had done, why didn't he just take her out and bury her where she wouldn't be found?' Jinny asked.

'Or throw her in the sea?' I asked the question gently, not wanting to offend Paul who was, after all, trying to be helpful. I didn't feel inclined to tell him he was going over ground we had already covered, considering hypotheses I had rejected.

'Where's the planted evidence?' This was Fiona, mild as ever, but certainly sceptical.

Jinny returned to the attack. 'Why assume it's a he?'

'Nobody could have put her in the rug by themselves.' I said.

Paul raised his hands to silence us. 'It was only a suggestion. It's back to the drawing board for me.'

'Do let's talk about something else for a bit. How did you come here in the first place, Paul?' Virginia asked. Fiona looked at Paul as if she thought the questions would pain him, but he was wistfully contemplating the fire. He looked as though, if he gazed hard enough, he would see something beyond the fireplace, beyond Sealsay; a kingdom far, far, away.

Three years ago, Paul and his wife Martha had come to the island in the summer, for the first time, and rented a holiday cottage. They had walked a good deal and fished in the lochs half-way up Ben Moray, and fallen a little in love with the place. Paul had been due to retire in a year or so from his job as a pathologist at a small hospital in Inveraray, near the top of Loch

Fyne. He had chosen the spot of all places in the British Isles to work, because he loved the area. 'Everything from the kippers from Loch Fyne, to the views from Rest and Be Thankful on the rising road from Tarbert to the west.' He loved walking in the hills, climbing in the mountains, fishing in the lochs. And Martha loved the people of the strange town, with its imposing eighteenth-century castle. 'I love just driving down the lochs, down through Carradale to Campbeltown in Kintyre, or over to Oban by Loch Etive. I miss it.'

He raised his empty glass to David, who half filled it, until Paul coaxed him into pouring more.

'Anyway, so here we were, having a jolly time and the laird and his wife send us a note, inviting us to dinner. We walk over, have a lovely evening, eat a marvellous dinner – well, a very good one, anyway – and then we set off home. And on the way . . .' He paused, a sob catching in his throat.

'You don't need to do this, Paul.' Fiona's voice was kind.

'She had a stroke. That's all. So I wrapped her up and ran down to the house and we fetched her in their Range Rover and took her into the house. They called the coastguard helicopter to come and fetch us out. But by the time we got to the hospital in Oban, she was gone. That was it.' He breathed out hard, blowing up his cheeks, and looked away from the fire for the first time since he had started speaking.

Paul wiped a tear from his eye. And then he drew himself up in his chair, and settled back into it with a faraway look again, raising the whisky once more to his lips. 'Well, I came back to clear up, fetch the car and so on, a week later and Iona was very kind. She had me to stay in the house. I started drinking. And one night, I told her that I couldn't go back to the house in Inveraray without Martha and she said, without batting an eyelid, without pausing, "Actually, Paul, we need a doctor on the island here."' He sniffed a little again. 'And, as we now know, she was right. Wonderful woman, Iona Rundle, you know, Patrick. Extraordinarily kind.'

It was after noon when we got back to the house. Paul popped in to see how Angela was and Iona had no difficulty persuading him he should stay for lunch. Virginia and I went upstairs to change into dry clothes before eating. We discussed plans for the afternoon. Things were beginning to move rather more smoothly now. Very soon, I felt sure, we should know all. It was time to push things along.

When we had changed, I told Virginia that I thought we should make a little trip back to the room where Letitia had spent her last night.

'You see, I've been thinking. When Alistair took us up there, I noticed the cupboard in that room had been moved recently. But I couldn't think why. Then Alistair said emphatically that there wasn't another way up, so I forgot about it for a while. But I was still puzzled about why Letitia should have chosen *that* room, of all the rooms in the tower. And why didn't she use a room in the other tower, over Colin and Iona and Alistair and Marie-Hélène? But then, as I was thinking about Letitia's movements last night, it occurred to me that the ideal room for her would have a staircase that didn't go into the main corridor. I mean, we'd been assuming that Letitia went into Justin's room just so as to avoid passing *our* door. But she would still have had to go past the nanny and the au pair. So then I wondered if the cupboard mightn't have been moved to cover the door to a staircase.'

When we arrived in the drawing-room a quarter of an hour later, our curiosity had been satisfied.

15

As we filed back into the drawing-room after lunch for coffee, I said to Paul quietly, 'I need your help.' He looked at me expectantly. 'I would like you not to contradict any claims I make about the autopsy . . . even if they aren't exactly true.'

'Is it fun being a detective? All this deception?' he whispered. I gathered the question was rhetorical. Various members of the family handed me pieces of paper describing what they remembered of the night of Letitia's death. I looked through them briefly, while the family collected their coffee, and then took my place in front of the fireplace. It was time to address the assembled company. All the adult Rundles were present. Colin and Iona sat at opposite ends of the long sofa by the fireplace, their faces composed and uncommunicative. Alistair and Marie-Hélène sat across from each other, on either end of a small table by one of the windows, holding hands. Jonathan was standing by the fireplace, chatting to Emma, with Marie watching them nervously.

As I took my place facing the company, with the windows behind me, Angela and Jessica settled in a large armchair, with Jessica on the arm. Gavin stood behind them, and cast me an amused glance when the two women caught my eye.

'I've made a good deal of progress in the last day or so towards understanding what happened in Letitia's last hours. We all know she was stabbed. But, as Dr Crawford – Paul – has discovered, that was not what killed her.' The effect of this news was a satisfying hush, followed by a buzz of questions. I raised my hand to quell the hubbub. So far as I could tell, everyone was equally surprised. Iona's response, as was now habitual, was the most extreme. She paled a good deal and then raised her hand to her forehead. But *everybody* seemed utterly nonplussed.

'Are you really sure of this?' Colin asked.

'I repeat. When Letitia was stabbed, she was already dead. There are only two serious reasons why you would stab someone who was already dead. The first is that you might not know she was dead. It was dark that night. Someone might have gone up to the tower intending to kill Letitia and done so in the dark. The second possibility is that he or she intended us to think she was stabbed to death, thus distracting our attention from the way she was actually killed. This second possibility is not very likely. No one who planned a murder as carefully as Letitia's was planned would have relied on an attempt to confuse an autopsy that was bound to fail. If I am right, then, one or perhaps several people in this room planned to murder Letitia, and another person tried to kill her independently.

'So what *did* Letitia die of? I am not yet able to provide you with certain details. But I can tell you that she was poisoned with phenobarbitone, and that it was given to her after the meal she ate in the kitchen the night before last, sometime after two in the morning.' I noticed that this news prompted Emma to look at Colin with a cold suspicion. I wondered whether the dumbshow was intended for my consumption. 'She didn't eat alone. I assume that those of you that *were* there will tell me who you were, so that we can then move on to the process of elimination.'

Jessica spoke. 'It's all on the piece of paper I gave you. Gavin and I were there; Alistair and Marie-Hélène and Father.'

'And this was at about two in the morning?'

'We met at about half-past one. But Letitia probably didn't start eating for half an hour and she went on eating and drinking until we all went upstairs at about half-past two.'

'Who knew about this meeting?'

'Those of us who were there,' Marie-Hélène said, shrugging her shoulders.

'Plus me. Jessica and me, we 'ave no secrets from each other,' Angela Horseman said.

Once Jessica had opened the floodgates, others spoke, adding bits and pieces of information.

Alistair and Marie-Hélène had arrived first in the kitchen. Since everyone had eaten modestly at dinner, to keep up the fiction that they were mourning Letitia, they had taken various cheeses and cold meat from the fridge and some bread from the larder and Marie-Hélène had made them a couple of sandwiches. Colin and then Jessica arrived not long after this and Marie-Hélène made sandwiches for them also.

Colin was convinced that the plan was not going to work. 'He said that somebody was bound to see Letitia eventually, even if she stayed in and around Sealsay House,' Jessica reported.

In the midst of a rather vigorous whispered debate on this issue, Letitia arrived and Marie-Hélène offered to make her a sandwich also. 'Two. I'm famished,' Letitia said loudly. Then she sat down and asked, 'What's happened since I died?'

It was in the silence that greeted this question that Gavin arrived, 'looking', Jessica said, 'a good deal closer to death than Letitia.' He had fallen into a restless alcohol-induced sleep, and, though his father had shaken him awake, he had drifted off again for a while before waking fully and realising that he was late for their 2 a.m. rendezvous.

The storm was by now very noisy and their voices were no longer whispered. 'We assumed that no one could hear,' Gavin said.

Between them they went through what had happened since Letitia's disappearance, their voices raised to be heard over the sounds of the storm against the kitchen windows. Gavin also told them that he had planted the story about old Sir Henry's incest. 'You'd better tell Patrick that story tomorrow, too, Colin,' Alistair had said.

As Jessica explained this, all the Rundle men made to speak. I raised my hand to silence them. It was not the time for apologies or excuses. 'How did Letitia seem?' I addressed the question to no one in particular.

'Rather agitated, actually,' Jessica answered me decisively. 'I'd been up to see her earlier and she seemed more nervy than usual. I thought she needed to calm down a little.'

'I think we'd all formed the same impression,' Colin added. 'But there wasn't much we could do.'

'I offered to make her some cocoa,' Marie-Hélène said, 'but she wouldn't have any. So I made a cup of cocoa for Ali and me.'

When I asked if anyone had made coffee, they all shook their heads. 'No,' Alistair said, 'we all went up more or less together at about a quarter past two.'

'But Letitia did pick up her flask. It was sitting on the kitchen table, where Mary always put it,' Jessica said.

'Mary didn't put it there,' I said. 'She thought Letitia had died on the cliffs. And I don't suppose any of you know who did fill it?'

There was a general shaking of heads.

'It was there when we arrived,' Alistair said. 'I'm afraid it didn't occur to me that it was odd that Mary had made coffee for Letitia even though she thought my sister was dead. I suppose I thought it was just force of habit.'

'Perhaps she knew Letitia wasn't dead,' I said. 'It seems to have been a pretty open secret.'

'We did not tell her about our plans,' Colin said firmly.

'Who turned out the lights?' I asked.

Marie-Hélène said, 'We did, Alistair and I.'

'Do you know where Letitia went?'

'She went into her bedroom. We'd agreed she wouldn't go along the corridor past your room. Instead she went through the bathroom and Justin's bedroom,' Colin said.

'And through the nursery and up the hidden staircase in the tower?' I asked.

'Probably,' Colin said casually.

'What staircase?' Emma asked, obviously surprised that the house had secrets she had not been let in on.

'The one from the nursery into the tower room where Letitia was hiding,' I said. 'The doorway's now covered by a large cupboard. But anyone who knew about the staircase could have got into Letitia's room, gone through Justin's room and into the cupboard in the nursery and climbed the stairs with no risk of being seen by anyone but a very tired child. And somebody did take that route. Because Justin's ghost didn't go out of his door and into the corridor, he went, as Justin said, "through the wall" into the nursery. I notice that none of these pieces of paper you have given me mentions such a trip . . . and some of you haven't left me a note at all. If anyone wants to put that right privately, I shall be in the study this afternoon.'

'Do you think that whoever it was gave Letitia the poisoned coffee?' Horace asked.

'I imagine it was the coffee in the thermos that was drugged.'

'You know, of course, that Letitia used phenobarbitone as a sleeping draught,' Colin said.

'Indeed.'

'If you knew she had all that phenobarbitone herself, Sir Patrick, why were you so sure she didn't just take an overdose?' Emma asked.

'Because it would make no sense at all to stage a suicide on the cliffs and then go home and kill yourself,' Horace said, glancing at me for approval.

'Horace is right, of course,' I said.

'I suppose you know I take phenobarbitone for my insomnia,' Jessica said evenly.

'Indeed.'

'But I didn't use it to drug Aunt Letitia.'

'Really, Jessica,' Iona said, fidgeting with her pearls, 'no one thinks you did.'

'Sir Patrick thinks that one of us did it.'

'Don't be silly, Jessica,' Iona went on. 'Are you really sure that Letitia was dead when she was stabbed?'

'Indeed.'

'For the record,' Marie-Hélène chimed in, 'Jessica gave a couple of pills to me a few nights ago to help me sleep; but I'm sure it wasn't enough to knock anybody out.'

'Do you have those pills still?' I asked.

'No. I used some the night she gave them to me and I used the rest last night. I mean, after what happened to Letitia, it was hard to sleep.'

For just a moment, I thought Jessica was going to say something; but she obviously thought better of it.

'What did Letitia say when she left?'

'"I think I shall sleep in tomorrow,"' Colin's voice was shaking. 'She said, "I think I'll sleep in . . ."' His voice broke.

For a while no one spoke. In the lull in the conversation that followed this remark, we all of us noticed that the storm had quietened somewhat.

'Perhaps we shall have a calmer night tonight than for the last few nights,' Iona said, looking meditatively out of the drawing-room windows. Her hands were trembling. Everyone understood that she was talking about the weather.

I needed to try to confirm some of the suspicions that had been raised in our conversation with David Sealsay, and so I wandered over to the corner where Horace was puffing away quietly on his pipe and consuming the mint chocolates that had arrived with the coffee. 'Horace,' I began 'did Letitia ever tell you anything about her mother's death?'

'Only what was in her book.'

'What book?'

'The one that Alistair mentioned yesterday.'

This remark came as something of a surprise. 'But Alistair said that the stuff in the book was made up to give her a motive for suicide.' I noticed that Alistair had looked up when his name was mentioned. As my conversation with Horace continued, he, Colin and Gavin drifted over to join us.

'Well, the only allegations I read in the book were about her father.'

'There were equally imaginary and equally defamatory stories about my mother,' Alistair said, joining in. 'The manuscript confirms, at least, that my sister was mad.'

'And this book was destroyed?'

'Yes,' Horace said. 'I destroyed the copy she left with me on Sir Colin's instructions before I came here. That was a matter for the executor. I must say I thought it was the right decision.'

'It was evidence relevant to her death.'

'Which I then thought was a suicide. It was entirely fabricated.'

'It would have revealed her state of mind.'

'Her suicide revealed her state of mind,' Colin said.

'But she didn't commit suicide.'

'If I'd known that, Sir Patrick, I wouldn't have destroyed the manuscript,' Horace replied.

'Was there anything in the book that would, if true, have been sufficiently embarrassing to any living person for him or her to want to see Letitia dead?'

'What an odious question,' Gavin said.

His uncle rebuked him. 'Sir Patrick is asking exactly the questions he needs to ask if we're to find Letitia's killer.'

As we spoke, Strachan puffed on his pipe and scratched his belly thoughtfully. Out of the corner of my eye, I saw Paul Crawford say farewell to Iona, with whom he had been talking quietly, and take his leave.

Horace began thoughtfully. 'I suppose there was a great deal in the book that any of the family would rather was kept secret. Let me see. I shall have to go and sit somewhere quiet with a notepad. Fortunately I have a rather good memory. With time I suppose I could reconstruct the whole manuscript.'

At this moment the telephone rang on the desk, and Colin walked over and picked up the receiver. It was Inspector MacAlister for me.

'Tell him I'll take it in the study,' I said. And I rushed off down the corridor to speak to him. I had, after all, a fair amount of news.

It turned out that he, too, had news for me.

'They tell me we'll be able to get over to the isle in the morning. We'll leave from the port in Oban as soon as it gets light. Should be on the island by mid-morning. Is there anything you're short of?'

'Evidence.'

He laughed. 'By the way, you've got a mole over there.'

'A mole?'

'A spy, I mean. The story's splashed all over the newspapers. It's in the *Glasgow Herald* and the *Independent*. It's probably in a lot of the others.'

'What does it say?'

'Famed sleuth seeks solution to island mystery. That sort of thing. No details. Nothing about the autopsy or anything.'

'Good. Still, it's interesting. I'd have thought the only person here with those sorts of journalistic connections is Emma Gale. And if she was involved in the murder, you'd have thought she wouldn't have wanted the story to get out.'

MacAlister said nothing for a moment. 'Mebbe. Mebbe . . . Well, just thought I'd pass it on.'

We parted with a promise to talk again later that night.

When I had finished talking to MacAlister, I opened the door to the study to find Jonathan leaning against the opposite wall of the corridor, head down, trying unsuccessfully to look nonchalant. When he saw me he cast an eye over me, his chin still lowered on his chest, glancing upwards like a shy child. He looked frankly rather sheepish. 'I've a confession to make,' he began. I looked sharply at him. 'Oh, no,' he went on quickly, 'I had nothing to do with killing her. It's something else entirely. But I'd rather not write it down.'

Bashfully, Jonathan revealed that he was engaging in the oldest trick in the book: he was sleeping with the Scandinavian au pair. Not, I should say at once, that this was the direct object of his confession. He got this out of the way as quickly as he could in order to explain why it was that he had been peering out from behind the door of Marit's room at a little after half-past three in the morning.

His visit to Marit had achieved its purpose. And he was about to leave her and return to the bedroom where his loving wife and infant son were sleeping, when the handle on the door to the bedroom opposite, where Justin slept, was turned slowly. Not wishing to be detected in his adulterous adventures, Jonathan retreated behind the door, keeping it open a crack to see who came out. 'Normally, you can hear people coming because the boards creak. But there was so much noise from the storm last night, that I hadn't heard a thing.'

Jonathan's nervousness was understandable. There was, after all, the distinct possibility that it was Justin, a child who would certainly have broadcast his sighting of his uncle to the world. So Jonathan was relieved when the figure that appeared was someone else, namely Monica Smythe, 'carrying, as it happens, a teddy bear. I suppose she was checking on her ward.'

'Then, as I walked down the hall to my own bedroom, I thought I detected the odour of a very feminine perfume on the landing outside Aunt Letitia's room. Nothing that Aunt Letitia would have worn . . . But none of this seems likely to have anything to do with the other business, so I was hoping it wouldn't have to, you know . . .'

I thanked him for the information and told him I would keep it to myself. I wasn't sure if this did have anything to do with the murder. But it might do. One thing Monica Smythe couldn't have been doing was checking on the child. Because Justin had been moved into the other bed in her room after his scare with the "ghost". And none of the women had admitted that they had walked along the landing towards Emma Gale's room (and the room where Jonathan and Maria slept with their infant child).

I settled down once more with the scraps of paper on which the household had written their night-time stories. MacAlister had taken down the contents of all of them as I had dictated them over the phone. But I hadn't had much time yet to think about them myself. Now I wanted to consider how much of a timetable I could construct for Letitia's last hours.

Iona's note was simple, written in her clear and generous script.
After Colin and I went upstairs, we changed into pyjamas, brushed our teeth and went to bed. It must have been quite early, about half-

past ten. I was awakened somewhat after half-past one by the sound of Colin leaving the room. (I turned on the light and looked at my watch.) I wasn't surprised by this, I'm afraid. I assumed he'd gone to see his mistress, Miss Gale. Colin came back at about three – I didn't really get back to sleep while he was gone, the storm was so noisy. I asked him where he'd been. He said he was in the kitchen, talking to Ali and Marie-Hélène and Gavin and Jess. Given the general disruption of the household, it didn't occur to me to ask why they had gathered there in the middle of the night. (And, anyway, Colin didn't seem eager to discuss it.) Then he got into his bed and said good-night to me. I slept until about half-past seven in the morning.

Marie-Hélène and Alistair both began by admitting that they had gone up to see Letitia in the tower earlier on in the evening. But the rest of what was in their notes simply repeated much of what they had told me earlier about the conversation in the kitchen, and said they had gone to sleep when they got back upstairs. Alistair had provided simply a listed chronology. Marie-Hélène's note was chatty: *Once we were upstairs again*, her note ended, *all the sounds we heard were of the storm.*

Gavin said he had returned to his room via the drawing-room where he poured himself a large whisky, which he sipped intermittently in his room for a few minutes, before turning the light out and going to sleep. (This struck me as cleverly plausible, whether or not it was true.)

Joanna and Christopher reported the episode with Justin, but otherwise had nothing to relate. Jessica repeated the fact that she had also visited Letitia earlier in the evening, sometime before dinner. And then she gave a detailed account of the party in the kitchen and said that she went back up to the room she shared with Angela. They stayed there, Jessica said, till she came down for breakfast. Angela, naturally, confirmed this.

Emma's note was a good deal less chatty than Jessica's. She had written: *The Place: Sealsay. The Time: the night of the murder, about eleven o'clock. The Action: the beautiful, high-powered journalist has just fallen asleep. Something wakes her in the middle of the night – perhaps at about two, though she doesn't look at her watch – and she wakens, stretches, glances about the room, before going to the bedroom door and looking out. There is nothing in the corridor and so she goes back to bed. And she sleeps well, waking up again a little before she comes down, refreshed, to breakfast. (Not too much for you here, I fear, Sir P.)*

That was all I had and it didn't amount to much. And I knew that not all of it was true. Clearly, it was urgent now to talk to Colin, who, as I say, had still not provided me with an account of his movements.

I marched down the corridor once more to the drawing-room.

Only Iona and her daughters were in there, huddled together by the fire, talking quietly.

'I'm sorry to butt in,' I said, 'but do you know where Colin is?'

'In the library,' Iona said. 'And Alistair and Marie-Hélène have taken Gavin for a walk.'

'And Horace?'

'Went up to his room, I think,' Jessica said.

I found Colin in the library, sitting in front of the great fireplace, with its logs unlit, reading a book. It was one of Letitia's, *That Dark Inn*.

'Extraordinary woman, my sister,' Colin said. He looked haggard, older than I had ever seen him, and deeply sad. I found it hard at that moment to think that he might have played a part in planning her murder.

'Wasn't there a Canaletto in here once?' I asked, as I settled down opposite the laird.

'There was, but Gavin advised us that it was a good time to get rid of it. He thought that Canaletto had rather reached his peak. And having it to sell was rather a coup in setting up his dealership, apparently.'

'I hadn't realised there was a risk of anyone's losing interest in Canaletto. I should have expected to pay a very great deal for a painting like that.'

'You'll have to ask Gavin about why these things move in and out of fashion. It's a very strange business, art.'

'You know, of course, that the sale of the paintings makes it less easy to believe your claim that you are not short of money. The paintings that are missing since I was last here would have raised a good half a million pounds.'

Colin snorted humourlessly. 'That was not a guess, was it? You don't know anything about the art market. Who told you? Gavin? Emma?'

'Yes, Emma,' I said. It was, after all, part of the truth.

'Alistair told me he and Marie-Hélène explained to you the point of Letitia's fake suicide. So you know I'm short of money. I lost a good deal as a Lloyd's name a few years ago . . . and *Glitz* is an expensive hobby.' He snorted again and nibbled his lip. 'Emma tells me that it's a natural process in magazine start-ups. A year or so after it breaks even, we shall be rolling in money. Till then . . . But I wouldn't have killed my sister for the money, Patrick.'

I nodded.

Colin looked at me gloomily, knowing that I was going to ask him more questions that he didn't want to answer. And then he turned his eyes to the fireplace and sighed in resignation.

'I *am* sorry to have to do this, Colin, but you didn't give me a chronology of your movements the night before last after you came up from the kitchen at half-past two. and I do need to know. Iona tells me you got back at about three. So I assume that, in the interim, you were with Emma?' He nodded. 'She *is* flirtatious, isn't she?'

Colin looked at me wearily, as if he thought the remark was beneath me.

'I apologise,' I said. 'Let's get on with last night. You went to see Emma?'

'I did. I told her that my sister was insisting that we separate and that I might have to appear to do so. Naturally, she was not pleased.'

'Did she tell you she was going to go up to see Letitia after you left?'

'You won't catch me out like that, Patrick. I know she didn't go up there.'

'Because she told you so?'

'Why should she? She couldn't have poisoned Letitia. Letitia knew I would have told Emma about the will. Why would she have drunk coffee brought up by Emma? She'd have been suspicious. And anyway she had her thermos already.'

'I agree. But I have to tell you something now that I very much hope you won't tell Emma. Letitia didn't die from the phenobarbitone. She was smothered with a pillow some time after three in the morning.'

For a long time, neither of us said anything. Now Colin was even greyer, older, more anguished.

'If Emma went up there not long after three,' I said, 'she may well have suffocated your sister.'

Still he said nothing.

'Did she know about the phenobarbitone.'

'No.' Colin spoke suddenly, with a certain firmness. 'How could she have known? I didn't know. Look here, Patrick, it's all very well trying to pin this business on Emma. I know she does have a motive of sorts. But I give you my word that she did not go up into the tower and kill Letitia. And if Emma had killed her, I wouldn't want her to get away with it.'

Altogether it was a most convincing performance.

I pushed on. 'When you returned from Emma's room to your own, you had a conversation with Iona.'

'Not really a conversation. She asked where I'd been. I said I'd been with some of the family in the kitchen.'

'Didn't she enquire further?'

'No.'

'Didn't you think that was odd?'

'I was simply glad she didn't press.'

'Did you stay up?'

'No. We went to sleep almost immediately.'

'And slept till . . .?'

'We slept undisturbed till about seven in the morning.'

I left the library and went on up to our bedroom, assuming – correctly, as it turned out – that I should find Virginia there. I told her that MacAlister was hoping to be here with a couple of men over on the island by the next morning. 'A fine way to start the New Year,' Jinny said. 'So, where are we with all this business?'

As we talked through the facts we knew, things began to slip into place. We had several solid enough motives for murder. I listed them for Virginia. 'There's Colin, who cares a good deal for his family's reputation. He would hardly have wanted Letitia publishing the accusation that his father had murdered his mother because his brother was illegitimate. Then there's Alistair and his wife: they both must know that a scandal of this sort would hurt any chances of Alistair's moving up in the party. And, last but not least, there's Gavin.'

'Why should Gavin want Letitia dead?'

'You remember that Jim FitzG. told me that Gavin had sold rather more than £800,000 worth of pictures?' Jinny nodded. Her memory is nothing if not reliable. 'Well, this morning, Emma told me that the value of the sales was about half a million pounds, and I got Colin to confirm the figure just now. I'd say that young Gavin, our plausible playboy, has been cheating his father out of a fair portion of the proceeds of the picture sales. If Letitia had found out, she might have been holding this knowledge over young Gavin: perhaps that was why he went along with her suicide plan in the first place. It's rather out of character for Gavin to have put himself out so thoroughly for her.'

'Don't you think that it would have been easier just to own up to his father?'

'Maybe. But £300,000 is a lot of money, even for a Rundle. A sum like that might come between a young man and his inheritance.'

'All right. What about the others?' I took it from my wife's tone that she was not expecting me to spend breath answering this question, since she was now ready to contribute herself. I was right. 'Emma Gale,' Jinny said. *'there's* a very determined girl with every reason to want Letitia out of the way.'

'I agree. As for the rest, Iona only really has a motive in the money, and the way Letitia's will is set up, it's not clear that she'd get it.'

'You are an unsentimental old thing, Patrick. Has it occurred to you that once Letitia was dead, she might get her husband back?'

'She wasn't any more likely to get him back with Letitia dead. In fact, with Letitia able to blow the whistle at any time and obsessed with keeping Emma out of Colin's life, I'd have thought Iona would want her alive.'

'Well, that still leaves a good number of people who might have wanted to kill Letitia,' Jinny concluded. I felt bound to agree.

'We may dig up some other things. Jonathan is carrying on with the au pair. It's the sort of thing Letitia might have used against him, I suppose.'

'The problem isn't going to be motive or opportunity.'

'It probably isn't going to be working out who did what, either. Sooner or later, it'll fall into place. What worries me is whether I'm going to be able to prove any of it, once I know.'

'Darling, when have you ever failed?' Such moments in a marriage are worth treasuring. It boosts a chap's confidence tremendously to learn that his good wife has such utter faith in him. And so I chose to ignore Virginia's mumbled qualification, which went, if I recall aright, 'Of course, you've never been completely without police help before.'

After half an hour of rest, Virginia and I decided that we needed some fresh air. We had grown used to fighting against the gale each time we went out, so the fact that there were still wind and rain beating at the windows did not deter us. We needed to get out of the house, away from the Rundles with all their infidelities and deceptions. I suggested that we might pop in on David and Fiona and see whether they would offer us tea. We dressed up for the storm and made our way down the drive.

Though it was still raining hard, the wind had fallen a good deal once more, so that we could walk without being blown about. The trees around the house – trees that had roared in the wind and given up the leaves and the occasional branches that lay on the lawn and the drive – were now still. It was reassuring to walk hand in hand with my wife, away from a house full of people I could no longer trust. 'It's all rather depressing,' I grumbled into Virginia's ear.

'Never mind, darling, David and Fiona will cheer us up.'

We rang the door bell and heard it ring in the back kitchen, and a few moments later Niall appeared at the door. 'Hallo,' he said smiling, 'what are you two doing out in this weather?'

'We were rather hoping to be invited into the warmth of your grandparents' parlour,' Jinny said.

'Well, come on in and get dry,' Niall said. 'We're all in the back.' As we struggled out of our coats and unbooted ourselves, Niall said, 'Actually, it's a guid thing you came. I've a strange piece of news to pass on to you. It was something Annie told me. I was just telling ma grandfaither.'

We followed him into the parlour, and Niall said to his grandparents, 'It's Sir Patrick and Lady Virginia.'

'Welcome, welcome,' Fiona said. 'Will you take some tea?'

'Lovely,' Virginia said.

'I was just telling 'em about what Annie told me.'

'Och. You *do* that,' David said.

On Friday, Annie and Elizabeth had been dropped off at Sealsay House, as usual, at about six in the morning, to begin the day's work. It was still dark, of course, and the weather was awful, so Annie's father had driven them up in his van. In the main hall, the lights were on. They were usually off when the girls arrived, but at this time of year with all the family in the house, it wasn't unusual to find them on. So Annie thought nothing of that. But she also noticed that there was a light on in Letitia's room. And that did puzzle her, since everybody knew that Letitia had drowned. The drive does not go past the kitchen door, and so the girls had been dropped off not far from the front porch and they had run in their heavy overcoats, their heads covered with scarves, from there to the kitchen door. As Elizabeth struggled with the great handle – the door was never locked – Annie glanced backwards because she thought she glimpsed something out of the corner of her eye, and saw through the window of the main hall, Alistair and Gavin appearing from the corridor and making their way up the stairs.

'Was there anyone else?' I asked.

'Not that Annie saw.'

'Why didn't she tell me earlier?'

'She was shy, Sir Patrick . . . and a wee bit scared. I mean, Mr Gavin was in the room there. She thought he might have seen them too in the morning and he could have been angry if she told you what she'd seen.'

'But when she told Niall, he told her that he had to pass it on to you,' David said.

'And she agreed, of course,' Niall said. 'She asked me to tell you she was sorry.'

'No harm done,' I said.

'Well now, here's the tea,' Fiona said. She put a full steaming mug in front of each of us and offered us some sugar. Niall waited until we declined and then reached over to grab the sugar bowl. 'I wouldna take any more, if you dinna want an overdose,' Fiona said to him sharply. 'I've already put in your three lumps.'

Something about what she said caught my attention: in a second it clicked. I took a swig of tea. 'You know,' I said to the assembled company, 'I think when all this is over, it will turn out that those Rundles are not such a bad lot after all.'

We spent a pleasant late afternoon at the home farm with Fiona and David and their grandson, chatting and making plans for the evening and the party at Sealsay House.

16

As the evening came, the weather improved further. The winds had diminished in the afternoon; by evening the rain had stopped falling altogether. The clouds blew away to the east and the sun set magnificently over Ben Moray. Virginia and I walked back from the farm as the sun disappeared behind the hills. I told her what I thought we had learned at the Mackintoshes. And she found my reasoning plausible. 'But there's nothing concrete enough for the police, is there?' she said. I was forced to agree.

The servants bustling about the house, setting up the buffet in the dining-room and seating around the hall, finally brought it home to me that it was New Year's Eve. As Jinny and I dressed upstairs in the Green Room, I found myself reminiscing about earlier New Year's Eves in Scotland. 'It's normally such fun up here at this time of year. It's terribly upsetting to have to go drearily through the formalities when we should be having a wonderful time.'

I was thinking of my first Hogmanay on Sealsay, not long after the war. Then, as now, the house was set up for a party.

But then the library was cleared, with chairs all around the walls and a gramophone set up to play reels interspersed with waltzes for us Sassenachs.

I had worn tails, which these days one is so rarely called upon to wear, but had envied Colin his wonderful MacIver tartan, worn by the Rundles courtesy of the Dukes of Kintyre. Both of us were sure we cut a pretty dashing figure . . . both of us, judging by the looks we got from the ladies, were right. Letitia was about thirty then. She was handsome and severe – like Glenda Jackson as the young Queen Elizabeth the first. She sat with the family and its guests in the drawing-room as the islanders came in in twos and threes to bid us good evening, nodding at each one who passed and saying nothing. I remember a couple of young men had tried to persuade her to dance; and she had turned them down. When I asked her, at Colin's bidding, approaching her with Colin at my right hand, she said only, 'Colin, don't be silly.' And so we flirted with the island girls as I danced the reels that Colin and Alistair had spent the past two days teaching me. I cannot remember the names now, but I can remember the steps and I can remember feeling young and strong and lucky to be alive as we stepped our way down lines of dancers, one hand on hip, one in the air.

And then, when the dancing at the great house was done, and we had sung in the New Year with 'Auld Lang Syne', Colin and I had set out first-footing. The idea is simple enough. You go from door to door through the early morning, bringing a greeting to your neighbours and getting from them a wee dram to help you to the next door. You carry a lump of coal to bring good luck to every house where you are the first guest of the year.

On that night I had seen into the lives of the other islanders. They lived in their tiny crofts, in cottages of two or three rooms, where they scraped a living off their smallholdings. But on this night of the year, they put behind them the cares of their harsh lives and they drank whisky and tea and sang songs and told tales. Colin, after years of this, knew better than I did how to regulate his consumption. The last thing I recall was a young woman, the daughter of the house we were in, back from the mainland where she worked as a maid in an hotel, gently topping up my teacup with a whisky as raw as any I have ever tasted until the cup was not tea, with a drop of whisky, but whisky with a drop of tea. I suppose I passed out. Colin roused me a little before lunchtime the next day. 'I think', he said, 'that my father will believe all the rumours spreading about the island about your behaviour last night, if you fail to appear for luncheon.' He handed me a steaming cup of bouillon laced with brandy. 'Drink this. And if I were you, I'd keep away from whisky for a few days.'

I was roused from these remembrances by Virginia. 'Don't you think you ought to talk to MacAlister, now, before the party gets going?'

'You're absolutely right.' I adjusted my tie, organised my cummerbund, which seemed to have shrunk somewhat in recent years, and dragged on my dinner jacket. I turned from admiring the results in the mirror to see a vision of elegance that still delights my heart after all these many years: Jinny in a smart evening dress – what, in the *Tatler*, would almost certainly be called a gown – of reds of various hues, her steel-grey hair piled elegantly on her elegant head, and pinned with a series of elegant hairpins. Years of experience have taught me that this is a moment to resist the urge to crush my dear wife in an embrace. But I was unable to resist leaning forward, so as not to crush her skirt, and kissing her gently on the lips. 'Gorgeous, ravishing, exquisite, pulchritudinous . . .'

'I don't need a recitation from Roget's Thesaurus, darling. But I do need you to help me into this black sash. I can't go around dressed as if I hadn't noticed Letitia was dead.'

'May I ask in what spirit you brought this with you? Were you *expecting* to attend a wake?'

'Don't be silly, darling. Marie-Hélène and I made some up earlier for all of us girls from an old dress of Iona's.'

'I wonder how Iona is.'

'Well, if you phone MacAlister, I'll go and find out.'

MacAlister was not particularly happy with my speculations. 'Now I'm no saying that *I* dinna believe you, Sir Patrick, but you've no' got enough for a jury, now have you?'

'I entirely agree. But I think I can produce a few more witnesses for you this evening. At the moment they're all sticking to their stories because they don't know what really happened. Once they do, I think they may begin to change their minds. The other thing is that there may still be something to be found by your forensic people when they get here.'

'Not likely. They've had days to clear up, now.'

'Still, it'll be worth bringing a search warrant and some specialists.'

'We'll all be there, Sir Patrick. And in the mean time, do take care. I mean, once the murderer finds out you know, you'll be a target.'

There was a knock on the door.

'Hold on, Inspector, there's someone trying to get in here.' I put down the receiver and went over to the door. 'Ah, Colin, I was just reporting to the inspector. I won't be much longer.' He smiled slightly and waved me back to the phone. I obeyed. 'It's Sir Colin.'

'Well, give him my very good wishes for the New Year,' Inspector MacAlister said. It was not, I think, a request to be taken seriously.

'Good-night.' I returned the handset to the cradle.

'When will they be here?' Colin asked.

'Not till tomorrow, I'm afraid. Though they may get in a little earlier than they'd planned, because the weather's cleared faster than they expected.'

'Good. I don't like the thought of Letitia being left in the doctor's freezer indefinitely. We're gathering in the drawing-room. We'll have a little to eat at about eight and the islanders will start arriving after about half-past nine.'

'How's Iona?'

'All right. She'll be here to greet them, of course, but then she'll want to go upstairs. I was going to phone Crawford and ask him to bring up something to help her sleep.'

I left Colin alone in his office and walked down the corridor towards the drawing-room. It sounded as though everyone was down. And the party was more cheerful than it had been for several days. It occurred to me that this might be a good moment to slip back upstairs and pop into a couple of the rooms I had not yet seen: Letitia's, in particular. But when I arrived outside it, it was locked. Then I remembered the other route. I walked down to Justin's room and knocked. There was no one there. One can't keep an eight-year-old upstairs for Hogmanay. I walked through his bathroom and into Letitia's room. I opened the cupboards. It took me a few minutes, but I found what I was after.

I had one other place to look before I returned to our bedroom. I sat, for a moment, at the desk. I wanted to see if I could imagine it all. Five minutes later, when I went downstairs, there were only a couple more questions I needed to ask. I picked up the copy of *A Tender Magic* that was on Jinny's bedside table, and found the passage we had read to David earlier, marking it with a slip of paper. Then I popped it into my jacket pocket. It might come in useful later.

I joined the family in the drawing-room where we all had drinks. I transferred Letitia's book from my pocket to Jinny's slightly more capacious handbag. The mood was restrained rather than festive, but the family seemed, on the whole, to have recovered its spirits. Iona was still pale and nervous-looking, still more affected, apparently, than the others by the events of the past few days. But while she said little and was too distracted most of the time to follow much of the conversation, she did her duty as hostess, making sure that Gavin kept our glasses filled and announcing, at about eight, that it was time for us to serve ourselves from the buffet in the dining-room.

I chatted with Horace as we stood at the buffet, astonished by the amounts of food he was piling on his plate. He was particularly keen on the steaming haggises, eyeing them first, and then carving himself a couple of enormous slices. Emma's mood had improved a good deal since this morning and she was now rather cheerful; she chatted to a group that included Maria, Gavin and Virginia, ignoring my wife's rather less than subtle indications that Emma was not her favourite person. Jinny has never had much time for women who come between men and their wives.

Iona put on her plate only the absolute minimum required to establish that it needed washing up, and then picked at it perfunctorily. She studiously avoided Colin – who was, in any case, rather preoccupied, and kept staring out through the windows into the dark – and was obviously unwilling to join the group that included Emma; and so she ended up chatting to Joanna and Jessica for a while, before joining Horace and me.

'I'm glad the weather's cleared up,' she said. 'It will be so much less unpleasant for the islanders to get up here now it isn't raining. I wonder if they'll come, given what's happened?'

'If I were a betting man,' Horace opined grandly, 'I should stake everything on their coming in large numbers. They'll be curious; and, in any a case, the New Year festivities always start in the big house.'

'Well, we shall see,' Iona said vaguely, her eye wandering over to where Colin and Emma were talking animatedly by the window. A look of pain crossed her face and then she smiled at us wanly. 'Ah what fools we mortals be.'

'*A Midsummer Night's Dream*, if I recall aright,' Horace said. 'Never seen the point of that play – have you, Sir Patrick? All that gadding about in the woods with fairies and so on. Rather hard to take seriously.' But he did not await my answer, excusing himself with a slight inclination of his head, and setting off once more to the groaning sideboard.

It was a sight that would normally have brought me pleasure, too. There were beautiful glazed hams; several large turkeys, splendidly browned in Mary's kitchen; even the haggises looked tempting. And there were enormous bowls of potato salad – a great favourite, Gavin had once assured me, with the islanders. On the other side of the room, the dining-table was laden with tempting desserts: trifles, chocolate cakes, a lemon pudding or two, and a plum pudding, crowned with holly, as a concession to the foreigners from England. Cream, brandy butter . . . every conceivable excuse for a heart attack abounded. I have never before resisted with such ease so much that would normally have tempted me.

By about a quarter to nine we were ready to drift back into the drawing-room. The children, who had been fed in the kitchen, were all there with Monica and Marit. When Virginia and I arrived, Iona was holding little Marietta, her grandchild, on her lap and gazing mournfully out of the windows. She turned towards us as we entered and gave me a sad, wistful smile. I reciprocated grimly, trying to inject into my look a levity I did not feel. I caught sight of the resulting expression in a mirror across the room and adjusted my face into an equally unnatural but larger smile. 'Patrick, darling,' Virginia whispered, 'I know that this is a wake, but I think we should try and look a little less mournful.'

I still needed to find out one or two more things from Horace, and so, when he appeared – as usual he was the last to finish eating – I collared him, and Jinny and I took him back into the hall.

'Horace,' I began, 'you were going to think through that manuscript of Letitia's and decide if there was anything troublesome in it about Lady Lorna.'

'I've run through it all, but I can't think of anything.'

'Let me read you something,' Jinny said. And she removed from her handbag the copy of *A Tender Magic* and opened it at the place I had marked. Quickly she read it to him. 'Any of that ring a bell?'

'It's one of her fantasies,' Horace said. 'Nothing to do with the real family. There was absolutely nothing of that sort in her manuscript.'

'You read it all.'

'Once I realised how scandalous it was, I naturally read it very carefully so that I could consider what advice to give Letitia and her family. I can assure you there was nothing so preposterous as a suggestion that her father had killed her mother.'

'But there was a suggestion that she had been molested by her father.'

'Indeed.'

'And you believe that was purely imaginary?'

'I think it was all part of this plot to give herself a motive for suicide.' I wondered if it was Colin or Gavin that had convinced him of this theory. 'A woman like that, you know, one who writes novels, obviously has an unreliable imagination.' With Virginia around remarks of this sort were skating on rather thin ice, but I didn't want to interrupt him in full flow. 'I think she just became so obsessed with this faked suicide that she overdid it a bit.'

'It might suggest – at least to someone like myself, a woman who writes novels and therefore has an unreliable imagination – that she didn't much like her father.' My wife was not amused by Horace Strachan's aspersions.

'Oh good Lord, Lady Scott, I meant nothing by that. I was thinking of Letitia. I mean *she* lived in a fantasy world. But, of course, you may be right, she may not have liked her father. Who knows? But she certainly didn't accuse him of murder.'

We chatted on for a couple more minutes and so we were in the hall when the first of the islanders rang the bell. Parsons opened the door to them and wished them a good evening. They knew the routine. They waved at us cheerily and then went down the corridor towards the kitchen, to the room next to Colin's estate office, where they left their coats. Then they made their way back up towards the drawing-room on their way to greet – and, this time, to offer their condolences to – the family.

The two older men in the first group that arrived were in kilts. They were accompanied by a cheerfully spherical woman in late middle age and a young man dressed in black trousers and a tweed coat, with a tie uncomfortably lodged around a collar that was obviously usually left unbuttoned. I recognised the two older men vaguely from earlier visits to the island and was struggling to recover their names from my ageing brain, when Horace introduced them to Virginia and to me.

'Patrick, Virginia, these are the Campbells. This is Ian, their patriarch, and his wife Sarah; his brother Andrew . . . and his son David.'

'I believe we've met before, Mr Campbell,' I said.

'Och, yes, more than once. But I've no had the pleasure of meeting your guid lady.'

'Delighted to meet you all,' Jinny said, in her best village fête manner, and they passed on in to see the family.

We followed after.

By ten o'clock there were at least eighty of the island people in the house. From time to time, above the din, I could hear Colin's voice booming out another tale of life up the Amazon, or down the Congo. Once it was a thirty-foot anaconda, apparently a formidable creature with which to wrestle; a second time I heard him say, 'The mouth of your average Congo crocodile has a pretty firm grip.' But he sounded each time more and more like a caricature of himself, as if he was struggling to live up to the islanders' expectations.

The Wrigleys had come up from the hotel and Paul had arrived, dressed in a dinner jacket that competed with mine in antiquity. Once he had got himself a hefty glass of whisky, he brought them over to where Virginia and I were standing in the hall.

'Nice to see you again, Sir Patrick. Can't keep you away, then, can we?' Wendy Wrigley said, adding, beneath her breath, 'Terrible business with Miss Letitia. I do hope you can clear it all up soon. It's so unnerving not knowing, isn't it?'

'You're not supposed to know about that, Wendy, because I shouldn't have told you,' Paul said laughing.

'It's not of any great consequence now,' I said.

'Ah ha, so you've solved the mystery,' Paul said.

'Almost. There's the odd piece still to work out.'

'Will you have it all wrapped up on a plate for the police when they get here?'

'Of course he will,' Peter Wrigley said. 'Sir Patrick always gets his man.'

'Or woman,' Paul said.

At this point the Wrigleys were dragged away by somebody and we were left alone with Paul.

'I'm rather worried about Iona,' I said.

'She doesn't look too hot.'

'She's under a great deal of strain. Did Colin ask you to bring up something to help her sleep?'

'Yes, he did, actually. But she's got a decent quantity of sleeping pills already. She wasn't sleeping very well *before* all this business.'

'Look, Paul,' I said, 'I don't think she should have anything she could do herself any harm with. She's in a very fragile condition.'

'Why is that?' His voice was solicitous, but it had a hard edge to it, as if I had accused him of something.

'Because of Colin's fling with Emma, and because of Letitia's death, and because . . .' I was about to tell him what I thought was really worrying Iona. But I wondered how easy he would find it to keep his tongue from wagging. I held back. 'It's rather trying, I should think, holding a party when your sister-in-law's murder remains unsolved.'

Paul knocked back the glass he was carrying. 'Extraordinary woman, Iona. Wonderful woman. Do you know, I think I may be a little bit in love with her.' He laughed heartily. 'He's a bastard, Colin, isn't he?'

'Indeed,' Jinny offered. 'But almost all men are.'

'If I may enter a defence of the comparative merits of my own sex, I should like to offer in evidence the lady who has diverted Sir Colin from the straight and narrow.' Jinny and I have these little discussions from time to time.

'She is a single woman who has not promised to love and to cherish.'

'Granted. But she did know he was married. And she certainly knew that she was taking advantage of him.'

'You would have resisted. Why couldn't Colin?'

'Colin was probably subjected to a protracted siege.'

'If I might just, for a moment, intrude, on this private discussion, I should like to observe that David and Fiona have arrived,' Paul said.

Virginia kissed me on the cheek, and as she did so whispered in my ear, 'Relax, my sweet, it'll all soon be over.'

'Sorry, Paul. Frightfully rude of us. Let's see if we can get over to have a word with them.'

An hour later everyone had had a chance to load up on food and drink from the dining-room. By now on a normal New Year's Eve, the dancing would have been in full swing. Instead, Parsons had set out an old gramophone on which he was playing rather mournful-sounding hymns. The younger children had fallen asleep on sofas in the drawing-room, but Justin was sitting up, beside his mother in the hall, looking decidedly bored.

'It's like a funeral parlour in Wigan.' Virginia's remark brought me back from my meditation on the cruelty of the very young.

'What do you know about funerals in Wigan?' Paul teased Jinny gently.

'There you have me.' She laughed.

'Well, I think I can cheer the place up a bit.' He went over and had a word with Parsons, who looked dubious, and then disappeared into the drawing-room. A moment later he reappeared with Colin, who went to the library and unlocked the door. Colin summoned a few of the men and together they all pushed the grand piano from the library into the hall.

A hush fell on the company and people who were still eating in the dining-room came out into the hall. Paul sat at the piano. Suddenly the drunken doctor disappeared. He breathed in deep, pushed out his chest and began to play marvellously. I am not a great judge of these things, but it seemed to me that it was a miraculous performance.

'It's one of Liszt's "Transcendental Études",' Virginia said. 'Fiendishly difficult. How can he do it when he's drunk?'

'How can he do it when he's sober?' I whispered in reply.

Paul's riveting performance broke the ice. After he finished, Andrew Campbell and David Sealsay stepped out and began to play a strangely moving dirge on the pipes. They had been carrying them to play later on as they went off first-footing; but the music they played was not the joyful dance music that sees out the old year, but the mournful mode that marks the end of a life. There were a few moist eyes when they finished; and into the applause that followed a single voice began to sing an old Gaelic song. The people of Sealsay were making a *ceilidh* for Letitia; and if she was listening somewhere, she must have thanked these people who had shared her strange life.

At five minutes to midnight, Colin broke off from a tale of capturing a tiger single-handed in Nepal, to ask everyone to charge their cups, and Parsons and the girls rushed around filling empty glasses with mulled wine and with whisky. As the great clock in the hall chimed midnight, the singing of 'Auld Lang Syne' began: and at the end of it the laird shouted, 'A happy New Year to you all.'

I took the opportunity to kiss Virginia, and she whispered

sweetly, 'Another lovely year together, darling.' I confess that, swept up in the moment, my own eyes moistened somewhat.

Paul, who happened to be nearby at that moment, reached over to me and clapped me on the shoulder. 'Glad to see you're an old sentimentalist at heart. Happy New Year. And many more of them.'

Colin made a small speech in the grandest feudal manner to the islanders, thanking them for another year of working together, wishing them well on his behalf, and for all the Rundles. He told them that Letitia, whom they had all known for so long – 'know', here, was something of an overstatement – was dead, as he was sure they were all aware. 'We do not know how she died exactly. Sir Patrick is looking into the matter and he tells me that he will be able to inform us soon. The police will take over as soon as they can get here. But there is no need to worry about it. It is all in good hands. Letitia would not want you to mourn her too long. She lived a surprisingly full life here on Sealsay. I am sure she would want you to celebrate the New Year for her, since she cannot be here with us. Happy New Year to you all.'

Ian Campbell made a brief speech of thanks to the laird, and offered, too, the condolences of all of them. The islanders raised their glasses once more to him in a Gaelic toast of their own. And then, in twos and threes, they fetched their coats and came to bid farewell. It was time now for them to set out on their night's adventures. The Wrigleys left immediately, driving down to set up the dancing at the hotel. Horace told me cheerfully that he had arranged to be driven down there, too. 'I do hope the family doesn't think it inappropriate, but I don't feel the year is really underway if I haven't been first-footing.'

I was keeping my eye open for David Sealsay, with whom I needed to make some plans before he left. When I saw him approaching the door, I hurried over to him and followed him out into the night.

'David,' I said, 'can you spare a moment?' It took me only a few minutes to explain what I wanted of him.

It was a lovely night. The storm was over. The moon was high and bright. I breathed in the fresh cold air and thought about what I had to do on this first day of the year of Our Lord nineteen hundred and eighty-nine. I was not looking forward to it. As I entered the hall, I found Virginia waiting for me. 'Iona's gone up. Paul gave her a fairly hefty tranquilliser. But everyone else is still downstairs. They're saying good-night to the children.'

Paul came down the stairs as we were talking. 'I've put her to bed. She'll be all right once she's rested.'

'Paul,' I said, 'I have a favour to ask you.'

'Anything.'

'Would you go to David Sealsay's house, straight away. He told me he wanted to see you.'

'All right. So I'll see you in the morning. I suppose the police will want Letitia and my autopsy report when they arrive.'

I shook his hand and Virginia kissed him good-night. 'I don't think I'll bother going into the drawing-room again,' he said as he waved to us from the door. 'If anybody asks, you can tell them I've left.'

'It's time,' Virginia said, and we entered the drawing-room. Justin was still in the midst of saying good-night to the family. He was obviously rather over-excited. The sight of his nanny, Monica Smythe, reminded me that I still had not asked her about her trip to Justin's room on the night before last. I reminded Virginia that I needed to check up on this and sidled over to Miss Smythe, who was standing by the door to the conservatory, engaged in conversation with Jessica. As I joined them, she dropped her gaze primly, and moved back, as if assuming that I could only have come to talk to Jessica. 'I'm sorry to intrude, Miss Smythe,' I said. 'And I realise that you must take Justin to bed soon, but I did just need to ask you a few questions about the night that Justin saw his ghost.'

'Right, then, I'll leave you to it,' Jessica said, returning to the small sofa where Angela was ensconced, looking as usual both cheerful and uncomfortable in equal measure.

'Perhaps we could slip out into the conservatory, where we can be more private,' I said.

I had not been in the conservatory since we arrived. The smell of tropical flowers was overwhelming. Sealsay had not been showing itself at its best since we had arrived, but, because the island is in the Gulf Stream and because it sits in the eastern Atlantic, it gets a good deal of warm weather much of the year and a great deal of sunlight. As a result the Rundles had managed over the years to develop, in this conservatory, a collection of flowers with the abundance of a tropical rain forest. In the absence of Virginia, my capacity to identify plants is extremely limited. (When she *is* present, I rely on the old trick of burbling, 'Isn't that a mumble-mumble *grandiflora*?' knowing that the reply will be something like, 'Don't be silly, Paddy, that's *Pisum sativum* probably *indica*.') I was reduced, therefore, always to appreciating the extraordinary beauty of the flowers and their fragrances without being able to comment on them.

'A fine fragrance,' I observed unpoetically. Miss Smythe was not impressed. 'Well,' I went on, 'I suppose we should get down to business. As you know, I've been asked to investigate the death of Sir Colin's sister, Letitia.'

She nodded.

'And I am now tying up various loose ends of the investigation.'

'Do you know who did it?'

'Well, now, there you may be able to help me. I am considering a few possibilities still, and I think you may know something that will help me sort them out.'

'Really?'

'Yes. Let me see if I can help you remember. On Thursday night, Justin, your ward, woke up at about three in the morning and ran screaming into his parents' room, announcing that he had seen a ghost.'

Again, she nodded.

'His mother then returned him to your room, where he slept in the other bed.'

This time I waited until she said, 'Yes.'

'Justin told me that he saw a man.'

'He told me that, too.'

'Good. Now, here's the thing. At about a quarter to four, perhaps half an hour later, you went into Justin's room again.'

'How on earth did you know that?'

'Detection, Miss Smythe, is a matter of gathering your clues where you find them.' A nice line, which means, of course, nothing whatsoever. 'Did you indeed go back to his room?'

'Yes. But I didn't have anything to do with the other business.'

'Of course not. I didn't for a moment think you did. But may I ask what you were doing.'

'Justin wanted his teddy. He woke up again after I'd just got him off to sleep and insisted I go and fetch it.'

'So you did.'

'Yes.'

'And did you notice anything when you went?'

'What sort of thing?'

'I don't know. Anything unusual.' I breathed in the air deeply, enjoying the fragrance.

'Oh yes,' she said, 'of course, the smell.'

'Go on.'

'The room smelled of perfume. I thought that was odd because it definitely wasn't there when I put him to bed.'

'Could it have been his mother's perfume?'

'No. she always wears Yves Saint Laurent. This was something much more expensive.'

'I'd be very grateful if you could tell me if you happen to smell it again at the party tonight.'

'I already have,' she said.

'On whom?'

She told me.

As she made her way back into the drawing-room I made sure the outside door to the conservatory was unlocked. It was time to make the last move of the game.

17

The islanders had all left. Wearily the family gathered in the drawing-room, with only Angela Horseman and Iona (and, of course, the children and their nannies) absent. The Christmas tree with its hundred twinkling lights still blinking with mechanical regularity was out of place in this atmosphere of exhaustion, like a lone noisy reveller disturbing the peace of those whose parties have ended.

'I think that went rather well, considering,' Alistair sighed, 'don't you, Colin?'

'I suppose so.'

'And now we must face up to the business of Letitia's murder,' Alistair said. 'The police will be here in the morning, I gather, Patrick. Will you be able to tell them what happened?'

'What happened? Yes, I suppose I can tell them what happened. But I don't know that I can prove it to their satisfaction without your help.'

'Help?' Colin said.

'I now know who killed your sister.' I looked at Colin and then at Alistair. 'Your sister-in-law.' I turned to Marie-Hélène. 'Your aunt'. I surveyed the others. 'But I shall also need your help to make the case. So, let me tell you what I'm sure of.

'A curious case, this was. We begin, of course, with the fact that Virginia and I were invited here as part of a plot, laid by Letitia, to allow her to transfer her wealth to her brothers, without actually dying. But her plan also made it possible for someone else to kill her, while she was, so to speak, already dead.

'I was led astray to begin with by three crucial false assumptions. Letitia was poisoned, as I say, while the world thought she was already dead. And many of you had known for a long time about her plan. You all therefore had time to arrange to kill her once she had persuaded the world she was already dead.

'So I began by assuming that the stabbing was an unforeseen intervention in a plan that would have allowed whoever poisoned Letitia to take her body off early yesterday morning and bury it where it would never be found.

'If that was true then, as I say, it was almost certain that Letitia's death had been planned by some of you, her family. That was a painful thought. I have known some of you for all of my adult life. But the fact that you had all lied to me about the suicide, and kept lying later, made it easier for me to believe that you had conspired against Letitia.

'At first, I was reluctant to believe it, not only because I knew and liked you, but also because I couldn't see a motive. Letitia's suicide had been arranged to make sure that you, Colin, had enough money to keep the house and the island. Once it was clear that Letitia's trusts were unbreakable – you were asking for her, not for yourself, weren't you, Alistair? – you had agreed to fake her death. But then killing Letitia didn't make much sense, unless you thought her plot wasn't going to work. And if you thought it wasn't going to work, why did you all go along with the suicide plan in the first place?' I took a sip from my champagne glass. 'It was then that I found out the truth about how your mother died, Colin, and I thought that Letitia had made plans to publish the story.'

'What do you mean by "the truth about my mother's death"?' Alistair asked angrily.

'I discovered that your mother had had an affair with one of the islanders. Your father found out. Letitia was up there in the caves by the Moray cliffs when your father came upon your mother there and challenged her with it. He asked her who your father was, Alistair. She wouldn't tell him. And then he pushed your mother off the cliff.'

Alistair glared at me in silence. It was clear that most of the family had not known about this particular skeleton. There were stunned exclamations around the room.

'Didn't you all know this?' I asked.

'It's stuff and nonsense,' Colin said. 'Letitia's imagination.'

'I don't think so. There's corroboration.'

'From whom?' Colin asked.

'Let us start with the fact that your father left Alistair nothing in his will. But I don't think it really matters very much now I know, does it? As I said, this has nothing to do with Letitia's murder.'

'Well, why the hell did you bring it up, then?' Alistair asked, still angry. 'So far, Patrick, all you've told us is that you think my father murdered my mother because she was an adulteress. Do you wish to insult my family further? Or would you just like to tell us who killed Letitia?' He was now red-faced with rage.

I thought, *He's afraid that I know who his father is.* But I said, 'I *am* sorry. It really hadn't occurred to me that you didn't know. I mentioned it because it explained why I began to work out how you and your family could have poisoned Letitia with phenobarbitone. It was only when Horace told me this evening that the events I had uncovered were not in Letitia's manuscript that I realised I was wrong. I should apologise, now, for having been so easily led to think you capable of murdering your own flesh and blood.

'The reason I asked Horace was that I had realised this afternoon that I'd made a mis-step. A chance remark over tea at David and Fiona's house led me to see how the poisoning might have happened.

'Jessica, you filled the thermos flask that Letitia took to bed that night, did you not?'

'Of course not,' Jessica said without conviction.

'You filled it and you put in perhaps ten pills, about a gram, of phenobarbitone from your own supply. You'd been up early in the evening to see Letitia and she seemed very excitable and you thought she should get a good night's sleep. You did not know that the weather was going to make it impossible for the police and the coastguard to land. And so you had every reason to want to keep her quiet for the next day or so, while the investigation continued. It was a harmless way to keep your aunt out of the way. And you knew that even if she took a few pills herself, fifteen or even twenty would not be enough to kill her. You just wanted her to have a long sleep.

'Do you still deny it?'

'No . . . no . . . you're right. But what went wrong?' Jessica asked. She was sitting on a small sofa by the window.

'What went wrong was that Alistair and Marie-Hélène had the same idea. You had made up the thermos before you went to bed. When they arrived and found it there, they added the eight or so pills that Marie-Hélène had left. I knew, from the way you responded to Marie-Hélène's admission that you'd given her "a couple" of pills, that you had given her more than that.

'You see, this afternoon, Fiona had put sugar in Niall's tea and he was going to put in some more, when she warned him he was about to get an overdose of sugar. I realised then that if several people had given Letitia phenobarbitone she could have received an overdose, even though nobody meant to harm her. I found the flask in Letitia's room earlier this evening; the police will be able to confirm that it's loaded with phenobarbitone.

'But not only did none of the family set out to poison Letitia, it wasn't actually the phenobarbitone that killed her. You did not kill your aunt, even by mistake. She might have died from phenobarbitone poisoning some time later that morning, but she might not have. The amount you gave her was over the smallest lethal dose, but she might have survived.'

'Well, so much for poor Aunt Letty,' Jessica said stolidly. It was borne in on me again how exactly true it was that nobody liked Letitia.

'Doesn't anybody care that Letitia was murdered?'

'We are not here to answer questions about our feelings,' Colin said brusquely. 'Are you or are you not proposing to tell us how you think my sister died?'

'Very well. The reason Letitia didn't survive was that she was comatose from the combination of her own pills and the doses Jessica and Marie-Hélène gave her. And that made it easy for someone to suffocate her.'

'Suffocate?' Alistair said. 'First I've heard of suffocation.'

'Indeed. It's the first *any* of you have heard of suffocation, save Colin, whom I told yesterday . . . and the person who did it.

'For a while, I was not sure who that was. You see, even if the family as a whole had no motive to kill Letitia, there were several people who might have wanted Letitia dead. There was Gavin, for example, who had dealings to hide that his aunt might have found out about.'

'What dealings?' Colin said. Gavin looked shiftily about him.

'I think you'd better ask your son,' I said.

'I haven't the faintest idea what he's talking about, Father.'

'What was your commission on the sale of your father's paintings?'

'That's none of your business.'

'Or is "commission" even the right word here? Perhaps "peculation" is apter. And if Letitia had told your father about that—'

Colin interrupted me. 'Are you saying that Gavin killed Letitia to keep her from telling *me* something?'

'I am simply explaining why he might have had a motive. I haven't said he killed Letitia. Any more than I've said that Alistair killed Letitia because she knew who his real father was.'

Alistair bristled again, but Colin stopped him from speaking with a wave of his hand. 'It simply gave Letitia something to hold over each of them.'

I went on. 'These are matters that can be kept away from the police, because, as it turned out, they were red herrings. You see, I had made a second false assumption. I had assumed that Letitia was suffocated in the tower. It was only yesterday afternoon that I realised that there was no reason to assume this. Letitia was supposed to be planning to spend many days hidden in the tower, yet there was nothing of hers up there. The bed she was supposed to sleep in was untouched. It could have been remade – that was what I assumed at first. But when I learned that the light to Letitia's bedroom was on at six this morning, I drew the obvious conclusion. Letitia could retreat to the tower, through Justin's room and the nursery, but she didn't need to give up using her room. She'd deliberately scared Justin by pretending to be a ghost, knowing that he'd be put to bed in Monica's bedroom. That gave her free passage all night. Which meant she might have been suffocated in her own bed, once the phenobarbitone had knocked her out. But why?

'It was then that I began to think about the stab wounds again. Someone had stabbed Letitia after she was already dead from suffocation. Who would do that? Only someone who was very nervous. Someone acting in the dark, who did not notice that Letitia was already dead. I simply couldn't think of anyone who would want Letitia dead enough to stab her, but was nervous enough to do it that way.

'And then I realised I had made my third false assumption. I had assumed that the person who had stabbed Letitia was trying to kill *her*. Someone who didn't notice that she was already dead might well not have known even whose body it was. It was very dark last night. It was very noisy. You wouldn't have heard someone breathing even if they had been alive.

'*So suppose that the person who stabbed Letitia had meant to kill someone else?* That would mean that Letitia's body would have had to have been in that person's bed, of course.

'The more I thought about it, the clearer it was to me that only one person fitted the profile. And that was Iona.'

There was a stunned silence for a few seconds, into which Iona's children eventually expressed their scepticism.

'Rubbish,' said Gavin.

'Mother wouldn't hurt a fly,' Maria said.

'Ridiculous,' said Jessica.

'You can't expect us to take that suggestion seriously,' said Christopher, holding Joanna's hand, as she shook her head emphatically in agreement.

I continued: 'That's why Iona fainted when she saw Emma come down to breakfast the morning after Letitia was killed. She fainted because she thought she had killed Emma. We all know that she had every reason to loathe her husband's mistress. We all saw how upset she was about her presence here. But if she stabbed Letitia thinking she was Emma, that meant that Letitia was in Emma's bed.

'Now why was that, I asked myself. What was Letitia doing in Emma's bed?'

'I suppose', Emma drawled, her voice tinged with a slight edge of alcohol, 'that you think I was having an affair with her.'

'No, that was not a possibility I considered. But the fact that her body was in your room did suggest to me another possibility. That it was you that suffocated her.'

'It's preposterous, of course.'

I ignored her interruption. 'You had, of course, a motive. Letitia wanted Colin to stop seeing you, and now that she was in on a plot with the family to pretend she was dead, she had a great deal of power to threaten everyone with exposure. Her will gave Colin a quarter of a million pounds if he stopped supporting your magazine. If he didn't, the money went to Iona. You may have hoped that with Letitia dead, Iona could be persuaded to take that money and leave. Or you may have hoped that, with Letitia dead, it would be relatively easy to get around that provision.'

'You can't prove any of this.' Emma was dismissive.

'Not by myself, I admit. But Gavin and Alistair took the body from your bed this morning, thinking that they were concealing Iona's accidental murder of Letitia. It's not too hard to work out what happened after you found Letitia stabbed in your bed. You went to Colin and Iona's room. Iona had taken a sleeping draught when she got back to her room and so she was unconscious. You persuaded Colin that she had killed Letitia:

and he must have got Alistair and Gavin to dispose of the body.'

'Did you tell him?' Colin asked Alistair, who merely shook his head.

'No, he didn't. They were seen in the hall in the early morning when the girls arrived to work in the house. And Emma, of course, was bound to ask you for help. They would hardly have done it for her. What puzzles me is how Emma explained the fact that Iona had killed Letitia in *her* bed. I'd have thought that might have made you suspicious.'

'She told me the truth,' Colin spoke firmly.

'Be quiet,' Emma said. 'Don't tell him anything.'

'Why not? The truth is clear enough. As you said, Letitia came to your room to gloat. To tell you that she was going to make sure I stopped supporting the magazine.' He turned away from Emma and spoke directly to me. 'The drugs knocked Letitia out while she was talking to Emma. When Emma realised Letitia was woozy from drugs, she went downstairs to make some coffee to help wake Letitia up. And while she was away Iona came in, thinking that it was Emma in the bed.'

'That's what she told you, and I'm sure you believed it. And so', I said, 'you told Alistair and Gavin what had happened and asked them to deal with the body. They were going to take Letitia's body out and bury her, but when they heard the car bringing the servants, they realised it was too late. So they hurriedly put the body into the rug, intending to bury it later, presumably about now, after the New Year's Eve guests had gone on their drunken ways. Unfortunately, they neglected to pass this information on to you, Colin. And, since neither of them was still at breakfast when you announced that we were going to put back the carpet, you were as surprised as the rest of us when the body made its dramatic reappearance.

'And, as I say, you were all acting on the assumption that you were concealing a terrible mistake of Iona's. The question is whether you should go along with Miss Gale now you know that you were concealing not Iona's murder but Emma's.'

'Mother stabbed a corpse?' Gavin said slowly.

And Alistair glowered at Colin. 'You might have told us.'

'Gavin. Alistair.' Colin was irritated but his voice was firm. 'Leave this to me. Patrick is just wrong. You can't leave matters in the hands of a man who trumpets it about that one of you's a thief and the other's a bastard. Patrick, I'm very grateful that you have cleared up what happened. I am sure we are all grateful. But even if you were right, I couldn't have all this business dragged out in the press. For one thing, it would ruin Alistair's career. It would also be extremely damaging to the rest of the family. I really can't allow it. You see, if we permit you to have Emma charged with murder, she will, I am certain, make sure that all the rest of the story gets out, won't you, dear?'

Emma nodded, smiling a sickly smile. 'You bet.'

'So you see, my family and its interests coincide here with Emma's. We cannot have this story getting out.'

'Would you say that if you knew why I was sure that it was Emma that killed your sister?'

Colin said nothing. He looked at Emma and then he spoke slowly. 'I believe the woman I love.'

'Ask yourself why Iona would have first suffocated the person in the bed and then stabbed the body.'

'Ask Iona,' Colin said. 'She did it. That's why she fainted when Emma appeared at breakfast; she thought she'd killed her.'

'Indeed she did. But Iona will tell you that she only stabbed the body in the bed. And the autopsy shows that when the body was stabbed, Letitia was already dead from suffocation. So, who suffocated your sister?'

Colin's face betrayed indecision. I could tell that he was beginning to doubt Emma's story. And so could Emma. She moved swiftly to the writing-desk where Alistair and Marie-Hélène were seated, opened it and removed what looked like an old service revolver.

'Tut, tut, Colin. How could you doubt me?' She strode towards the conservatory door with the revolver in her hand, and Jonathan and Maria moved back into the room out of her way. 'I think we are all going to have to think a little more clearly about what we will say to the police. Iona stabbed Letitia. Patrick, for some reason, wants them to think *I* suffocated her first. He just can't believe poor sweet Iona would have done it. But she did. I don't know why she did it, but she did. And if we stick to that story – stick to the *truth*, Patrick –

Iona will get her just deserts and the rest of us will be able to pick up our shattered lives. If, on the other hand, you pursue this line, Patrick, then, as Colin says, I shall have to defend myself by pointing to some of the tawdrier details of Rundle life. And that wouldn't suit anybody. Have you any idea how big a splash my trial would make?' Emma concluded. 'Every sordid secret of the house of Rundle, including the ones you've uncovered, Patrick, would feature prominently.'

'May I ask what you plan to do with that gun?' Alistair enquired. He was trying – unsuccessfully – not to sound nervous.

'I'm just keeping everybody calm while we sort out what to do.'

'I know you did it, Miss Gale. Do you want to know how? I found the pillow.' I spoke slowly and clearly. It was time to provide the final piece of evidence.

'What do you mean?' Colin asked.

'It's a theoretical possibility that the same person first suffocated and then stabbed Letitia. But why?' I paused and looked straight at Colin. 'Paul's autopsy showed that the pillow that killed Letitia wasn't a down pillow.'

'Emma's allergic to down,' Colin said in a dull voice. 'She has a foam pillow.'

'If Iona had suffocated Letitia, she'd presumably have used Emma's pillow. And if she stabbed her immediately after suffocating her, wouldn't there have been a pillow somewhere with blood on it?'

'There wasn't a pillow on the bed at all,' Gavin said.

'Where is it, Miss Gale?'

'If you're so clever, Sir Patrick, why don't you tell me?'

'I checked a little earlier. It's on your bed, now. Which means you must have fetched it from where you left it the night you killed Letitia.'

Emma said nothing.

I went on. 'After you killed her you left the room with the pillow in your hand and went up to the tower. You were looking for somewhere to put the body.'

'How the hell do you know that?' Colin's voice was raised in anger.

'Jonathan told me he had smelled perfume outside Letitia's

room and on the landing beyond it. Monica smelled the same perfume in Justin's room – and she said it was Emma's. So then I knew that Emma had been into Letitia's room and through into Justin's on the way up to the tower at about a quarter to four on Friday morning. When we went up to the attic yesterday afternoon, there was a foam-filled pillow on the bed. Jinny tidied it away under the bedspread. Why would Iona have removed the pillow with which she thought she had suffocated you and taken it up to the attic?'

'I don't know. Ask her.'

'How did the pillow get back to your bedroom?' Emma said nothing. 'How did you know where to find it? How did you know where to look?'

I could see all of them, including Colin, now believed me. They were all eyeing the revolver uneasily. Colin looked stunned: for a moment or two, his face was utterly blank, as if he was taking nothing in.

In the mean while, Emma addressed me coolly. 'Very clever, Paddy boy. You caught me out there. But I doubt that that'll do much to persuade a jury. And the fact is, it'll be Iona's word against mine.'

'It'll be the word of Iona and her family against yours,' Colin said, his voice quivering. He was angry, now, and you could see that he was dispirited, and very, very tired.

'You fool,' Emma said. 'We can be rid of her! All you have to do is stick with my story.'

'You killed my sister.' Colin pronounced these words with the weight of a final judgement. He did not have to say that, however tiresome Letitia had been, he could not forgive Emma for murdering her. 'Give me the gun.'

He stepped towards her slowly. She kept her eyes firmly on his and gave no ground. I thought, *He wants her to shoot him*. And for a moment, I thought she was going to do it.

Then my wife sneezed.

Virginia was seated near where Emma was standing and the sound focused all attention on her. Colin stopped moving. Emma glared angrily at Jinny, who shrugged apologetically, looked down, and began to open her handbag.

'Hold on a minute,' Emma said, waving the gun nervously in her direction. 'What are you getting out of there?'

'Just this?' Jinny said, holding up a small bottle. As Emma bent down and peered at it, Jinny sprayed the contents into her eyes, and swung her handbag up fairly efficiently into Emma's hand, dislodging the gun. It fell to the floor a few feet from where Emma was standing. In the mad rush that followed, I heard the voice I had been waiting for, bellowing from the door of the conservatory.

'I'll shoot the first pairson that touches that revolver,' David Seasay said. 'I mean it. I'm a damn guid shot.'

18

I wasn't sure that Inspector MacAlister would be keen on getting a call at one on New Year's morning. But he was exceedingly genial when I woke him.

'And a happy New Year to you, Sir Patrick. I was just getting my beauty sleep to prepare for the trip over tomorrow,' he said sleepily. 'But I'll listen to you, if you don't mind me being a wee bit edgy in the morning.'

I gave him a report of the evening's events. I was speaking on the phone in the drawing-room, where David and Niall were keeping Emma under surveillance. I had been uneasy about telling the family what I knew with nobody to appeal to if things got difficult and so I had asked David to make his way back into the conservatory with his shotgun to make sure that all went well. 'Don't come in, if you don't need to,' I had told him.

Paul had come, too, and he stood now in the doorway to the conservatory. He looked utterly drained. When he had arrived at David's house an hour ago, saying that I had sent him to help, David explained the situation to him, sobered him up a little, and prepared him to back me up, too. But what he had heard had obviously upset him a great deal. I assumed that what had hurt him most was discovering that it was Iona who had stabbed Letitia.

I spoke to MacAlister on the phone in the drawing-room because I wanted Emma and the family to be clear that the police knew everything. It would make them less likely to try and escape from us.

'We'll keep guard until you arrive,' I ended. 'But I'd be grateful if that was soon.'

'I think, in the circumstances, that I can get a helicopter from the coastguard. We'll be there in a few hours.'

'Thank you, Inspector.'

'I think I should be thanking you and your merry men.'

'And my Maid Marian. Without her, I would never have worked it out.'

Niall and David agreed to take the first watch. Virginia and I took Paul into the hall, and I asked him if he wanted to join us as we told Iona what had happened.

He nodded sadly. 'I suppose they'll lock her away.'

'I don't think so. She was sorely provoked and she didn't actually kill anybody.'

When we reached Colin and Iona's bedroom, Jinny knocked quietly and went in. A minute later she fetched the two of us. 'She's a bit groggy, I'm afraid.'

'She would be,' Paul said. 'I gave her a pretty hefty sedative.'

Quietly, the three of us explained what had happened downstairs. Iona said nothing, looking always down towards her bed covers, or over beyond Colin's bed into the darkness outside the window. All the time tears fell down her cheeks, but she did not cry. Not a sob passed her lips. When we had finished, she said, 'It's lucky Letitia didn't have to suffer.' Then, for the first time, she broke down in sobs. 'God, I wish I weren't so feeble. I couldn't even stab the right bloody person.'

Virginia took her hand and Paul, who had watched in anguish, knelt beside the bed and spoke to her: 'If you need anything, just ask. I'll do anything I can.'

After a while, she calmed down. 'I suppose you want me to tell you what happened.'

'Only if you feel up to it.'

'Yes, I feel up to it. It's all so silly really. I mean, Colin went off in the middle of the night and it just enraged me. He'd brought her here, that woman, to our house and I thought, now he's corridor-creeping like a stupid teenager. He hadn't let me in on his stupid plot with Letitia, so I didn't know there was any other reason for him to be creeping around. When I thought he was asleep, I just got up and took the screwdriver . . . He'd been adjusting the door to our bathroom and he'd left the screwdriver on my bedside table. I just slipped out of the room and walked into her room. It was very dark. But I knew where the bed was. I just went over to the bed. And then . . .' She closed her eyes, as if trying to shut out the horror. 'I just struck out at the bed. I couldn't look . . . not that I'd have seen anything. I just brought the screwdriver down again and again, where I thought her heart would be. I must have missed; she must have been further over than I realised, so I hit the wrong side of her body. But I knew I was striking flesh.' She paused again, shuddering a little, before she continued. 'The noise was horrible. I went on till I was sure she must be dead. After a while, there was no response. So I left.'

'What did you do with the screwdriver?'

'I put it back on the bedside table. Then I went into the bathroom and changed my night-dress. I was surprised how little blood there was. But, of course, now I know why. And then I was very tired.

'I took a few sleeping pills and eventually I fell asleep. I was fairly woozy when Emma knocked on the door and Colin left the room. But I didn't hear any voices; and it didn't worry me anyway, because I thought Emma was dead. I assumed it was Alistair or one of the children.

'When I awoke, I turned on my light and saw that the screwdriver was gone. I went to the bathroom and my night-dress was gone from the laundry basket. For a moment, I wondered if I had dreamed it all. And then Colin spoke. He was still in bed. He didn't look at me. He just said, "We've cleared up your mess. Alistair and Gavin and I." That was all he said. So, of course, I thought they'd buried Emma. I was terrified and . . . delighted.'

Iona laughed humourlessly. 'So you can imagine what I felt when that woman came in to breakfast. Colin assumed that I had just been pretending to be asleep when they made their plans in the doorway of the room. He thought I knew what had really happened. That's what comes of not talking to your wife.'

'I think you should rest, now,' Paul said. 'Here, take some of these.' He took a couple of pills from the bottle by her bed.

'Would you sit with me until I fall asleep?' Iona asked.

'Of course,' Paul said. 'Of course I will.'

'We'll just go and take a little rest ourselves,' Virginia said, and we retired to the Green Room for the last time.

'It's horrible to imagine Iona driven to do something so desperate. I still can't quite believe it.'

'She must have stood by the bed, above Letitia's right arm. That way, if Letitia was in the middle of the bed and Iona brought the screwdriver down with her right hand, she would have hit the body on the right-hand side of the neck.'

'Really, Patrick. I didn't mean I needed a mechanical explanation. It's her state of mind I don't understand.'

'Remember, she knew nothing of Letitia's plot. As far as she knew Letitia had jumped over the cliff. Emma was taking Colin from her. And they'd already had more than a week of tension over her presence in the house. She was under an enormous strain.'

'I suppose it makes sense. Certainly, she had every right to want Emma out of the way. Now, *she's* a nasty piece of work, isn't she?'

I agreed.

'Oh God, I've just thought of something.'

'What?'

'Horace will be back from first-footing at some point. We'd better head him off. Otherwise he'll charge into the drawing-room looking for a drink.'

Reluctantly, we made our way back downstairs and into the drawing-room. Maria was making tea for David and Niall. 'We'd forgotten about Horace. He'll be back eventually. He may be a bit surprised to find you two in here guarding Emma.'

'I locked the front door,' David said. 'He'll ring to get in.'

'Or he might come in through the conservatory or the kitchen.'

'Why don't you just telephone him?' Maria asked sweetly.

'He'll be at the hotel. He always spends the early morning of New Year's Day in the bar there.'

'Thank you, my dear,' I said.

When I got Horace on the phone, I asked him if he was sitting down. 'Of course, old boy. If you weigh as much as I do, you don't stand unless it's absolutely necessary.'

'I'm afraid that Miss Gale is now in the drawing-room under the watchful eyes of David and Niall Sealsay, both of whom have guns.'

'Well, we must rescue her at once.'

'She's under arrest, Horace. David and Niall are guarding her.'

'Do you mean she did it?'

'No. Yes. Well, not exactly. Letitia was suffocated by Emma Gale. That's what killed her. The stab wounds were the result of an attack by Iona, who thought she was killing Emma.'

'What?'

'I really haven't the time to explain everything now, Horace. The point is, I think it would be best if you stayed at the hotel tonight. The police will be here in a few hours.'

'But they'll need a lawyer, Sir Patrick. I shall come up at once.' He slammed the telephone down immediately.

By the time we had settled Horace down and he had consulted with the family, it was half-past four.

Paul joined the rest of us once Iona was asleep. 'Do you think we could perhaps just not mention Iona's involvement?'

'Paul, I don't think she's likely to be prosecuted. The only witnesses against her would be Emma and Colin: and Colin can't testify against her and Emma's testimony would be obviously unreliable. But I've already told MacAlister what happened . . . and I don't think Iona's going to want to lie anyway.'

'You're right there. She kept saying how much better she felt now everybody knew.'

'I think the main thing she's going to need is someone to help her start again,' Jinny said.

Paul smiled.

'You lot go and sleep,' David said. 'An old shepherd like mysel' has no need of sleep. Fiona will be over in a wee while with some coffee.'

'And the old drunken doctor will sleep beside the shepherd, ready to wake at a moment's notice to do his bidding.'

'Why don't you get some rest too, Paul?' David said. 'You can take the next watch with Sir Patrick. You can sleep at our house. I'll send Niall over for you when the time comes.'

It was agreed.

'Good-night, Paul,' Jinny said, kissing him on the forehead. 'Good-night, David, Niall. And thank you both. Thank you for saving our lives.'

All day, as each piece of evidence had come in, I had thought it through with the instrument of my imagination. That was how, each time, I had escaped from the false assumptions that had led me astray. As we fell asleep, Letitia invaded my imagination for the last time.

Letitia is excited. Very, very excited. The plan she has been designing for so long has come to fruition and it is working. She sits in the tower all evening, visited first by Jessica, then by Alistair. To each of them she displays her excitement, striding around the room, gesticulating wildly. And later, when she comes back up from eating with them in the middle of the night, she is still excited. She waits in her room. This too she has planned; she has planned every moment of it. Living romance is so much better than just writing it.

Colin comes up to see her – and Justin, woken when his grandfather makes his way through the room, sees his 'ghost'. The child – a child she does not much care for – screams and runs, still screaming, to his parents. She can return to her room, lock the door, lie in her own bed. The boy will sleep with his nanny now. Her way is clear.

Now it is time to sleep. She takes a few pills from the pillbox on her bedside table and opens up the flask. She pours herself a cup of the coffee and knocks back five pills. Then she thinks, I do not need to be up tomorrow morning. I should keep out of the way. I do not want to spoil my perfect plan. And so she takes another cup of the bitter coffee and another few pills. She is about to set off upstairs to the tower, where she is supposed to sleep. But then she thinks, this stuff never works straight away. She thinks, I have time to go and talk to that woman. To tell her that I have won, that she will have to go now, leave Colin alone. He promised he wouldn't tell her about the plan, but I knew he would. She has him under her spell.

She opens the door to her bedroom. There is no one out there. All she hears is the noise of the storm. She walks down to Emma's room and opens the door. She turns on the light and waits for Emma to awaken. And then she says, 'Go away. Leave him alone. We don't need you.'

Emma is cautious. She knows that she must be careful with Letitia or Colin will lose his money and the plan will fail. At first, she pretends not to know what Letitia is talking about. But Letitia says, 'I'm not a fool.' And so Emma decides to play along with her. 'All right, you've won,' she says.

But then she notices that Letitia's hands are to her face, that she is swaying. She staggers towards the bed. 'What's the matter?'

'Something's wrong,' Letitia says, grabbing at the bedside table. But she isn't able to keep standing. She loses consciousness, mumbling all the time, 'Something's wrong.' And she slithers down on to the bed.

Emma looks at her for a moment, this ridiculous old woman who stands in her way. Then she makes up her mind. She covers her with the counterpane and takes the pillow out from under her head. She holds it over the old woman's face and keeps it there until the body no longer shudders.

19

It wasn't much fun saying farewell to the Rundles. Colin was shattered. Paul – who had been jolted sober – told MacAlister that Iona was too out-of-sorts to fly out in the helicopter, and the inspector agreed to leave a sergeant to guard her and let her come the next day by ferry. And the rest of the family, faced now with the truth of what had happened, were in various stages of shock. Only Horace seemed relatively cheerful, as he waved us off. 'I'll travel over with Iona, tomorrow. She'll need a lawyer with her while they decide what to charge her with.'

Jinny and I travelled back to Oban in the helicopter with an impassive Emma and a friendly Inspector MacAlister. He turned out to be an entertaining companion. As we left him in Oban, he thanked us again. 'If you're up in these parts again, I'd like to introduce you to ma wife.'

We took the train to Glasgow and flew back to London. Sebastian had left Catharine, his wife, and their daughter Hermione down at Chewton Ampney, and driven to Heathrow to meet us. I was frankly touched by this display of filial piety, and by his insistence that we join them in the country. He and Catharine had been expecting to have some time to themselves, after the sociability of their New Year. Sebastian's medical life doesn't allow him many uninterrupted holidays with Catharine.

As we drove west on the M4, he quizzed us about what had happened. I sat in the front, next to him; and Jinny sat behind, chipping in with the odd remark to fill out the story.

'What'll happen to them all?' he asked.

'Emma will go to jail for a very long time. I don't think Iona will get more than a few years of probation. The rest of them will probably get off altogether, even though they did try to cover up a murder. I told MacAlister that we wouldn't give evidence against them. They've suffered enough.'

'That seems awfully generous.' Seb sounded reproachful.

'Colin was only protecting his family.'

Sebastian said, 'You're very brave, aren't you, you two? Did it ever occur to you that you might be taking a serious risk?'

'To tell you the truth, the sight of Emma with a service revolver pointed in my direction did rather shake me up,' I said. 'I was thinking how terrible it was that I had led your mother into this trap. I'd got Paul waiting in the conservatory, but I hadn't expected the gun. I thought Emma might get one of us before Paul could do anything, and I was hoping it would be me.'

'Very chivalrous, I'm sure,' Sebastian said. 'And I'm sure Mother would have been delighted to be left behind. But *I'd* have been very cross with you.' He glanced away from the road and smiled ruefully at me. 'I don't know if I've ever mentioned this to you, Father, but I do actually prefer you alive.' My son paused for a moment. He was obviously struggling to express himself. 'Family *is* very important,' he went on slowly.

I felt Jinny's hand gently pressing on my shoulder.

'That's what Letitia said,' I told him.

'Well, it's true. Maybe nobody liked Letitia, but you can't say she didn't care about her family.'

Nobody spoke for a while, and we turned off the Swindon exit towards Cirencester. It was good to be back in the ancestral vales. Good, too, to know that my son was feeling what I had felt: that we had time left to get to know each other and that it was not time to waste.

I made a promise *in pectore* never to take so foolish a risk again. And as I did so, I caught Jinny's eye in the mirror of the lowered visor. She smiled and said to our son, 'Your father has his pious look. That means that he is soberly promising himself to keep out of harm's way in the future. But I can tell you right now that if another murder comes his way, he'll be after it like a bat out of hell.'

'Just be careful, Father. I mean it.' Sebastian spoke with an unfamiliar sternness. 'Hermione needs her grandfather.'

It is hard for an Englishman of my son's generation to tell his father how he feels about him. It is harder still for an Englishman of my generation to respond when he does. But after the tensions and fissures of the Rundles, the sheer good luck I had had in my own smaller family overwhelmed me. Which is how it came about that I found myself telling my son for the first time in his adult life that I loved him.

I don't know which of us was more surprised.

JB	